Broken Love

A SAFE Security Trilogy

Mercenary Hearts 2

Michele Zurlo

www.michelezurloauthor.com

Broken Love (A SAFE Security Trilogy: Mercenary Hearts 2)
Copyright © July 2018 by Michele Zurlo
ISBN: 978-1-942414-50-6

Editor: Nicoline Tiernan
Cover Artist: Anne Kay

Published by Lost Goddess Publishing LLC
www.michelezurloauthor.com

This book is a work of fiction. While reference might be made to actual historical events or existing locations, the names, characters, places and incidents are either the product of the author's imagination or are used fictitiously, and any resemblance to actual persons, living or dead, business establishments, events, or locales is entirely coincidental.

Warning: This book contains sexually explicit scenes and adult language and may be considered offensive to some readers. It is not meant for underage readers.

DISCLAIMER: Education and training are necessary in order to learn safe BDSM practices. Lost Goddess Publishing LLC is not responsible for any loss, harm, injury or death resulting from use of the information contained in any of its titles. This is a work of fiction, and license has been taken with regard to BDSM practices.

Broken Love (Mercenary Hearts 2)

"I'd wanted the fairy tale, and somewhere along the line I'd forgotten that everyone in a fairy tale paid a price."

Jesse: Four months after Jessica walked away from me, I returned to find that she'd removed herself from my life as much as possible—even from her art studio and storefront on the first floor of the SAFE Security building. She couldn't run far since she was carrying my child, and one night of playing nice landed me in her bed. While it didn't repair the broken love between us, it renewed my determination to win her back.

Jessica: Ending up in the back of Jesse's truck while he was on vacation wasn't what I'd intended, but it gave us time to talk in a way we hadn't before. Now that he understood I wasn't a submissive, maybe we had a chance to be friends and co-parents? I just wish I could stop yearning for his touch.

A Note to Readers:

The Mercenary Hearts trilogy begins in the prequel, Forging Love, and it's meant to be read in order:

Forging Love (alternating viewpoints)

Drawing on Love (Jessica's viewpoint)

Broken Love (Mostly Jesse's viewpoint)

Shards of Love (alternating viewpoints)

Chapter 1—Jesse

Automatic machine gun fire came from my left, so I zagged right. Behind me, Frankie shot off a few rounds before joining me. We ducked behind a junk pile and plastered our backs against the building. Though we both wore vests, impact from ammo like that would not only hurt like a bitch, it would do some damage.

I reloaded my weapon, an M16 rifle I'd taken from a guard I'd knocked out, and I checked to make sure the thing would work.

"How many left?"

"Seven," Frankie said. She glanced around, her keen gaze taking in our surroundings, noting the same things mine had noted seconds before. Frankie Sikara was one of the finest soldiers I'd ever known. We'd been working together for more years than I could remember, and she was one of my three closest friends.

On the other side of the junk in front of us was a scene from a post-apocalyptic movie. Hard sand and scrubby growth went on for miles. This place was protected on all sides by wasteland. Getting in without being seen had been difficult enough. Now that they knew we were there, getting out was going to make our entrance look downright easy. "We're pinned down."

"So much for a quick in-and-out." She snorted a laugh, which told me that she had observed our surroundings enough to devise a plan.

Working so closely for so long, I knew exactly what she was thinking. We'd been in situations like this before. "Fuel is in the building behind us."

"I can't resist a toasty bonfire." She grinned, and I pried loose an edge of an aluminum panel.

The sheet cut into my fingers as I held it open for Frankie to slide through first. As soon as she was inside, she pushed all her weight against it so that I could shimmy my larger ass through. Once I was inside the storage facility, she eased the panel back gently because a loud bang would have alerted our pursuers as to our escape path.

1

Unlike in my favorite action movies, there weren't barrels of stored gasoline for us to blow up. However, that wasn't going to stop us from blowing stuff up. Three sport utility vehicles were parked inside, and the walls were lined with various types of equipment. Across the way, I spied an old sofa with the stuffing half torn out, which was useless. Next to it was a pile of old farming equipment, which made me wonder if this land had ever been arable. I leaned toward not, and I wondered how all that junk had come to be here.

This was not where they stored munitions. It was a glorified junk yard.

I found cans of paint and stain on a shelf. I pried them open and stuffed them with rags while Frankie hotwired one of the cars.

Also not something that happens in real life—cars don't tend to explode in a fire. They melt. I positioned my incendiary devices strategically in the driver's seat and jammed under the rear wheel well. The chances of explosion were still minimal, but the chances of them being able to extinguish the fire and also still be able to use the vehicles were nonexistent.

The engine on Frankie's car started, so I lit the fuses I'd created from rags. Then I jumped into the passenger seat. She peeled out of there.

We exited the garage to a hail of bullets. It was a good thing some paranoid drug lord had the foresight to armor plate the SUV. Frankie kept her eyes on the path to freedom while I watched our six. She busted through an electrified fence, and the car bounced along the uneven terrain.

Once we were clear of the compound and near a driving path, we picked up two more cars. They fired shots as the makeshift path became a pot-holed road. I climbed into the backseat and put my Delta Force training to good use. A bend in the road was coming up. I lowered the window on the back passenger side and used the frame to steady my aim. Then, when Frankie took that corner on two wheels, I squeezed off a few rounds. The lead car spun out of control and hit the turn violently. It flipped over and smacked into a tangle of hardy brush lining the dirt road in the middle of nowhere.

A split second decision saved the second car from crashing into the first. The road was too serpentine for me to time another shot the same way as the first, so I leaned out of the car and sprayed bullets into their radiator.

They shot back. I ducked out of range by sliding my head back into the car. Through the spiderweb of broken glass on the back window, I watched them lose speed and stutter to a halt.

"We lost them," I said.

"Keep watch for more." Frankie's speed didn't slow one tiny bit. She wove around curves and barreled through intersections. Nobody lived in this part of the world, and so oncoming traffic wasn't a problem. She floored it until we approached the edges of civilization, and then she modulated her driving to blend in with the local population.

"I think it's safe to say we weren't followed." It was also safe to say that the drug cartel from which we'd escaped was unaware that we weren't after drugs. They probably thought they'd chased us off before we could do any damage.

We hadn't been after drugs, just their list of contacts on the American side of the border so that our client—a man looking to climb through the ranks of the DEA—could have intel the rest of law enforcement had failed to find.

"We're about an hour outside of Caborca," Frankie said. "We'll trade out for a new ride, and then we'll head to Nogales to cross back into the good old U.S.A."

In Caborca, we traded in our bulletproof vests and work clothes for togs befitting a couple of tourists looking to get away from their everyday lives. We procured a car at a rental place, and Frankie changed out the license plate for a New Mexican one. I offered to trade driving duty, but she declined.

"You drive too slowly."

Point of fact: I was a speed demon, but Frankie made me look like a Sunday driver.

"We don't want to tangle with local police," I reminded her. "Mexican law enforcement isn't known for their love of foreign drivers."

She shot me a warning glance. Frankie had been one of the finest Special Forces agents, and the CIA was still actively trying to recruit her for clandestine services. She was smart, brave, and she spoke three languages. But since one of them was Farsi, she figured she'd end up working in the Middle East, which she didn't want to do. Like me, she much preferred to stay in the Western hemisphere. Jobs in Central or South America were no problem, but she routinely turned down anything that might take her to Iraq, Iran, or Afghanistan. We'd had our fill of that region when we were stationed there. Plus, working closer to home meant we could take on jobs more frequently and still have adequate time at home.

Knowing when to shut up was one of my better qualities. I turned on my phone and it dinged with a dozen notifications. Three of them were David telling me that I'd missed checking in.

"Whoops. Forgot to let everyone know we're okay." I fired off a couple of texts to let the rest of the team know that our mission had been successful and that we were on our way back to Kansas City.

Miles disappeared beneath the tires, and I looked over the next scheduled mission. "You know, we could stop off and take care of recon for the Houston job. It's on the way."

Frankie pressed her lips together.

"C'mon. It'll be fun. We can get ice cream. You love ice cream."

"One would think you're avoiding going home." She turned off the main road and headed into a small town.

"From the looks of it, you're avoiding heading home." The car stopped in front of a small café, and I remembered how much Frankie liked discovering out-of-the-way restaurants. "Or you just want lunch."

"It's closer to dinner time." She undid her seat belt and exited the car, leaving me no choice but to follow.

I wasn't particularly hungry. It was amazing how losing everything that ever meant anything washed the color and flavor out of one's life.

Frankie didn't wait for me to catch up. Her long strides took her into the café. I remained on the sidewalk and looked around, my practiced gaze roaming the street for possible sources of danger. In our line of work, being careful was a matter of life and death, especially when we were still in a foreign country for what basically amounted to illicit and unsanctioned activity. If our client could get this information through official channels, he would have.

That's where we came in. SAFE Security did dangerous but necessary work to keep our corner of the world safe.

Once I'd established the relative security of our environment, I headed inside.

Frankie stood, hand on hip, and stared down a group of four men. At 5'11, my partner was a tall woman—three inches taller than me— and her lithe build disguised her true strength. The men in question were her size or taller, and they looked like they spent a lot of time in the local gym.

As I came inside, one of them threw a dismissive glance in my direction. I didn't take it personally.

Rather than intrude on what was going to be a moment of truth for someone in this establishment, I skirted the edge of the group. They probably thought I was avoiding confrontation, but I was positioning myself to be of service if needed. While I had every confidence that Frankie could take on all four, I was prepared to split the workload.

"You want help?" This served as a warning to the men. If they were smart, they'd realize that if I was at all concerned about her safety, I wouldn't have asked. I would have simply stepped in.

"Nope. I got this."

I could kick ass, but I'd learned pretty much everything I knew from Frankie. She was proficient in six forms of martial arts, and she was the deadliest person I'd ever seen in close-quarters combat. Though I could hold my own, I was technically the team nerd. Computers and programming were my passion. I selected a table in the corner with a good view out the storefront.

Though she'd said she didn't need me, I kept watch. Frankie knew I had her back. One of the men put his hand on her arm, probably with the intention of jerking her toward him, but he didn't get far. Frankie twisted out of the hold and used the momentum to palm-heel his nose. He went down hard.

Yeah, this was going to be over quickly.

I called over the din. "How many empanadas do you want?" I knew what she liked, but I didn't know how hungry she was.

"Eight." She took down the next one the second he moved to defend his buddy. "And dessert. See if they have good churros. I'm hungry."

I opened a menu and hoped for pictures. No such luck. Though I could pick out some of the more common food words, I couldn't read in Spanish.

Jessica could. If she was here, she'd translate and then she'd happily charm the server while she ordered for us.

I pinched the bridge of my nose to chase away thoughts of the woman I'd loved and lost.

The men stumbled out the front door, each holding onto a body part that was going to hurt for a while. Frankie, finished dealing with men who had more muscles than brains, plopped down across from me. "Did you order?"

The server hadn't stopped by yet, probably due to the fact a woman was being accosted by four men in the mostly empty dining room, and they didn't want to witness anything that might get them killed. As soon as they cleared out, an old woman brought out glasses of water.

She shot me a look, and she smiled at Frankie. She patted Frankie's hand and spoke in rapid-fire Spanish.

"No hablo español," she supplied. She knew fighting phrases, like, "Come at me, bro," and "I'll shove your balls up your ass." Nothing appropriate for this situation.

Though I didn't fare much better, I pointed to Frankie. "*Ocho empanadas y quatro churros.*" Then I pointed to myself. "Fajita con carne."

Yeah, I probably sounded like an idiot, but high school Spanish had been a long time ago.

The server smiled. "*Señora* wants eight empanadas and four churros, and *señor* wants a steak fajita. Anything else?"

"Lemonade," I supplied, relieved that she spoke English because I didn't know the Spanish equivalent.

"Is there a rest room?" Frankie lifted her hands. "I need to wash up."

When Frankie was gone, the old woman frowned mightily at me. "You did not defend your wife's honor."

I didn't bother to correct her assumption that Frankie was my wife, but I would be remiss in not pointing out that she'd handled it just fine without me. "She doesn't need a man to defend her honor."

The ancient lady leaned down. Her bony fingers dug into my shoulder. "A beautiful woman may not need a man to defend her, but she needs to know he will."

"Noted." This was like arguing with my mother. No matter what I said, I was in the wrong.

Frankie returned, and the server shot me a meaningful look from across the room. Frankie lifted her brows. "What was that about?"

"Apparently I'm lacking as a husband because I didn't rush to your defense."

"Ah." She sipped her water.

"That's it? You're not going to disagree?"

She shrugged. "You're not really what I'd look for in a husband because I couldn't wear heels when we went out."

Though she'd meant to kid me, her assertion struck a direct blow. Four months ago, the woman I loved more than anything in the world had ended our relationship. I'd been preparing to propose marriage and find a house where we could raise a passel of kids, when she'd decided our relationship was over.

Frankie's hand closed over mine, squeezing reassurance through my flesh with her firm grip. "I'm sorry, Jesse. I shouldn't have said that. It was a bad, bad joke. You're a wonderful friend and partner. I know you have my six. If I'd needed help, you wouldn't have hesitated."

I swallowed down the grief threatening to choke the life out of me. "I'm fine."

"You're not fine. You've been working yourself ragged for months."

6

"I like my job." Making the world safer was a noble endeavor, but I would be lying if I denied that the covert and dangerous aspects didn't appeal to me just as much. Of course, I usually balanced field work with office work and software development. Since Jessica had walked out of my life, I'd thrown myself into field work.

"You're running away from her. You're doing everything you can to avoid her."

With a casual lift of my shoulder, I dismissed Frankie's assertion.

"I can't believe you're giving up."

"Woman says no, man obeys. That's just common decency." I didn't mention all the times I'd pushed her to open up, to give me more, to be my submissive. It had all backfired, and when I let my guard down, that last image of her face—mired in misery and twisted with agonizing grief—tattooed itself on the inside of my eyelids. For a moment, I felt guilty, but mostly I was angry. I'd done everything I could to make her happy, and she'd thrown it all in my face.

"She has PTSD. She needs time."

I'd given her over a year of time. Yeah, I'd pushed her, but only because she needed to be pushed. That was my job as a Dom—to help her be a better version of herself.

Jessica wasn't a topic I'd discussed with any of my friends, though they all found opportunities to bring her up. I scooted my hand away from Frankie's well-meaning clutches and took a long drink from my lemonade. It was sweeter than I liked. Jessica would have liked it.

I shook away the thought. "She has all the time in the world now."

"She's having your baby."

This conversation wasn't one I wanted to have. "Do you have a point?"

"I'm not taking sides on this, Jesse. You're both my friends."

While I didn't want anyone to vilify Jessica, Frankie's admission took me by surprise. "You've been one of my best friends for over two decades, and you're not on my side?"

"I'm Switzerland," she said.

The old woman came back with two plates piled high with food. She set both down in front of me. A younger man came out with a plate of empanadas and a basket of churros for Frankie.

"*Gracias*," I said.

Frankie smiled. "Thanks. This smells really good."

It smelled great, but Frankie's claim of neutrality stunk. "You've known her for a little over a year, and you've never really liked her."

"I like her just fine. She's hard to get to know, but I'm doing it." Frankie dug into her first empanada and moaned. "God, these are good."

Rather than let Frankie know exactly how much her lack of loyalty hurt, I busied myself loading up my flour tortilla with fixings.

"You know, she reminds me a lot of you after Josie died."

If there was one thing to say that was guaranteed to piss me off, Frankie hit the bull's-eye posted on my back with a perfect throw of her dagger. She fucking nailed it. Rage unfurled in my gut, and I struggled to contain it. "Don't fucking go there."

She cut her next empanada into bite-sized pieces while regarding me stoically. "Closed-off, terrified to take chances, feeling guilty about things beyond your control."

"Frankie." I growled one last warning.

"Of course, you tried to take on every bad guy in the world to fill that emotional hole. You jumped out of planes, volunteered for perilous missions, and put yourself through hellish training."

"So did you." That's where we'd become friends.

She ignored my interjections. "At least she's seeking more of a creative outlet."

At least she wasn't fixated on Josie. If there was one thing I refused to discuss, it was the tragic end of my first marriage. I pushed aside thoughts of Josie and concentrated on picking apart Frankie's argument. "Jessica isn't closed off. She's willing to take chances, often reckless ones, and she's in therapy to help her cope with guilt and anger and whatever else crops up."

"Yeah, you're right." Frankie flashed a grin. "She's definitely got her mental house in order."

"I didn't say that." Jessica had come so far in such a short time. I'd wanted to believe that she had moved past the worst of it, but she hadn't. Deep down, she was still a liar and a con artist, and I'd been her latest con job. I stabbed at an onion that had fallen out of my fajita, and I ate it from the fork. "But when things got real, she ran away. She's a fucking coward."

That was one thing I hadn't counted on. I thought that if she really loved me, nothing would tear her from my side. If she really loved me, then she would have wanted to work through our differences. I was wrong.

"You're still mostly angry." Frankie wolfed down her fourth empanada before I finished one fajita. "Hopefully it won't take you years to move past it so that you can do the healing you need to do."

I wanted to say that it hadn't taken me years to get over the guilt and anger I felt about Josie's death, but the truth was I still felt like it was my fault.

If I hadn't joined the Army...

If I hadn't signed up for an additional tour in Afghanistan...

If I hadn't fought with her on the phone the night before...

If I had been there, we wouldn't have fought. If we hadn't fought, she wouldn't have been on the road that night. If she hadn't been on the road, she wouldn't have been in that crash. She'd be alive, and I'd be living a completely different life. Of course, if she hadn't been fucking that guy from her math class, she probably wouldn't have been on the road that night either. That was a hunch on my part. I had no proof to back it up.

I'd also never told another soul that the night before she died, Josie had asked me for a divorce. I'd never said a word to anyone about the man who'd showed up at her funeral, a stranger who was every bit as upset and bereft as I had been.

Frankie was quiet, watching me while morose thoughts rattled around in my head.

For the rest of the drive home, we talked about other things—my mother and sisters, her parents and brother, and some of our upcoming cases.

SAFE Security headquarters had a gym and showers. I showered and shaved the moment we returned, and then Frankie and I met David and Brea in the conference room for the debrief.

Like Frankie, David was one of my best friends. We'd met while assigned to a Special Forces unit made up of Army and Marine troops. David was a big guy. He had an intense way about him, but he somehow managed to have a friendly and affable nature. He was golden with explosives, both making and defusing them.

Brea was his wife, but she had badass credentials of her own. She'd never met a lock she couldn't pick or a safe she couldn't crack. Raised by a con artist to be a con artist, she had spent a lifetime honing skills I'd never even begun to master. She was also Jessica's sister, which meant I had to be on my guard around her. I wasn't sure where she fell on the breakup spectrum. It was natural that her sympathies would lie with her sister, and I didn't know where that left me.

Technically I hadn't done anything wrong.

Brea had warned me Jessica would use me and toss me aside—and I'd dismissed her concern. I'd been confident I could handle Jessica.

Of course, life was never as simple as that, was it?

"Where's Dean?" Of everyone in my SAFE Security family, Dean was the one who was unequivocally on my side.

"Houston," Brea said. "He decided to take on the job you were supposed to do next week. We all got together and decided that you need some vacation time." She followed the news with a sad smile and a plate of muffins.

When she wasn't running around learning the ropes of mercenary work, she was also a badass in the kitchen. At one point in her life, she'd considered opening a bakery. Judging from the way she baked, it would have been wildly successful.

But I didn't want vacation time, and I sure as hell didn't want to be told when to take it. "He went alone?"

"We contracted with Malcolm for the job." Brea softened the blow with a sympathetic smile and a soft hand on my wrist.

Malcolm Legato was a former FBI agent that David had come to know while working a job in Michigan. It was the same one where he'd met Brea—the person responsible for bringing Jessica into my life. Malcolm was a good guy and a great partner in the field. Dean was in capable hands, but he was supposed to have gone with me. We were scheduled to leave the day after tomorrow.

To say I was pissed was an understatement.

"I can do my fucking job."

"I know," Brea said. "But all you've been doing is working. You've taken on so much extra work that we've exceeded last year's quarterly profit margins already."

I didn't fucking care about money. "Some of that has to do with you joining us. More people means we can take more jobs."

David tapped his pen against the table. "Not so many that you're in danger of working yourself into an early grave. Take the time off. You're due for a visit to your mother in Florida. Stay a few extra days."

"Don't fucking tell me what to do."

"You're swearing a lot more than usual." David leaned forward. "Take the days, Jesse. You need time off."

I looked over at Frankie to see if she was part of the conspiracy. She shrugged, which meant she hadn't been involved, but she wasn't against the idea. "Now isn't the time to be fucking Switzerland. Grow a pair of ovaries, will ya?"

She said something in Farsi or Hindi that I couldn't translate, but I knew she was essentially telling me to go fuck myself. Then she folded her hands on the table. "I don't care if you take a vacation or not, but you need a few days off. You can't work four months straight without going a little crazy. Schedule some time with your subs. You need an outlet for all the shit you're going through right now."

Being outnumbered meant I didn't have a leg to stand on. It looked like Dean was out of town right now because he agreed with the rest of them, and he'd left David and Brea to break it to me because he knew how convincing Brea could be.

Well, fuck that, and fuck manipulative women.

I closed my eyes. That wasn't fair. Brea was only doing what she thought was right, and Jessica had been up front with me about her struggles with that particular habit. I'd told her not to worry about it. I'd told her I'd handle that burden.

It was yet another way I'd failed her.

"You didn't fail her." That gem came from David.

I looked up to find them all staring at me. I hadn't uttered my thoughts aloud. The vast majority of what I thought didn't make it into verbal form. I wasn't much of a talker. I waited for David to continue. Being married and enlightened and all that shit, he was into communicating.

Okay, maybe I stared at David, passive-aggressively challenging him to explain.

He pursed his lips, a sure sign he was going to wait me out. Fucker.

"Will the two of you stop it?" Brea exhaled her impatience. "Jesse, we know you blame yourself."

I turned my venom on her. "Because it's not my fault? Because there's nothing I couldn't have done differently? I don't blame myself as much as I'm pissed at her for jerking me around. You said that's what she'd do, and I didn't believe you. I fell for her con."

She crossed her arms and set her jaw hard. "It's a little bit your fault, a little bit her fault, and a little bit the fault of factors neither of you can control. Is that what you wanted to hear?"

"Sugar, don't." David set a hand on her wrist. "We're staying out of this, remember?"

She rolled her eyes, but before she could huff out something caustic, Frankie intervened. "How about we do this debrief? Even if Jesse is against taking a day off, I'm not. I'm tired, and I have things to do."

Frankie wasn't insensitive or impatient, and for her to be at this point meant I was less than no fun to be around. In the twenty-one years we'd been friends, I could count the number of times I'd annoyed her on one hand.

"Sorry," I said. "Let's do this."

An hour later, I declined an offer from David to hang out and get wasted even though it was probably the only thing that had a snowball's chance of making me feel better. The sun was setting, and the streetlights weren't yet on. A winter wind blew in from the direction of the river. I stuck my hands in my pockets and skulked around the side of the building. I lived walking distance from the office. Frankie had offered to drive me home, but I wanted to linger at some of the empty fountains that reflected the way I felt inside.

More than that, it gave me an excuse to walk by Unexpected Treasures, the shop Jessica ran on the ground floor of the building SAFE Security owned. Maybe she'd be there. Maybe she'd be hard at work transforming a flea market find into something remarkable. She was a talented artist. Though her skills had taken a beating due to a head injury from a car accident, she still had an amazing talent for reproducing works she'd seen elsewhere.

It tore at her that she couldn't create the visions she saw in her head. Or maybe she'd lied, and she cared as little about painting as she did about me.

Maybe she'd be inside, chatting with a customer who was gushing over something she made. She'd wear her flirty smile because that's how she manipulated people into paying the price she wanted.

Though I'd hoped to see her, I was surprised to actually see her. Carrying a rather large cardboard box, she emerged from the shop. Remnants of sunlight hit her dark brown hair. Her back was to me, and my gaze roamed her delectable curves. She wore jeans and a jacket, but I knew that she probably had on an old black T-shirt underneath the jacket.

I fought the urge to take the box from her. She was pregnant with my child, and I didn't want her doing any heavy lifting.

"Hey, I can get that." A man's voice drew my attention to the open rear door of an SUV parked on the street. Leon Zinn, Jessica and Brea's younger brother, rushed to take the box.

"It's not heavy, and the doctor said I had no restrictions. Stop treating me like I'm going to break." Annoyance huffed from Jessica, a whole lot of attitude wrapped in a bratty tone.

Searing pain shot through my heart. I wasn't ready to face her. My gaze automatically went to my surroundings, assessing for danger.

That's when I noticed her shop was empty. Was she moving out of the storefront just to spite me? Fuck that.

It was best to rip off the bandage quickly. I forced myself to stop lurking. Stepping out of the shadow, I waited for her to notice me.

Leon stowed the box in the car and closed the hatch. "Is that everything?"

"Yeah. Thanks for helping me pack up and move."

"That's what brothers are for." He handed a cane to her, and I recognized the elegant design of the carved cobra Frankie had given her. I'd originally bought it for Frankie when she'd been recovering from an injury, and Frankie had passed it to Jessica last summer.

She stepped onto the curb without turning around.

I couldn't let her leave without seeing her face, without looking into her eyes. I needed to hear her say she was fleeing to punish me. "Jessica."

She froze.

Leon stepped between us. "Jesse, we didn't know you were back yet."

My gaze remained pinned to a woman who wouldn't turn around. "What's going on?"

"Just helping Jessica move the last of the boxes." He smiled, but it conveyed a distinct lack of warmth. Like the rest of the Zinns, Leon had dark brown hair and brilliant green eyes. His eyes, happy or not, weren't the ones haunting my dreams.

"The last of the boxes?" I sidestepped Leon and touched Jessica's shoulder.

She turned slightly, enough for me to see that her eyes were puffy and red. She'd been crying.

My heart seized, and somehow the anger fell away. "Darlin'? What's going on?"

She flinched at the term of endearment. "It's for the best."

"What is?"

Leon opened the passenger door and motioned for Jessica to get inside. "The cost of the lease isn't worth the hassle anymore."

I was part owner of the building. We'd been renting the space to Jessica and Brea for a dollar a month. I blinked uncomprehendingly. Maybe she didn't want to operate a storefront, but this was great studio space. She needed this more than she needed the physical therapy that allowed her to live independently. Why the fuck would she target herself so vindictively?

She wouldn't. This was part of her con game. She was lying to Leon the same way she lied to me and everybody else whenever it was convenient.

Jessica slipped out of my grasp and got into the car.

I followed her, but she stared straight ahead. Habit rushed to the fore, and I was ready to combat her stubbornness. "You don't have to do this."

Leon closed the door and faced me with firm resolve. "She's not mad at you."

She had no fucking reason to be mad at me. She was doing this, not me. My anger came back with a vengeance.

I tapped on the window, and she hit the button to roll it down. Those unforgettable green eyes pointed no higher than my chin.

"This is stupid. Where will you paint?"

"I've given up on painting." Her gaze slid away.

If I was still her Dom, I'd haul her ass out of the car and make her tell the truth. I'd force it out of her any way I could. She responded to bondage in a very profound way. I'd found she couldn't lie when I tied her up. On the other hand, keeping her from slipping into subspace was nearly impossible, and so that limited the efficacy of questioning her under those circumstances.

And following that line of reasoning wasn't going to get me anywhere.

I grunted. "Jessica—"

She closed her eyes, and a tear squeezed out. "Don't, Jesse. Please don't say anything. Like I said, this is for the best. My PT and medical care have been transferred to a place closer to my parents' house."

She was leaving the city just to get away from me, taking herself as far out of my life as she could.

There was nothing I could think to say that wouldn't communicate the depth of my anger and the vitriol I felt toward the mother of my child, and so I kept my mouth shut. With my child in her body, there was only so far she could run. If she tried to keep my baby from me, I'd fucking destroy her.

I watched Leon's SUV merge into traffic. I kept my gaze on the tail lights until they turned on the street that would take them to the freeway.

Anger poisoned my view.

Chapter 2—Jesse

Frankie was right—I needed to get back to my routine. I needed to do something normal, and I sought refuge in the things I'd done since before Jessica had tied me in knots. If there was any fucking tying to be done, I needed to be the one who did it.

I scheduled sessions with two of my subs who lived nearby. A few hours with Damon would give me an outlet for the corrosive fury that ate at me. Then Wendy, my sweet submissive, would benefit from my finesse with the flogger and my skill with the rope.

Yes, normalcy was exactly what I needed.

Once both subs confirmed their agreement to my summons, I found myself alone in my loft with the skeletons of half-built tech equipment and the ghosts of my memories of Jessica.

The U-shaped leather sofa that dominated my living room had once been a favorite place to sit, but now when I looked at it, I saw Jessica all over it. I saw the place where she'd fallen asleep. I'd lifted her gently, careful because she was exhausted and sore from a session of physical therapy, and I'd carried her to my bed.

I saw all the places she'd lounged, the spot where she'd sat on my lap, and the various places we'd made out.

The kitchen was better because Jessica was not a cook. She'd been in that part of my wide-open place the least. But the kitchen was also not a place where I cared to be unless I was cooking.

That left what was supposed to be the dining room or bedroom. I'd long ago purchased the loft next door, and that's where I had my bedroom and play spaces. For years, this portion of the loft had been dedicated to my love of building and programming tech. I had a bank of monitors. Tables and shelves were littered with parts and pieces, each a component of a project in progress.

When I'd asked Jessica to move in with me, I'd promised to clear out this area so she could have studio space for her art—whichever medium she chose. But I hadn't touched it. I hadn't moved a single thing. Maybe that was one reason she'd never felt like this was her home?

I shook the thought away. She hadn't left because I hadn't made time to make room for her. She'd made her reasons for ending our relationship crystal clear—I wasn't the man for her.

Wandering into the bedroom was almost worse. This was where I'd made love to her. This was where I'd bound and flogged her. This was where she'd submitted to my dominance.

My bed was unmade, the comforter thrown in a heap at the foot, which I knew bothered her. She'd mentioned it when I'd had her immobilized by rope. When she was bound, she said things that were true and significant, but she never gave context, and so I didn't always know what she was talking about.

I found myself slumped in the seating area in front of the bank of windows at one end of my bedroom. Jessica hadn't spent much time here. I couldn't recall a time when she'd sat down in either of the chairs or on the sofa. I couldn't think of an instance when she'd used the sliding glass doors to the balcony.

She'd given me so many signs she didn't feel like she belonged here, and I'd ignored them.

And now she was gone.

Half a bottle of Scotch later, I called her.

She picked up, which wasn't something she always did. Even when we'd been together, she often didn't answer her phone when I called. I hadn't taken it personally because she was in the habit of shutting her phone off and not turning it back on.

"Hey. What's wrong?"

"Something has to be wrong?" My response was automatic. I needed to hear her voice. Maybe that was wrong, but I didn't feel like being right.

"Jesse, it's late, and you're drunk."

"Little bit." I must have been slurring my words. "I wanted to know why the bed not being made bothers you."

She sighed. I imagined her eyes closed and the back of her hand rubbing her forehead, like she did when she was on the verge of exasperation. "It doesn't matter."

"It does too."

"Why are you really calling?"

I missed her. She was everywhere and nowhere, leaving behind a hole in my heart and an ache in my gut, but I wasn't drunk and pathetic enough to admit it. "I haven't seen you in a while. How's the baby doing?"

"The baby is fine. I had a checkup two weeks ago, and the doctor said everything is normal."

A selfish part of me wanted there to be a problem so she would need me to be there for her, but the better half of me was relieved my child was healthy. My saturated brain jumped to a new topic. "Where are you going to do your art? You didn't have to leave just to get away from me."

"Jesse, let it go. It's for the best."

How could she say that? Art meant everything to her. Losing her ability to paint and draw the way she used to had left her devastated and depressed. I'd been there for the worst of it, so I knew firsthand how much it killed her soul not to able to put her vision on canvas.

"It's bullshit, Brat." I defaulted to my nickname for her, from when she was my bratty, headstrong sub. "I was right—you're a coward. You're running away from me, and it's stupid."

Through the phone, I heard her sudden intake of breath. "Jesse, I'm not talking to you when you're drunk. Sleep it off. Good night."

The call disconnected because she hung up on me.

She was right to end the call. I was being an ass because I wanted her back and I didn't know how to make her want to be with me. I'd tried my hardest. I'd been the best Dom I knew how to be, but it hadn't been enough.

I closed my eyes and willed my brain to focus on a problem I could fix. It obliged by jumping to an idea for coding a silent stalker virus that could guide a user's internet activity toward a particular end. It had hundreds of nefarious applications, and I was sure I could use it in a covert mission.

The next morning, I awoke to the ringing of my phone. With a groan, I rolled over and cracked open an eyelid. My head felt cottony, but at least I didn't have a headache. The generic ringtone didn't tell me who was calling, so I let it go to voicemail. Another hour of sleep would clear away the cotton.

Just as I was drifting off, the damn thing rang again, but this time it was David's ringtone. Instantly the cotton cleared from my head. David had headed out this morning for a mission. It was his first with Brea, and so Frankie and I had put ourselves on-call in case something should go south. Brea was great at a lot of things, but she lacked the close-combat fighting skills the rest of us had spent years honing.

The phone was on the floor next to the chair where I'd parked myself to explore the depths of that bottle of Scotch. I flung aside the comforter and rushed to answer before it went to voicemail.

"David, what's wrong?"

"This is Brea."

I'd looked at the display before answering, so I knew she was calling from David's phone. Immediately my brain went to worst-case scenario situations. "Is David in trouble?"

"No. We're fine." She laughed a little, the nervous kind. It was out of character for her, so the feeling something wasn't right didn't go away. "That's not why I'm calling."

"Okay." I waited. My gut was rarely wrong, but I figured this wasn't life-or-death, otherwise Brea wouldn't be nervous. She'd be barreling through the information I needed in order to mount a rescue mission.

"It's about Jessica."

I flopped onto the sofa and sighed. Yes, my drunken call had been ill-advised, but it hadn't been that bad—more on the pathetic/whiny side than anything else. Certainly it was nothing for Jessica to get her panties in a twist about. "What about her?"

"She's stuck at physical therapy. Warren was on his way to pick her up, but there was an accident on the freeway, and it's going to take him at least another two hours to get into the city."

Both Brea and Jessica referred to their biological parents by their first names because they'd only met them a little over a year ago. They'd been kidnapped as children and raised by their kidnapper, which was the source of most of Jessica's emotional problems. If the fucker was alive today, I'd beat him back into the grave.

If Jessica and I had been together, this would have been my problem. I would have been the one slated to drive her to PT and pick her up. But we weren't together, and something wasn't making sense.

"I thought she changed her PT doctor to a place closer to your parents?"

"She did, but they didn't have an opening to start until next week." Brea laughed again, a nervous one. "Look, I'm obviously out of town, and so is David, so we can't help out. Leon can't get there until the afternoon at the earliest. Frankie somehow turned up here with us, and Dean won't have anything to do with Jessica. Can you pick her up? You can take her to my place so she can have lunch and take a nap while she's waiting for Warren."

It looked like Frankie had decided to be proactive as a backup measure. Since I'd been working almost nonstop for the past four months—I'd taken the holidays off to spend with my family—I understood why she felt the need to keep me from responding to a call for help. Brea had to be pissed that Frankie didn't trust her to have David's six.

"Frankie's there? Are you guys in trouble?"

"No." The tightness of her voice confirmed my suspicion. "Can you go get Jessica or not? I'd hate to have to call Dean, but I will if you'd rather continue to avoid her."

I wasn't avoiding her. If anything, she was avoiding me. Moving her business out of my building and transferring her medical care away from me were pretty powerful indicators that she didn't want to be near me. "I don't think she wants to see me."

Brea snorted. "The two of you need to talk so you can learn to be friends again, and I know for a fact she and Dean shouldn't be alone together."

Dean hadn't said anything to me about Jessica, so I wasn't sure what Brea meant. Channeling the cowardice I'd accused Jessica of having last night, I refrained from asking. Dean had been clear about being on my side from the beginning. He'd threatened Jessica that if she broke me, he'd break her. So far, he'd honored my request to he stay out of it.

"I'll go get her." I didn't have to ask how much time I had before her PT ended because I knew her schedule by heart. I had time for a quick shower, and I threw together a sandwich to eat on the way out.

The medical complex was nowhere near the waterfront, so there was no way Jessica would be able to walk from there to Brea's place. I found a parking place in the structure close to the door leading to the PT office. After a session, Jessica was often sore, and I wanted to minimize how much she'd be on her feet afterward.

The lady at the front desk buzzed me into the back where the magic happened. I wound my way through a maze of people with various levels of physical problems. Some were recovering from surgery, others sported injuries. I found Jessica in the back, lying on a padded table. She wore black yoga pants and a light blue cotton shirt with a dolphin on the front. The smallest swell rounded her stomach. I'd thought she'd be bigger. My calculations put her at five months pregnant. Wasn't she supposed to have a larger baby bump by now?

Though her eyes were closed, she wasn't resting. She held an ice pack to her hip, and her lips were pressed together in an effort to suppress a grimace. Traces of sweat dotted her brow.

She liked to tell me that she was going to run a 5K, and I believed that she eventually would. A year ago, she hadn't been able to sit up for very long without it taxing all of her strength. She'd needed help with everything from eating to using the bathroom. In a year's time, she'd come so far. Every obstacle she'd conquered took strength and tenacity, and it was one of the reasons I'd fallen in love with her.

"This is the PT you complain wipes you out?"

Jessica's eyes flew open, and she sat up halfway. Surprise widened her brilliant green eyes, and her gaze roamed my body, drinking it in with a hint of desperation. Her breaths came faster, and she froze, which I knew meant she was combating an urge to move toward me. This was the first time I'd been alone with her since she'd ended our relationship, and it was heartening to see that I still had an effect on her.

Then she got herself under control. Her nostrils flared and her lip curled, and she settled back on the table. "What are you doing here?"

"Your dad is stuck in traffic."

"Warren called *you*?"

I tried not to take her umbrage personally even though her entire objection was based on personal reasons. "Brea called. She's on a mission with David and Frankie, and Leon can't leave work. It was me or Dean. Brea said you and Dean aren't getting along."

Her gaze sidled away, and her lips pressed together so hard they turned white. Then she exhaled. "We're fine."

I knew she was lying, so I lifted my eyebrows and took my phone from my pocket. "Did you want me to call him so you don't have to deal with me?"

"You're already here." She glanced away, turning the nervous tell into a sweep of the room. "Malik should be back in a minute."

That must be her physical therapist. No reply was required, so I said nothing. It didn't take long for the silence to wear on her nerves.

"Are you taking me home?"

"If you want." Traffic might be tied up on the freeway, but I knew other ways out of the city.

She took a deep breath. "What are my options?"

"Home or Brea's place."

Irritation flashed in her eyes. "I'll go to Brea's."

I nodded as a tall, athletic man wearing sweatpants and a polo shirt came over to her. He had the physique of a man who worked out but who knew nothing about combat. His clothes had the logo of the place on them, so I figured he was her physical therapist.

He didn't seem to notice me because his gaze was on Jessica. He smiled and took the ice pack. "That's enough icing it for now." He tossed the pack onto the empty therapy table behind him. Then he put his hands on Jessica's hip. He dug into her flesh, and she hissed at the pain.

My gaze went to her face where new beads of sweat were breaking out.

Malik didn't seem to notice her discomfort. "Swelling has gone down some. Okay, you're going to ice it for twenty minutes every hour for the next four hours."

His gaze lifted, and he seemed to notice me. He flashed a polite smile. I nodded in return.

Jessica grunted as she sat up and swung her legs down. "Malik, this is Jesse. He's a friend of the family who drew the short straw on giving me a ride home. Jesse, this is Malik, the sadist who spends several hours each week torturing me."

Malik's polite façade didn't crack. "Hi, Jesse. It's nice to meet you."

I figured that she must not tell him much about her personal life, which made sense. Jessica wasn't open with many people, even when she liked them. Before I could respond, she piped up again.

"Jesse doesn't talk much." Her lips curled slyly. "He's shy."

I flashed a warning without using words. When Jessica was agitated or felt vulnerable, she lashed out verbally. Right now, it seemed she was playing offense.

"The strong, silent type," she continued, ignoring my warning. "Really, he can speak, but years of steroids have made his voice falsetto, so he rarely says anything until he gets to know someone. Don't take it personally."

With a curious frown, Malik looked me up and down.

I worked out in the gym and in the field. Though Malik was taller than me, he was not bigger. He looked like a teenage boy compared to me.

In my regular, deep voice, I said, "She's full of shit."

Malik's face softened, and he laughed. "I know. She likes to tease." His attention returned to Jessica. "You're progressing well. I've sent your records over to your new place. Your new therapist is a friend of mine. You'll be in good hands." Malik handed her a thick elastic band. "Same homework as before, which I know you'll do."

"Damn right I will."

Malik grinned. "You did amazing today. Don't push it too much. No more running until tomorrow, and only moderate exercise."

I walked her to the cubbies where patients kept their stuff. She grabbed her bag and cane. I knew she was exhausted when she didn't complain about me getting the door for her.

We slowly made our way to the parking garage, and I searched my brain for acceptable topics of conversation, but I came up empty. My heart screamed at me to talk to her. Brea had said Jessica and I needed to reestablish our friendship. I knew it needed to be done, but right now I was too busy vacillating between anger and the urge to throw myself at her feet and beg for another chance.

When we got into my truck, Jessica leaned her head back and closed her eyes, a clear signal that she didn't want to talk to me.

Perhaps neither of us was ready.

I stopped outside David and Brea's building. "Do you need help getting upstairs?"

She ran the tip of her finger over the head of her cane. "I can do it."

"Jessica, it's okay to ask me for stuff. Just because we're not—" Breaking off, I scrubbed a hand over the stubble on my jaw. One of the reasons she'd ended our relationship was because I didn't listen to what she was saying. "Warren should be along in a couple of hours."

Her gaze lifted, landing on me briefly like a doe unsure of the danger. She swallowed. "Thank you."

Not sure if she was thanking me for the ride or for honoring her assertion, I nodded. "Anytime."

I watched, holding up traffic, until she was safely inside the building. Being with her, even for a half hour, was a bittersweet experience. The heaviness of all the things we couldn't say hung between us. It stung that I'd lost a friend as well as a lover. I wanted to hold her hand, kiss her cheek, and touch the small swell of her abdomen. Acid burned in my stomach because I had to watch the mother of my child walk away. It cleared the way for the anger churning in my gut to return, but this time it failed to make me feel better. Too much grief and guilt had seeped into the mix.

Back at my place, I got ready for Wendy's visit. I'd met Wendy eight years before when I'd consulted with the KCPD on a case. When she'd decided she wanted to try out a D/s relationship but her husband had no interest, they'd asked me to be her Dom.

My bondage equipment was set up in the bedroom half of my loft. Since Wendy and I weren't romantically or sexually involved, I made sure to keep her away from my bed. I'd set down a hard limit right off about nobody being allowed to touch the bed. In fact, the half of my room with the bed was elevated from the part with my dungeon equipment, and so nobody was even allowed up the single step.

I set out a sturdy cot and put a waterproof cover over it. While I cleaned my equipment after each use, I kept separate equipment for each of my subs. Inside the storage closet, I ran my hand along the rim of the laundry basket filled with Jessica's items. It was the only basket that contained sex toys. Lifting out a vibrator, I recalled how her body had writhed when I'd tied her to my bed and forced her to orgasm.

She'd loved it.

And then the next day, she'd changed her mind. Or lied. I don't think she even knew which she'd done.

Shaking off the malaise threatening to overtake me, I grabbed Wendy's basket. It held three different floggers, a cat, two rattan canes, and six lengths of rope. Additionally, a smaller bag inside contained the aftercare lotions she preferred. I set out two floggers, the cat, and a cane. Then I checked the rope to make sure it was smooth and unbroken.

A knock sounded at the door at the scheduled time. I opened it up to find Wendy on the other side. Her gaze was lowered submissively, and her husband, Marc, stood next to her. Wendy was younger than me by ten years, as was Marc. She had an average build, dirty blonde hair that she'd twisted in a knot on top of her head, and light brown eyes. I'd be lying if I said I didn't think she was pretty, but I didn't find her attractive. Other than being a submissive, she was not at all my type.

"Hey, guys. How are you?" I shook hands with Marc and hugged Wendy.

"Great." Marc chuckled. "She's been looking forward to this all week."

I closed the door and frowned. When I'd talked to her the night before, she hadn't mentioned anything. "Tough week?"

"Tough couple of weeks, Sir." Wendy's subdued tone had the perfect amount of subservience to it, a submissive addressing her Dom.

"Do you want to sit and talk first?" I motioned toward the sofa, which was neutral territory. Sometimes it was difficult to get a sub to subspace when they were too stressed. Wendy and Marc often talked with me before a scene.

"That's not necessary." Wendy's gaze locked on the floor.

Marc rubbed a hand up and down her back. "She's okay. She just needs to relax and let all the stress drain out."

"Sure." I faced Wendy. "If you need to stop, use your safeword."

"Yes, Sir."

I spread my palm toward the sofa. "Marc, make yourself at home. Same routine as usual today."

He disliked watching the impact play, but he was fascinated by the Shibari designs I wove on Wendy. I'd offered to teach him, but he'd turned me down.

I escorted Wendy into the play space, and I closed the barn door behind me. Marc knew he was welcome to join us at any time, but I knew he preferred not to hear the flogger. As Wendy peeled out of her shoes, shirt, and pants, I heard the sound of voices on the television.

She knelt before me in plain white underwear and a tank top, her gaze lowered. Normally I would look her over, reveling in the power she surrendered to me, but today, something about this rang hollow.

Jessica had never knelt for me. She'd lowered her gaze, and she'd tried to be my submissive, but she'd never seemed to embrace it the way Wendy did. With Jessica, it often seemed like a role she was playing; with Wendy, it was the core of who she was.

Comparing them wasn't productive or fair. Shaking away thoughts of Jessica, I stroked a strand of hair away from Wendy's face. I needed to know she truly didn't want to talk first. Perhaps she wanted to say something to me in confidence? "What's your color?"

"Green, Sir."

"You know you can tell me anything, right?"

"Yes, Sir."

When she didn't elaborate, I gave the next order. "Go stand in front of the flogging wall."

Some people had a St. Andrew's Cross to bind a sub for flogging, but I had a series of two-by-fours nailed horizontally to the wall at heights suitable for binding a person at different levels.

Wendy positioned herself in front of it. She waited, facing the wall, with her legs spread shoulder-width apart and her hands clasped behind her neck. I took a moment to admire her perfect positioning, but I stopped when my brain superimposed Jessica's curves over Wendy's. The two women had very different builds, both beautiful, but nothing about Wendy should bring to mind anything about the woman who possessed my heart even though she didn't want it.

Plus, given her physical limitations, she couldn't handle being bound to a flogging wall. According to the doctor I'd consulted, it would aggravate her problem areas and set back her recovery—unless I used a body harness or something like that to take the pressure off her spine.

Back to Wendy. I needed to focus on my sub. I needed to lose myself in being her Dom because that would provide salve I sorely needed.

"Shirt."

A hard limit for Marc was that I not see or touch Wendy's breasts, but flogging was a better experience on bare flesh. Therefore, I had her face the wall before removing her shirt to expose her back. She lifted it over her head and tossed it to the side. Practice gave her good aim, and it landed on the cot.

I buckled leather cuffs around her wrists and above her knees. A spreader bar kept her from moving too much, and I used carabiners to attach her to the eye hooks of my flogging wall. Then I doubled up a thick rope and bound her waist to the wall so that she couldn't twist out of the way too much when I used the cane.

Once she was secure, I ran the falls of the heater over her flesh. She moaned, and a shiver of pleasure shook her body.

"You like that, sub?"

"Yes, Sir."

"What do you want?" Our scenes were highly scripted, and she liked to beg as much as I loved to hear it.

"Sir, please flog me."

"How badly do you want it?"

"Very much, Sir. I long to feel the kiss of your flogger. I'm begging for the sting of your Dominance. Please, Sir." Her tone communicated submissive need, and for the first time ever, it failed to sufficiently stoke the flames of my dominant nature.

Rather than force her to beg more, I stuck to the script. Deviations from the agreed-upon scene threw Wendy off and damaged the efficacy of our session. I didn't know why she was stressed, but she was, and it fell to me to help her deal with it.

I started lightly to warm her up before switching to something with more bite. As I got going, the clutter in my mind cleared. My world became this task. I took Wendy to a blissful place where pain turned to pleasure, and when she was flying, I delivered two strokes with the cane.

I freed her arms first, and I handed her a towel to wrap around her torso while I unbound her legs. Then I led her to the cot where she settled on her stomach. Aftercare was my favorite part. I massaged arnica cream into the sore muscles of her back and thighs. Another hard limit dictated I avoid flogging her ass. I was pretty sure it was due to the fact that Marc didn't want another man massaging his wife's ass, and I understood his position. Wendy and I may not have a romantic or sexual association, but a woman's ass could be an erogenous zone. It was for Jessica. She loved when I touched her ass, and she especially liked when I slapped it during sex.

How the fuck could she think she wasn't submissive?

My mind chose that moment to play with me. I heard her voice coming from the other room. There was no way in hell she would come here on her own, so I knew it was wishful thinking.

Still, as I approached the barn door to let Marc know it was time for his part of the aftercare, my heartbeat sped up in anticipation even though I knew full well it was doomed for disappointment.

Chapter 3—Jessica

After Jesse dropped me off, I heated up leftover Thai food from Brea's refrigerator. Since she planned to be gone for a couple of days, I didn't think she or David would care if I cleaned out food they'd have to toss once they returned home.

Her new place was beautiful. The building had been a bank back in the days when such structures were works of art. A developer had turned it into condos, and now my sister lived in a top-floor penthouse. Each room was large, and it had fourteen-foot ceilings throughout. Some of the walls even had marble inlays, and the vintage windows let in tons of light.

It was a perfect place for me to have an art studio.

But that would never happen. David and Brea had planned for me to come live with them when I got out of my rehab facility, but I'd chosen to move in with Warren and Sylvia instead. Though I hadn't known my birth parents all that well, they seemed like good people. And I thought it would be better to live with them than crash the pad of a newly married couple. Brea needed time alone with David.

In this new place of theirs, I had my own room. This was leftover from when Brea used to stay home while David was on missions, and I would stay with Brea when he was gone. Now that she was also working as a security specialist, I didn't know if I would be staying over as often.

But it was nice to have a place to go since Dean had effectively kicked me out of Unexpected Treasures. He knew I couldn't pay market rate for that storefront, and he'd known full well raising the rent that high would force me out. And I knew exactly why he'd done it—he wanted me as far away from Jesse as he could get me.

It would be easier for Jesse to get over me if I wasn't hanging around all the time.

If I was in Dean's shoes, I would have done the same thing to protect my friend. A huge part of me agreed with Dean, which was why I hadn't told anyone but Leon the real reason I'd moved all my stuff out of the store. I knew that Brea would go to war against Dean on my behalf. David and Frankie would agree with her, but that's only because they'd both sought me out separately to swear to me that they weren't taking sides.

David had said that Brea wasn't taking sides either, but she'd merely rolled her eyes at the idea. Of course she was on my side. Our whole lives, it had been us against the world. She wouldn't abandon me, not for any reason.

As I ate, I called Warren. "I'm at Brea's, and I'm having lunch."

"I'm still stuck in traffic."

I flipped on the television and checked out the local reports. "It's a chemical spill. They've closed the freeway." I sighed. "Head home. I'm going to take a nap, and I'm okay with hanging out here. Worst-case scenario, I stay the night."

"I don't like to leave you alone this long. What if you have a seizure?" He cleared his throat, which meant he was really worried.

"I've been seizure-free for nine months. I'm fine. I promise."

His sigh sounded a lot like a grunt. "Maybe you could call Jesse?"

I knew he'd already talked to Brea, and he knew Frankie and David were on a mission with her, and Dean and I weren't on friendly terms. We weren't enemies, but he'd made it clear where his loyalties lay. I respected that about him.

"If I need to, I will."

I napped in my room. An hour later, I woke up refreshed. I flung open the curtains to the balcony. Birds sang, and one landed on my outstretched finger. Okay, that's a lie. Brea didn't have curtains on the sliding door to the balcony, and the only bird-related activity involved me shooing away a seagull from perching on the ledge. But it was a beautiful winter day, and I didn't want to be a princess trapped in this lovely tower.

Waiting for a prince to come to her rescue...

Seeing Jesse without anyone around to run interference had been harder than I'd thought it would be. He'd been one of the few people I considered a friend. I longed to talk to him without the awkwardness, and I longed to feel his arms around me. Breaking up with him was the hardest thing I'd ever done, but I didn't regret it. I wasn't the kind of woman who could make him happy, and he wanted things from me that made me unhappy. Part of me would always love him. Okay, maybe all of me would always love him, but it didn't matter. I wasn't submissive, and I didn't want to be.

That left our baby as a connection. My next obstetric checkup was in two weeks, and they planned to do another ultrasound. That was the sort of thing Jesse should be present for, and I vowed to invite him. We also needed to discuss plans for the birth and what life would look like after the baby was born. Jesse had every intention of being fully involved in the raising of his child.

This was a conversation that needed to take place face-to-face.

Before my resolve could weaken—because I could talk myself out of it pretty easily—I borrowed a heavier jacket from Brea's closet. Jesse's loft wasn't far from Brea and David's new digs. I estimated a walk of a little over a mile. It wasn't bad. Definitely it was moderate exercise, which meant I wasn't disobeying Malik's rules.

I locked up and set out. My hip was still sore from PT, so I took my time, hobbling down the sidewalk and stopping at a couple winterized fountains to rest up. I missed the water and the warmer weather, though right now it wasn't as cold as a normal winter. By the time I exited the elevator in Jesse's building, I was tired again.

I paused at the door, hesitating because anxiety clogged my throat. What if he was still too angry and hurt to talk to me? What if he tried to seduce me? I wasn't sure I'd turn him down. The ache in my heart echoed painfully through my body. The flesh was definitely weak where he was concerned.

Girding my loins against whatever was coming my way, I knocked.

A few moments later, the door opened, and a man I'd never seen stood on the other side. I wasn't under the impression I knew all of Jesse's friends, but it was unusual for anyone but Jesse to answer his door.

"Hi." I smiled brightly. "Is Jesse home?"

He opened the door wider. I put him in his early thirties. The laugh lines around his mouth and eyes softened his features even when his smile was tentative. He was perhaps six feet tall, and he had an average build. "Is he expecting you?"

My nerves fired random warning shots. Jesse was not expecting me, and I was relatively sure he didn't want to see me at all. Affecting my best smile, I tilted my head and pushed past the guy into the loft that had almost been my home. "He won't be surprised to see me."

He'd be shocked as hell, but he'd hide his reaction because big, bad Dom-types didn't tip their hand.

Inside, I saw no one. Alarm bells sounded in my brain, but I wasn't sure what they meant. The door to Jesse's bedroom was closed, but that didn't mean much. When people were over, he usually kept it closed. That room was private.

That room held his bondage equipment.

Fuck.

I couldn't have picked a worse time for an unannounced visit.

Morbid curiosity overrode my need to flee. "You must be Marc."

Surprise flashed in his eyes. "Yes. I'm sorry, but I've never run into another person here before. Forgive me if this is a bit weird. Who are you?"

"Jessica." I pointed, indicating the other room. "Is Wendy just getting started?"

"It shouldn't be too much longer." He motioned for me to follow him to the living area. "You're Jesse's girlfriend, right? He told us about you a few months ago. I thought you were moving in?"

I sat down on the comfortable leather sofa and leaned my cane against the side. "We broke up."

"Oh." Marc chewed his lower lip, probably thinking he shouldn't have let me inside. "I'm sorry to hear that."

I waved away his concern. "We're better off as friends."

He assessed me with knowing brown eyes. "You're still his sub?"

I chuckled because the opposite was true. I'd never wanted to be his sub. "Hell, no. I don't go in for that kind of thing." I realized how that sounded, and I heard Brea's voice in my head, warning me against judging people who embraced the BDSM lifestyle. "No offense intended."

"None taken."

At no point in my life had I wanted to be around while Jesse was with one of his subs. Picturing him in there with another woman went a long way toward dowsing the little fires that started in my core at the prospect of seeing Jesse. It also hurt. When we were together, I'd spent a lot of time rationalizing his need to have subs in his life and the reasons I'd needed to shut up and accept it.

Now that we were broken up, my heart was free to feel only the pain. I'd fucking hated that I hadn't been enough for him. Perhaps coming here now was good for me. It only underlined the correctness of my decision and all the reasons Jesse and I were wrong together.

We could talk about the doctor's appointment later.

I'd send him a text. I reached into my pocket for my phone, but it wasn't there. It had been there when I'd left Brea's, and so I mentally retraced my steps. I hadn't removed it from my pocket once.

I looked to see if it had fallen out when I'd sat down.

"Lose something?"

"My phone. I was going to text Jesse and leave, but my phone seems to have gone AWOL."

Marc stuck his hands in the cushions near him, helping with the search. "I'm not into this stuff either. I tried years ago when Wendy expressed an interest, but I just couldn't find the joy in flogging my wife even though she loves it. And the D/s dynamic just isn't right for our relationship."

In the midst of digging between the back of the sofa and the seat, I paused. So many questions cruised through my mind, each crashing into a distinct desire to remain ignorant.

"If you have questions, just fire them off. I'm okay with talking to you about this. I know this setup is unconventional."

"It's none of my business."

He chuckled and sat down, giving up the search for my phone. "Jesse must have told you about Wendy and me."

"Nope." I resumed my search for the phone. He'd tried, but I hadn't wanted to hear it. Still didn't. "It's Jesse's life, not mine, and I'm not interested in the details. We're not buddies like that."

Marc kicked off his shoes and folded his legs. "But you used to be. What kind of buddies are you now?"

When had we turned into twelve-year-old girls who dished about this kind of crap? This was not the conversation I wanted to be having with a perfect stranger while Jesse flogged the man's wife in the next room. I'm sure my pain was evident in the scowl on my face. I opted for a partial truth. "Mercenary buddies. Last time, we went to San Tesoro where we carried out an op to stop a notorious hacker from releasing sensitive information about CIA operatives and the current administration."

I felt Marc's stare as I continued searching for my phone. Damn thing wasn't in the cushions. I knelt down to check to see if it had fallen under the sofa.

"Seriously?"

At Marc's incredulous question, I peeked up. It did my heart good to find the blood had drained from his face. "You didn't know Jesse was a merc? What the hell else did you think an ex-Special Forces guy who calls himself a 'security specialist' would do?"

"My—my wife is a sergeant for the KCPD."

"So she knows." Underneath the sofa was dark, and the clearance was low. If I had my phone, I could use the flashlight app to shed light on the situation. Irony sucked. Lowering down more, I stuck my arm under to feel around.

"No, she doesn't know. She'd never knowingly spend time with a criminal."

I took offense to that. Jesse didn't go around committing crimes for the fun of it. He did it if and when it was required to complete his mission. "He's not a criminal, and even if he was, the KCPD doesn't care. I mean, they totally enabled Brick Dixon for years. Why would they get their panties in a twist about a guy who does good things? We saved the lives of countless American undercover operatives around the world." We had also saved the asses of several people high up in political circles, though I cared less about them. The CIA operatives were people to whom I could relate. They led lives much like the one I had before, ones that involved different identities and questionable moral choices.

I found my phone. Barely grasping it with the tips of my fingers, I dragged it closer until I could get a better grip. Then I slid it out and tried to stand up. No go. Pain seared through my hip and my lower back, so I eased my body over, and I sat with my back against the sofa.

Marc cleared his throat. "I'm going to get some water. Are you thirsty?"

Now that he'd mentioned it, I was in need of fluids. "I could use some water."

He left, and I tried to move. Bracing my hands on the seat cushion, I tried to leverage myself up. Being on the floor was never a good thing. If I could get on the sofa, I had a better chance of being able to work out the problem. It was usually a pinched nerve. I moved an inch before spasms pummeled the base of my spine, so I eased myself back down. The spasms decreased in intensity.

Marc handed a glass to me. I got two coasters from the narrow drawer under the table and threw one across the way where Marc had once again taken his seat. It would serve Jesse right to come out to find rings on his wood.

"Thanks." He set his glass down. "So, you're a mercenary?"

I shrugged. "Sure." Mercenary, con artist—what was the difference?

"And you work for Jesse at SAFE Security?"

"Sometimes I work with him. Mostly I freelance." I sipped my water. I did not freelance. I did not work with Jesse. I could do all of those things, but I didn't want that kind of life. I wanted to be an artist. Though I couldn't quite remember my skills, I was working on developing new ones. My will would prevail over my brain damage. "Why? Are you looking to hire out a job?"

"No." He stumbled over his tongue to blurt out that denial. "No. Definitely not. I'm not sure what exactly a mercenary does besides kill people for money."

I arched a brow, affecting disdain through a withering glare. In the midst of all the pain I felt from being here and in this situation, it felt good to play a role. Lying and conning were two of the best treatments for what ailed me.

"You're thinking of an assassin, which is different. We don't kill people—for money or any other reason. We just do dangerous things, like rescue someone who has been kidnapped, guard people and their valuables when they are in danger, and save the government when they can't afford to be officially associated with the operation. Things like that."

He put his hand on his neck. "Is that where Jesse gets hurt? I noticed the stitches and the bandage when we were here last fall, and he had a shiner a couple months ago."

"Last fall, someone objected to us stealing their servers, so they tried to slit Jesse's throat." Marc's color returned with a vengeance. He'd gone from pale to purple, and he choked on his water.

I wiped my phone on my pants to dust the screen.

Marc held his water with two hands as if the clear liquid held answers to deep questions. After a few moments, he chuckled. "So, he's one of the good guys."

The last thing I needed was to give this guy the delusion that Jesse was a superhero. "He's human, with faults and all that."

"Has he ever saved your life?"

I'd be lying if I denied it. There was a better than even chance I'd be dead today if Jesse hadn't been in my life. "Yes, and I've saved his. Like I said—mercenary buddies."

We sipped in silence; Marc's was thoughtful, while mine was pensive. I really wanted to get out of here, but I was stuck until my lower back stopped spasming. Five more minutes, and I'd try again.

Marc looked at me and frowned. "Why are you sitting on the floor? You found your phone."

"I couldn't abandon this stimulating conversation."

A single brow arched. "Seriously—are you okay?"

I wrinkled my nose. "I'll be okay in a minute. I messed up my back, and sometimes I have to let it rest before I can get up."

"Can I help you?"

"I'll be fine. Happens all the time." It didn't happen all the time because I typically avoided sitting on the floor, but I was committed to the lies.

"If you change your mind, let me know."

"Are you in the medical field?" I didn't understand why he cared, unless he wanted to get rid of me because this afternoon was a private experience between him, his wife, and her Dom—though it seemed to primarily be between his wife and her Dom.

33

"Investment banker." He glanced around the room. "Do you mind if I turn up the TV? I'm not a huge fan of hearing the flogger." He grimaced to emphasize his point.

"Go ahead." I'd blocked out the sound, and the shape of the sofa had done a great job of deadening the noise in my current location. The remote was near me, so I tossed it to him.

I tried again to lift myself from the floor. The resulting spasms in my back had decreased in strength, so I took that as a good sign. I rolled, aiming to get on my hands and knees so I could better leverage myself to stand. My arms were strong, and so was one leg. I would prevail against my left leg and lower back if it killed me.

"She's in subspace now, but she won't be there for long. You weren't kidding when you said she was extra stressed."

So absorbed in moving slowly and fighting the pain, I hadn't heard Jesse come into the living room. Fuck. There went my plan for a smooth escape before he knew I was there.

Marc stood and drummed his fingers on his thigh. "Fifteen minutes?"

"I'll knock."

Though I heard this conversation, I didn't understand it, and I didn't much care to figure it out. I had other concerns. I braced one hand on the sofa and the other on the coffee table, grunting against the way the spasm intensified. If I could get past this point, I'd be fine.

"Jesus fucking Christ. What the hell are you doing?"

Jesse hauled me to my feet, and I cried out as pain stabbed through my back and down my leg. I gripped his biceps hard, digging my fingers into his flesh to mitigate the pain. "Too fast, you sadistic son of a bitch."

"What the hell are you doing here, and why didn't you ask Marc to come get me? How long have you been stuck and hurting?" He held me against him, his hands kneading my lower back while his breath fanned my cheek and sent shivers to compete with the pain.

The hardness of my abdomen pressed into his, and I wondered if he could feel the evidence of his child growing inside me. Tears pricked my eyes, traitorous shards that drove home just how weak and pathetic I was. Part of me wanted to melt into his embrace, but most of me wanted to punch him in the gut. I shoved against him. "I'm fine."

"Liar."

"Let go of me."

"Shut up, Brat." He lifted me and set me on the sofa so I was on my stomach. His warm hands kneaded and stretched, pushing and

34

pulling at my rebellious and fatigued muscles. He pressed his thumb against a spot that stole my ability to inhale.

"Fuck. Not there," I croaked.

The pressure eased. "It's your pinched nerve." He rubbed concentric circles around the area that marked the pinnacle of pain. "Breathe through it."

He'd probably told his sub to breathe through it as well. I huffed. "I'm fine. Help me up so I can leave."

"You came all this way just to leave?"

"It's not far. I went out for a walk, and I got tired. I stopped here because it was the closest place I could find."

"Hmm." His thumb moved to another knot. "You're slipping, Brat. You used to be a better liar."

I was a fucking fantastic liar. I'd spent the past ten minutes lying to a cop's husband, and he hadn't noticed. My back was feeling a ton better, and even if it wasn't, nothing was going to stop me from getting up—not a little pain or my own frailty. Planting my palms on the sofa, I pushed with all my might.

Jesse had leverage and weight on his side. He pressed down on my upper and lower back, and my spine crackled. Bones moved into place, startling us both. He eased the pressure. "Are you okay?"

The searing pain had vanished, but I tested my movements gingerly. I sat up with no problem, and then I stood. My spine felt loose and free of tension. I knew this feeling was temporary because my PT manipulated my bones during sessions. As long as I stayed off the floor, I'd be fine for a few hours.

Though it was a dangerous move, I met his gaze. I flashed a tight smile. "Peachy."

"Liar." His tone lacked heat but somehow managed to make the word sizzle with meaning.

Ready for battle, I squared my shoulders. "Jesse, I don't like when you call me names like 'liar' and 'brat.' It hurts my feelings. Please stop."

He arched one eyebrow and pursed his lips. "You're learning I-statements in therapy now?"

"Don't judge how I express my feelings." I bristled. Feelings were difficult for me to express, but they were often harder to identify or admit I felt them. I had come a long way, and I aimed to not lose my progress.

"You're full of shit, *Brat*, and if you don't want me to call you out on your lies, then stop lying. Actions have consequences. Have you learned that yet in therapy?"

I glared, throwing a punch with my eyes. "Don't make fun of me for going to therapy, jackass. You, of all people, know how much I need it."

"Don't call me a jackass."

Narrowing my eyes, I concentrated the full power of my glare. Anger rolled from me in waves, though Jesse didn't seem particularly upset. I hated that he was immune to my emotions. I hated that I had them where he was concerned. The fact he was keeping his cool while I battled the urge to punch him in the gut made this interaction harder. "Don't call me names, and I won't call you names."

His lips curved in a leonine smile, and my thighs quivered. "Well played." He stepped back and offered his hand. "Truce?"

I'd come here to find common ground. We needed it if we were going to raise a child together. I accepted his hand. "Truce."

"Why don't you watch this next part of the scene?" He kept his tone carefully neutral. "I think you'll like it."

My stomach dropped as I vividly remembered how much I'd loved bondage with Jesse. For some reason, being bound with rope sent me directly to subspace. I doused my tone with all the acid burning through my stomach. "If it's all the same to you, I really don't want to watch your sexcapades."

He pressed his lips together, probably an effort to not rehash things he'd already said. "Wendy is having sex with Marc right now. It's the reason I set up a bed and a private area for them."

"That's smart. I wouldn't want other people fucking in my bed either."

"I'm glad you approve." Sarcasm dripped like acid, and he scowled. "Ten minutes."

I closed my eyes. Would ten minutes of watching him work his magic on another woman be enough to cauterize the way my heart bled every time I looked at Jesse? Maybe it would help me move past the pain so I could focus on co-parenting with him? At best, it would limit the scenarios my imagination used for torturing me.

"Jesse?"

Marc's voice was a welcome reprieve. I turned away from Jesse to think about whether this was a good decision. Where he was concerned, I'd always made questionable choices.

"Is she ready?"

"Yeah. She's in position." Marc ducked back into the room.

I turned off the television, and the wrestling announcer ceased yelling about the cosplay. Jesse headed into the bedroom, and like a reluctant masochist, I followed.

Marc was seated on a chair he'd dragged over from the seating area near the windows. I perched on the edge of Jesse's bed.

"I'll get you a chair." Marc got up. "There's a rule about not touching the bed."

I glanced around, taking in the bed in which I'd experienced incredible ecstasy. It was no longer a place I was welcome. "Thanks."

Jesse ignored us. All his attention was on Wendy. I'd never seen her before. She was about my size and full of soft curves. Her breasts, hidden behind a plain camisole, were slightly smaller than mine. She had long blonde hair, where I had shorn my brown locks so they hung just below my ears. Wendy had rich brown eyes that had a sleepy, sated look to them. My green irises caught people's attention, but my iciness usually took care of anyone whose gaze lingered longer than I wanted.

Jesse walked around her, dragging his knowing gaze across her flesh. She wasn't naked. In addition to the cami, she wore underwear. These weren't sexy panties; they were cotton briefs. On her feet, she had plain white athletic footies to keep her feet warm. Wendy hadn't dressed to impress.

Once he was satisfied everything was the way he wanted, he snagged a coiled rope from a nearby table. He folded it in half and looped it around her ribs just under her breasts. Then he wound the lines over her shoulders. He went around back and manipulated the silky rope, and then he brought it around front by way of tying her upper arms in place.

The whole damned thing smacked of intimacy, especially the dreamy look in Wendy's eyes. Yeah, I'd made the right decision in staying away from this when we'd been together. Jealousy would have made me do and say horrible things. I felt the urge now, but I didn't have a need to act on it. Jesse wasn't mine, and he could do anything he wanted with anyone he wanted.

I glanced at Marc to see how he was handling watching another man touch his wife. Marc seemed to be doing fine. The expectant expression on his face promised some kind of bliss. I wasn't sure who was going to be in the receiving end of that bliss—Marc, Wendy, or Jesse, but I was sure no permutation of this scenario involved me.

Yeah, I felt left out.

Strangely, I was also inexorably pulled in, unable to look away to deliver a beat-down to the green-eyed monster festering in my core. I needed that beast to kill the love I still felt for a man who was completely wrong for me.

Over her chest, he wove a web. As I watched, he bent one arm up so her hand rested on the opposite shoulder, and he weaved it into the design. Unfinished as it was, the web was remarkably beautiful.

This was art.

When I'd been in Wendy's position, I'd known what he did was beautiful, but I hadn't been able to fully appreciate the visual aesthetic. Now I could.

He stopped every now and again to ask her how she was doing. Each time, she'd smile brilliantly and answer, "Green, Sir."

By now, my mind would have been long gone.

I stayed far longer than I'd intended, watching him weave a spell with each inch of his rope. A hush had fallen over the room, enveloping even the delicate horns from the soft jazz floateding around us, so that the music seemed to come from down a long hall in a black-and-white dream. The entirety of his focus was on her, on the ropes he wove over her reddened skin, on every breath and sigh, the soft moans that occasionally escaped from between her delicate, parted lips. Before my eyes, Jesse grew. He'd always dominated a room, but now he swelled so his presence overshadowed everything else. Wendy, Marc, and I were riveted on him, on what he was doing, and he funneled every ounce of that energy into Wendy. She positively glowed.

This was worse than watching Jesse have sex with another woman. I was watching him be intimate with another woman. I was watching him touch her, create art around her, weave her into the center of his masterpiece. It was beautiful and terrible, hypnotic and heartrending.

My pulse beat faster as I struggled to keep the panic at bay. I wanted this with him—the intimacy and the art—but I didn't want to be his submissive all the time. Bitterness constricted my lungs, and when I noticed the bulge at the apex of Jesse's pants, pain seared my chest. My heart stopped, and I couldn't breathe. Hands pressed to my heart, I fled on silent feet.

On the street in front of Jesse's building, I turned right. SAFE Security and Brea's place were to the left, and I didn't want to take the chance that Jesse would find me. I wanted to be alone to untangle the knots in the gut of my psyche. Aimless wandering was not something I did. Even when I didn't have a clear destination in mind, I'd been trained to appear like I did. *Walk like you belong,* BS used to say. So my feet took strong, resolute steps, even though I had no clue where I was going.

I'd wanted to eradicate Jesse from my heart, but all I'd done was shoot air holes to let the sting worsen. This wasn't supposed to happen. I wasn't supposed to care what he did and who he did it with.

The only thing I knew for certain was that I wasn't going to cry. I wasn't going to think about the near-rapture on Wendy's face or the way Jesse had looked at her and touched her. That wasn't what I wanted from him.

A chill wind snaked around the corner, reminding me I'd left my jacket at Jesse's place. I shivered through it, convincing myself I didn't need a coat. The breeze kicked up again, and I let it push me, invisible cords drawing me to my death.

Only it didn't kill me. When the wind died away, I found myself on the sidewalk in front of Art Attack, an art supply store. I hadn't been here in months, not since my art therapy sessions had stopped. Deshaun Johnson, the store owner, had taught the six-week course that had helped me regain some of my manual dexterity. I'd brought Brea here once to finger paint. Then she'd splurged, buying me a load of art supplies with the hope that I'd start painting again.

Given the fact that my brain wouldn't cooperate with my hand to put the vision in my mind onto canvas, the supplies were mostly useless. Thanks to Leon and, if I were being honest, Jesse, I was dabbling in other media. Leon had given me oil pastels and charcoals, and Warren had given me full access to his carpentry equipment. All of them encouraged me to try different things.

With Unexpected Treasures, I'd been steadily repurposing unwanted pieces. I made wine racks from old window frames, corner shelves from old doors, chairs from dressers, and tables from parts of old farm equipment. When I finished with them, the pieces looked new and chic, and I sold them fairly quickly.

When I'd found out I was losing the store, Leon and Sylvia had helped me build a website, and now I had online orders to fill. Though it wasn't the kind of art I wanted to do, it was still art. In the last few months, I'd devoted myself to finishing more pieces, and my dedication was beginning to pay off.

Maybe I wasn't fulfilling my dream, but I was getting by. Would that be enough to earn my child's respect? I wanted very badly to be a role model, but I wasn't sure I'd ever done anything all that worthwhile.

"It's not that bad."

The voice startled me. I pressed my hand to my heart. Given my normal hypervigilant state, it was rare for anyone to take me by surprise. Even so, I gathered my wits quickly. Painted on the store window was a scene depicting the outline of what might one day be a cupid.

I threw a smile at Deshaun, the man who'd taught a class at my PT place that helped people recover manual dexterity. He'd noticed my skill, and we'd talked a lot about art. I motioned to the outline. "It's not finished."

"You were scowling like you were thinking about throwing a punch. The glass is reinforced with some advanced tech that keeps it from shattering, but that just means it'll do some serious damage to your hand." His smile reached his eyes, as it always had. "And since I've seen your potential, I'd hate for you to wreck your hand."

As I had been during therapy, I was drawn to his inner glow. Calling it attraction was a bit of a stretch. Deshaun lived a life I envied. He spent every day focused on art, whether he was creating, teaching, or selling. That was the life I wanted—one where I did something profitable that also made me happy.

Right now, though, I just wanted the image of Jesse touching and looking at Wendy out of my mind, and in my fucked-up mind, yearning was yearning. I tilted my head and lifted a corner of my mouth in a flirty half-smile. "Deshaun. How have you been?"

"I've been well." He looked me up and down, his gaze lingering a few seconds longer on my chest. "You look like you could use some art."

The wind couldn't have done that much damage. I raked a hand through my short locks. "It's that bad?"

He didn't bother to assess the state of my hair. "It's that bad. I have an extra smock inside." Opening the door, he inclined his head to urge me forward. "Come on."

Powerless to turn him down, I went inside. A cluster of customers perused a selection of colored pencils, and a lone man stared at blank canvasses of various sizes, bewilderment making a choice impossible.

Deshaun led me to the back, and I waited while he dug through a stack of paint-stained cloth. "What are you expecting me to do?"

"Paint. I have a Valentine's display that needs to be finished, and you're the perfect woman for the job." Fishing out a smock, he held it out.

I stared, unsure and lost, like the guy trying to decide on a canvas. "You want me to finish painting your front window?"

"Yes. The mural needs hearts and flowers, and the other window needs to say 'Happy Valentine's Day,' or something equally welcoming."

Taking the smock, I hesitated. The dingy poly blend was heavier than I'd remembered a smock being. "Are you hiring me to work here?"

He shrugged, carelessly turning his palms upward. "I'm providing a place for you to practice therapeutic art. You get something, and I get something." Without waiting for me to decide, he donned another stained smock, picked up a two-sided carrier with paint pots lining both sides, and then he exited to the sales floor.

I hadn't come here to paint. Though I wasn't sure why I'd ended up in this place, the moment I recognized Deshaun on the sidewalk, I knew I was going to seduce him. Months ago, he'd showed extra interest in me. We'd flirted, and he'd invited me to visit his store anytime. Nothing had come of it because I'd sworn off men and relationships.

But Jesse had insisted I give it a try with him. That experiment had failed, and now I needed something to wash away the pain and misery. I glanced down, double-checking that my loose shirt covered emerging evidence of my pregnancy. Men, as a rule, didn't make out with women impregnated by another man. Right now, I just looked like I'd packed on a few pounds. I'd always been on the curvy side, and so what was one more curve? It looked like the result of excessive ice cream, not irresponsible sex.

I followed Deshaun, not because I wanted to paint, but because I wanted to stay close to my target. Hunting dick was a victimless type of con. He'd get laid, and I'd get to feed the parts of me best suited to deal with emotional pain. We'd both benefit.

The second I emerged from the back room, a customer smiled at me, probably because I was behind the cash register. He'd been the one staring at the canvasses. He had the rugged look of a man who spent a lot of time exploring the great outdoors. I placed him in his mid-fifties, and with a quick glance at his left hand, I also labeled him divorced.

His smile was open and welcoming, if a bit sheepish. "Hi, I was wondering if you could help me pick out a canvas?"

I scanned the store, on the lookout for Deshaun. It took but a second to find him on this side of the window. He'd moved a couple display racks to make room. Gesturing to the front of the store, I said, "I don't work here. You should ask Deshaun."

The man nodded absently. "I'm looking for my daughter. She's fifteen and taking this art class, and they're doing a portrait." He kept going, rambling like I'd confirmed my status as an employee instead of telling him I wasn't.

With an aggravated sigh, I marched to the shelving unit that held different sizes of blank canvasses, selected an eight-by-ten, and shoved it at him. "Here. Portrait size."

Then I continued to the front of the store. Smocks were not sexy wear. Deshaun had a nice body—hard, toned muscles, wide shoulders, and a nice ass between those narrow hips. We'd talked about running—his daily habit compared to the fact I hadn't been completely out of a wheelchair at that point—so I knew he was a serious fitness buff. With the exception of his shoulders, the smock hid everything that was visually appealing.

I stopped next to him, hands on hips. "There's a guy at the register with a canvas."

"Thanks." He handed me a paintbrush. "Go ahead and work your magic." With that, he went to help the customer.

Paints meant to be put on a window and washed off in a month were not a high quality product. I was essentially using tempera paint, something safe and non-toxic for the preschoolers who couldn't resist licking a window or two, and so I didn't feel like I needed a mask to protect my baby from fumes. I used one when I worked in the wood shop, though. Warren had bought them in bulk.

Deshaun had started with the outline of hearts bursting out of a basket, shooting like skeets into the air as targets for cupid. This kind of mindless art appealed to me just then. It didn't take long before I fell into a rhythm and didn't notice the passing of time until Deshaun locked the front door and unplugged the "OPEN" sign.

"Jessica, that looks incredible."

I stepped back to survey what I'd done. The hearts interspersed with paintbrushes and other art supplies, making it look festive while still advertising the store. The design spanned both front windows, and above it, I'd painted 'Be Mine' in curly lettering.

It didn't look incredible. It was blazingly mediocre. The tableau lacked style. This could have been made from clip art. Rather than let bitterness build in me, I channeled that energy toward better pursuits. I set down my brush and wiped my hands on my smock.

"How do you feel now?"

Like shit. Like a washed-up has-been trying to pretend I hadn't lost everything that had differentiated me from every other paint-by-number, wanna-be artist out there. Bitterness was difficult to keep at bay, but I was a master at denying my emotions. At least I'd stopped obsessing over Jesse for the afternoon. I turned a brilliant smile on him, one designed to make him feel like a hero about to be worshipped.

"Hungry." Unbuttoning my smock, I sauntered toward him. Maybe it was long past time for food, but I made it clear he was on my menu. I focused on his luscious lips, so different from Jesse's thinner ones that were often pressed together with disapproval. "How about you?"

His tongue darted out, wetting his lower lip, and I knew I had him. "There's a place down the street that has excellent ribs. How about I take you to dinner?"

I knew the place because Jesse had ordered takeout from there for me before. The comparisons kept coming. Deshaun was taller, but Jesse had broader shoulders and bigger muscles. To chase away images of Jesse—the way his eyes softened just before he kissed me or the reverent way his fingertips had skated across Wendy's skin—I closed the distance between Deshaun and me.

He'd removed his smock some time ago. I slid my fingers over the rough hemp of his striped shirt, increasing pressure so he could feel my caress through the thick fabric. His smile widened, and his eyelids fell to half-mast in eager approval of my intent.

Rising to my toes, I pressed my chest against his. Our lips met at the halfway point, and I felt his hands resting on my waist. He was a skilled kisser, and the soft glide of his lips became a bolder foray. Parting my lips, I invited him to deepen the kiss even more.

The hands on my hips migrated to my back, and soft caresses feathered up and down. From the way he kissed, I knew Deshaun would be a skilled lover. He was the kind of man who spent hours exploring and memorizing, a tactile artist in the bedroom.

I wanted this. I *needed* this.

My brain kept conjuring images of Jesse even though Deshaun's style of kiss was completely different. Everything was different, from the angle I had to tilt my neck to the way his body felt against mine. They were both rock hard, endless expanses of muscle, but Deshaun was streamlined, like a race car, where Jesse was more like a Humvee, built for the long haul over rough terrain.

To drive Jesse out of my brain, I threw myself into making out with Deshaun. I slid my palm along his neck and into his hair. He had a riot of small, shoulder-length braids, each terminating in a series of colorful beads that caressed my arm as they cascaded around it.

He moaned, and his kiss moved to trail down my neck where I was incredibly sensitive. It felt good, and my brain finally cooperated, allowing me to enjoy what Deshaun was doing. I let my head drop back to give him more access. Though it was a little forced on my part, the chemistry was there. We should take this to the back room or to his place where we could strip naked and let nature take its course. I did not want to have sex in the front window of an art supply store.

I opened my eyes, and my heart stopped. Standing on the other side of the window, glaring at me with a promise of murder in those pale blue depths, was Jesse Lee Foraker in all his Neanderthal glory. Fear flooded my bloodstream, and I stiffened.

Chapter 4—Jesse

The design I'd chosen for today was new to me. I'd been researching it for almost a year, and I'd watched a few dozen tutorials. I'd meant to try this out with Jessica. The spiderweb design would support her whole body, which would alleviate any stress on her hip or lower back.

But I had to settle for having Wendy as my practice model. As the design neared completion, I envisioned Jessica in Wendy's place. It was wrong to do, but I couldn't help it. Having her here, watching, meant I was taunting her with sweet memories. From the start, she'd responded to my ropes in a way no other person ever had. She was made for Shibari.

I saw her in the center of the web, her swollen belly large with child and her face relaxed and blissful. Mine to touch. Mine to love. As I pictured it, I became aware my cock was responding.

In six years of being Wendy's Dom, I'd never once popped a boner. While this had nothing to do with Wendy and everything to do with Jessica, I wasn't sure either Wendy or Marc would believe me. So I took pains to keep my body turned away from Marc. Wendy wasn't a concern because she was too focused on what she was feeling.

For the first time, it occurred to me that Wendy had never once asked me how I was doing. When I'd sat her down to tell her I had a girlfriend, she'd only asked if that meant I couldn't be her Dom. She hadn't been interested in me or my life. She hadn't noticed a difference in my affect when Jessica had broken off the relationship.

A pang ricocheted inside me. I wanted a sub who cared about me as much as I cared about her. I'd had that briefly with Jessica, and now it was gone.

I glanced over to see how this was affecting her, and that was when I noticed she was gone.

"She left a few minutes ago," Marc said. "I think she's going to text you."

My cock deflated, meaning I didn't have to angle my body away from him anymore. "Thanks."

Normally I would stand back and admire my handiwork, and then I'd begin the process of undoing the design. Marc snapped a couple of photos, and my phone dinged as it registered a text. He always shared one of them with me.

An hour later, Wendy emerged from the bathroom fully clothed. Marc and I discussed our favorite restaurants while we waited. We'd long ago found we had nothing in common except a love of good food, and so when we talked, the topic inevitably turned to a new dish one of us had discovered.

"We stopped because my buddy, Frankie, loves empanadas. Whenever we're south of the border, she has to stop for empanadas. It's her thing."

As Wendy approached, Marc sat forward, suddenly alert. He motioned for Wendy to join him.

Normally after a session, they went home. I liked that they didn't feel the need to linger. Scening usually pumped me with energy and left me invigorated. I often had a breakthrough in coding or software design afterward. Today the opposite had happened. I didn't know if it was due to the funk I was in over losing the woman I loved or if the fact that Jessica had left without a word had done it. No matter what, Jessica was the root of my problem.

Wendy sat down. She shot a frown at Marc.

He cleared his throat. "Jesse, last time we were here, you told Wendy and me that you were in a serious relationship. We're happy for you, and after talking with you, we weren't concerned. But after meeting Jessica today, I have to confess I have concerns."

I furrowed my brow, a foreboding look that mostly meant I was confused. "Jessica and I are no longer together."

"That's not what concerns me." He shot another glance at Wendy. "She said she's not into all this stuff, and then when she left in a hurry, I realized she's very uncomfortable with the whole thing. I get why you guys broke up."

Jessica wasn't uncomfortable with anything she'd seen. Of all the things we'd done, bondage had been the single thing that had put her in a state of bliss. I wasn't going to have a heart-to-heart with either of my guests, so I didn't bother to respond. I cut to the chase. "Two hours ago, you weren't concerned, and then you met Jessica. What did she say?"

"She said you were a mercenary. She said you met in that capacity, and your relationship revolved around dangerous activities."

I was sure Jessica had phrased things to tell the literal truth in a way that guaranteed misunderstandings—or, at least I hoped that was the case. With the distance between us, I didn't feel like I was in her head enough to be certain. I locked my gaze to Marc's. "You don't want Wendy to be my sub anymore because you think I'm a mercenary or because Jessica said something to make you personally uncomfortable?"

Wendy cleared her throat. "Marc, I met Sir when he helped the KCPD with a delicate matter. I know what he does. It's okay."

Marc pressed his lips together and glared at her.

This was a curious development. It appeared Wendy had obscured the true nature of my job in order to secure Marc's approval of me being her Dom. "It it that, or did Jessica say something? She can be misleading."

"Because she's also a mercenary?"

"Neither of us is a mercenary." I dug my heels in. Mercenaries were concerned with making money at the expense of ethics. I had a strong set of ethics, and I applied them to every case. "I'm sure that's not what Jessica said." She had the same reservations about the term—didn't she?

"She said you rescued kidnapped people and protected national security secrets." He wasn't going to let this go. "She said she sometimes helps out."

She also sometimes needed to be rescued, but I was sure she hadn't mentioned that. "I can't discuss cases. What I do is confidential."

"How do I know my wife is safe with you?"

I growled. "She's safer with me than she is every day when she goes to work."

Marc held up a placating hand. "I'm not attacking you, Jesse. I'm concerned."

Wendy gasped. "Marc, you did not discuss this with me."

"I didn't know about any of this before Jessica showed up." He rubbed his hands together. "I'm not comfortable with this anymore, not now that I know what you do. My top priority is Wendy and making sure she's safe. I don't know that I believe she can be safe with you."

Wendy jumped to her feet and clenched her fists at her hips. "Marc, you can't change your mind just because some twit shows up and says some inflammatory things. She's his ex-girlfriend. Ex-girlfriends can be evil and vindictive. That's all this is."

I couldn't sit here while they lampooned Jessica's character, not even if she had it coming. I rose to my feet, towering over both of them with a jetpack powered by my will. "She's neither evil nor vindictive. She's smart, witty, generous, and sensitive—and she's the mother of my child. I won't listen to either of you malign her character."

Marc rubbed at his jaw. "You're still in love with her." He got to his feet. "Seeing you with Wendy—I think she didn't handle that very well. She, um, she looked really upset when she left. Maybe it's best if this is the last scene you two do for the foreseeable future."

He took Wendy's hand and led her to the door. Like a good submissive, she submitted to his paltry dominance.

At the door, she turned back. "Sir, I wish you well. Maybe if you tell her you released me, she'll come back."

I shook my head. "She didn't have a problem with me having subs. In fact, she encouraged me to keep them. That's not what broke us up."

Though she didn't argue her point, the sympathy in Wendy's eyes said how little faith she put in my argument.

When they were gone, I called Jessica. Given the problem she had earlier with her back, I wouldn't be surprised if she had trouble getting to David's place. Perversely I also wanted to know if watching had impacted her the way Marc seemed to think. He wasn't the most observant person in the world. His wife had been lusting after me for years, right in front of his face, and my ethics were the only thing that had prevented anything physical from happening between us. A fucking mercenary wouldn't have cared. He would have taken what was offered and not cared about the immorality of it.

Okay, maybe that was a petty thought, but it didn't make it less true.

Not surprisingly, Jessica didn't answer her phone. A ringing coming from the direction of my living room showed that she'd left her phone on the coffee table and her jacket on the arm of the sofa. Briefly I toyed with the idea of going after her, but then I rejected it. She was a grown woman, capable of taking care of herself. If she needed my help, she'd ask for it.

But she'd come all the way over here, and she'd left without her things. She had to come back. The keys to Brea's house were in her jacket pocket. Unsatisfied curiosity might not kill me, but it ruined my afternoon. Worries about her vacillated with questions about why seeing me with one of my subs had upset her.

Did she still care? Maybe I could convince her to give us another chance?

A few hours later, my phone rang with a generic tone. If Jessica was going to call, it would be from an unfamiliar number. I picked it up. "Foraker."

"Jesse? This is Warren. Have you seen Jessica since you dropped her off at Brea's? I'm here to pick her up, and she's nowhere to be found. The concierge said she left around two and hasn't returned."

I glanced at her phone, and I saw that the battery had gone dead. He'd no doubt called her, and the phone had gone straight to voicemail. "She was here, but she left a few hours ago. She didn't say where she was going."

"Was she upset?" Warren sounded more curious than anything else. He trusted me with his daughter more than Jessica trusted me. I'd been there through the worst of everything. He knew what she meant to me.

"I had people over, so I didn't see her leave. We didn't really have a chance to talk, so I'm not sure why she came over."

"Oh." He sighed. "I'm not sure how to find her."

"I can." I booted up my computer. Unbeknownst to everyone, I'd microchipped her cane. When the going got tough, she had a tendency to disappear, and I wasn't going to take another chance she'd take off. The program I'd written showed her exact location. She was an at art store. Good for her. "She's not far from here. I'll get her and bring her to you."

"Thanks," Warren said. "I appreciate it. And, Jesse?"

"Yeah?"

"Flowers couldn't hurt."

The call ended, and I wasted a moment staring at the fading display. Jessica's dad was rooting for us?

I didn't agree with Warren that Jessica would want flowers from me. I remembered how perplexed she'd been by the rose I'd brought her on our first date. Jessica wasn't in a place where romantic gestures would win her over. She wanted something. She wouldn't have come to me otherwise.

Sometimes I was a clueless ass. I should have realized something was the matter when I found her crouched next to my sofa, but instead I'd continued my scene with Wendy.

No wonder my love life was in shambles.

Art Attack wasn't far from my loft. I tucked Jessica's phone in the pocket of her jacket and took it with me. Since I knew there would be no parking in that area, I left my truck in its spot and walked to where she was.

The store was easy to find. Someone had painted a huge cupid shooting at hearts and art supplies on the window. I tried the door, but it was locked, and that's when I noticed the sign. The place closed at seven, and it was a little after that time.

Lights were still on inside, and when I peered closer to block out the glare of the city lights reflecting from the window, my heart stopped.

Standing a few feet away, Jessica was wrapped in a man's arms. Their lips were locked together, and their hands wandered over one another's bodies. Some random fucking guy had his hands on my Brat. Rage boiled in my veins, and I struggled to contain it.

Jessica broke away and smiled up at the man. Then she noticed me. Our eyes locked, and hers widened as she recognized I was barely holding it together.

The guy noticed her attention had been diverted. He saw me, and his eyes narrowed. "What the hell is his problem?"

The sound of his voice carried through the glass. I heard him clear as a bell ringing at the other end of a long tunnel.

Jessica didn't move. She seemed frozen, in a sort-of trance, but not fearful.

The guy had his wits about him. "Go in the back." He shoved her behind him as he faced the window. "I'll take care of this."

Jessica seemed to come back to herself. She heaved a sigh. "No. I've got this."

He threw a frown over his shoulder. "No offense, but I don't think you can take him."

"Neither can you." She seemed curiously resigned, almost defeated. "He won't hurt me."

My rage had turned to open-faced fury. My hands rested at my sides, ready for anything. "Open the fucking door."

The guy pushed her away from the window, and I was almost impressed by his protectiveness. "I'll call the police."

She came to the door and put her hand on the lock. "Don't call the police. Jesse isn't going to stand there nicely and wait. If I don't come out, he'll come in."

Chivalry wasn't dead. The guy jerked her away from the door. "Is this an abusive ex?"

"No."

"Stalker?"

"No. Jesse is... hard to explain." She said something else, but it was too soft to penetrate the broken seal on the door.

The guy frowned while throwing another glance at me. "Explain, or you're not opening that door."

She sighed again. "He's a friend. He won't hurt me. He's not like that."

49

"He looks like the kind of guy who wouldn't hesitate to put a bullet in anyone who pissed him off, and you've pissed him off." Urgency colored the guy's tone, and for the second time that day, I was offended by someone's assessment of me. At least this guy was a stranger who was going by instinct and observation. Marc should have known better.

The guy continued. "He's the kind of guy who is carrying a gun under that jacket. I'm not going to let you open that door until I'm satisfied he won't hurt you."

I did have a gun under my jacket. I carried a firearm most of the time. She touched his cheek lightly. "Deshaun, you're a great guy, but you're in over your head right now. I'm going to unlock the door and go out there."

"Because if you don't, he'll bust in here and drag you out?"

She shrugged. She knew I would do exactly that. "Let me talk to him. I'll calm him down and send him away."

I wasn't going anywhere without her.

The guy brushed past her and opened the door. He tried to block me from coming inside by propping his foot against the bottom of the door. "Jessica doesn't want to leave with you."

I looked over the man who'd been kissing Jessica. He was moderately handsome. Both taller and thinner than me, he looked like an artist. He had butterscotch skin, thick lips, a flat nose, and a riot of braids in his weave. I could see where women might be attracted to his Bohemian style, but not Jessica. I'd seen the way she'd looked at me when she was turned on—lips parted, breaths coming faster and faster, her gaze roaming my body appreciatively.

She liked her men built for action—strong, decisive, able to take care of themselves and of her.

Then I remembered meeting Mateo, her first real boyfriend. Except that he was Hispanic instead of black, he had a lot more in common with this artsy guy than he did with me.

Perhaps being with me was the anomaly. She'd said over and over that we weren't compatible, but I'd dismissed her concerns. Maybe I should have fucking listened to her.

The burning in my chest argued against the idea she wasn't meant to be mine.

I fucking hated the knots she tied inside me.

I peered past this would-be knight to find Jessica. It was her decision whether she remained here or came with me. I couldn't keep the frost from my gaze, but that was her problem, not mine. "Your dad is at Brea's, waiting for you. You didn't answer your phone when he called."

"I was busy." Her gaze sidled to the artwork on the windows, and I realized she must have spent the afternoon painting.

It wasn't her best work, and I was pissed at her, so I didn't comment. "So I saw." The muscle on my jaw ticked with the effort not to growl and drag her out of there.

Her gaze fell. From the way she pressed her lips together, I knew she wasn't playing at being submissive. This was pouting, pure and simple.

An uncomfortable silence settled, and Deshaun cleared his throat. "She'll check in with her father."

I didn't acknowledge the boho, and I didn't cave to the urge to rip his face off. It wasn't his fault Jessica had targeted him. When she was bent on seducing someone, her target, especially one as innocent as this guy, didn't stand a chance.

Doing my best to affect a neutral demeanor, I said, "I told your dad I would bring you home."

She glanced back at the guy, and I knew she was looking for a good way to end this con. "Thank you for today. I didn't realize how much time had passed. My dad must be worried sick." She handed him the smock she'd been wearing, and when she kissed his cheek, I growled. "I'll come by when things settle down."

She'd better not fucking return here ever again.

The guy, for his part, didn't seem upset she was leaving.

The temperature outside was as frosty as I felt right then. She wrapped her arms around her body and fell into step next to me. I modulated my usual pace to match her slower gait, and handed over her jacket. "Put this on."

She slid her arms into the sleeves and jammed her hands into the pockets. She pulled out her cell phone and noted that it was dead. "How did you find me?"

If I told her about the chip in her cane, she'd burn it just to spite me.

"Good guess."

"Jesse."

"Don't, Jessica. Just fucking—don't."

I led her back to my place, cutting through two alleys to shorten the trip. As we approached the parking garage underneath my building, she huffed. "You have no right to be mad at me."

Incredulous, I looked over at her. She faced forward, so I noted the tight set of her jaw and the flash in her eye. If anyone was out of line here, it was not me. "You were making out with a guy in the front window of an art store."

"Are you pissed off I didn't invite you to watch me make out with Deshaun the same way you invited me to watch you feel up Wendy?"

That was not at all what had happened. I'd barely come into physical contact with her. She'd felt the kiss of my flogger and the whisper and press of rope on her skin—not the heat of my hand grasping her neck or the taste of my lips, all liberties Jessica had allowed that guy. "I didn't feel up Wendy. It's not even close to being the same as what you did."

She exhaled hard. "You're an idiot. I don't give a fuck what you do or who you do it with." Her voice shook the tiniest bit. Someone who didn't know her as well as I did would have missed it.

However I didn't know if it meant she was cold or upset—and it didn't tell me exactly why she was upset. "Obviously you do. You didn't hesitate to come in and watch me practice Shibari on Wendy. If you didn't care, you wouldn't have come in."

I struck a nerve, and she erupted. She swiveled to face me, and she smacked the flat of her hand against my chest. Her eyes flashed with green fire. "Fuck you, Jesse. I don't have to justify my actions to you. I'm not your sub, not now and not ever, and you don't get a say in anything I do. If I want to kiss Deshaun, then I'll kiss Deshaun. If you want to get off on feeling up Wendy while her husband watches, then you can get off on feeling up Wendy while her husband watches. We're not together."

We'd arrived at my truck. Rather than open the door, I leaned against it, trapping her between my body and the truck. "I didn't get off on feeling up Wendy. I've told you repeatedly that our relationship isn't sexual." It drove me nuts that she refused to listen to me. She had no reason to doubt me. I'd never lied to her, not once.

She snorted. "That's rich. You tell yourself whatever you need to believe, but I saw the hard-on bulging in your pants when you were tying her up. I saw the way you looked at her. Marc must be fucking blind to miss it—or maybe he gets off on watching you lust after his wife?"

Thoughts of Jessica had contributed to my arousal, and she had the nerve to throw it in my face? Fury bubbled over, and I leaned closer. "You told Marc I was a mercenary."

She shrugged and threw out a flippant response as she pressed both palms against my chest in a futile attempt to put distance between us. "I said we were mercenary buddies who used to fuck."

I couldn't remember a time I'd been this pissed at another human being. "You fucking, cold-hearted bitch. You can't stand the idea another sub might be able to give me the things you couldn't, so you came over today to sabotage it."

She flinched, and the angry disdain of her expression melted into a patronizing pout. "Whatsa matter, Jesse? Did your pretty little subbie dump you? Is that really why you're mad? You don't care that you saw me kissing Deshaun. You're just jealous because, sub or not, you don't have a handy piece of ass to screw."

Her mouth ran at a million miles an hour, and I could spend all day figuring out the ways in which she'd insulted and jeered at me, but I had better ways to spend my time. I seized on that last part and hit back. "So that's what that was? You found a handy piece of ass to screw? Does he give you free paintbrushes for whoring yourself out to him? If you're so hard up for art supplies, you could always just steal them."

She gasped and shoved against me, so I knew I'd scored a direct hit. "I hate you."

I leaned even closer, not stopping until my face was inches from hers. "Back at you, Brat."

She blinked, and I saw the tears she struggled to hold back. At that moment, I realized the enormity of what I'd said, and I felt like shit. Her kidnapper had forced her to seduce men for various purposes, and she'd already confided the pain and shame she still felt from those experiences. He'd abused her, and I'd just taunted her for it. Right now, I was in the running for lowest form of life on the planet. She'd been lashing out, and I'd responded with cruelty.

Backing off, I got out of her personal space. "Jessica, I didn't mean—"

She turned and walked away. "Don't follow me."

Figuring I'd been enough of an asshole for one night, I didn't follow her, but I did call Warren to come pick her up. Considering how this evening had turned out, I should have just bought her the fucking flowers. Her rejection of them would have stung less than the lost and bereft expression on her face just before she'd limped away from me.

Chapter 5—Jesse

A couple nights later, Dean picked me up. David and Brea were having a wine-tasting party at their new place. I hadn't planned to go, but Dean had pointed out I couldn't avoid Jessica forever. David was one of my closest friends, and Brea was Jessica's sister.

Also, there was the minor issue of the pregnancy. In a few months, I'd be seeing Jessica quite a bit. No matter what bad blood was between us, I knew she wouldn't keep me from my child.

Dean stood in the middle of my living room, lips pursed in disapproval. "You're wearing that?"

I looked down, taking in my jeans and the blue polo shirt. No stains. "What's wrong with it?"

"We're going to a wine-tasting. Most people would dress up." Dean wore slacks, a cardigan, and a jacket, which I thought was overkill.

Indicating the collar on my shirt, I said, "I did." It wasn't a T-shirt, which was my usual fare.

Dean rolled his eyes. "That's how you should dress for work. Don't you have slacks or a nice sweater? It's sweater weather."

It was February, but we were in the midst of a warm snap. I wasn't sure I'd worn a sweater since middle school, when my mother still had a voice in my wardrobe. "If I get cold, I can put on my jacket." Mine, unlike his, was black nylon with SAFE Security's emblem on the front. Jessica had designed it.

Running a fingertip along his lapel, he sighed. "I'm never going to get you to dress as nicely as I do, am I?"

"I'm not into overdressing for a simple party." I grinned to soften the blow. "Your title as the snappiest dresser will have to go undefeated."

He held up a folded bill. "Fifty dollars if you wear a suit."

I had several suits that I rarely donned. Snorting, I shook my head. "Fifty isn't even worth what I'm wearing right now."

"I'll also leave Jessica alone." He casually tossed that ante onto the table.

That was something I couldn't ignore. Dean had declared war on Jessica. Ever since we'd broken up, he'd been openly hostile toward her—even though I'd admonished him to leave her be. Just like in his wardrobe, Dean's attitude tended toward extremes. He was generous and solicitous toward those he liked, and he was merciless toward those who slighted him. Right now, Jessica occupied the top slot on his shit list.

When Brea answered the door at her new place, her jaw dropped. "Jesse, you look amazing." She beamed, as if I'd worn the suit for her. She threw her arms around me and kissed my cheek. "Thank you for coming tonight."

From her greeting, I surmised that Jessica hadn't confided the details of our last exchange. Otherwise, Brea's only greeting would be a glare.

I hugged her back. "Thanks for having me."

She turned to Dean next, and her attitude cooled slightly. "Dean, I'm trusting you to stick to our agreement."

"To the letter, Sugar." He one-upped me by kissing both of her cheeks.

Though I had my suspicions, I regarded Brea closely. "What agreement?"

"Just a little something to keep Dean on his best behavior tonight." She took our hands and drew us deeper into the foyer.

Narrowing my eyes, I threw Dean my best glare. He'd already promised Brea he'd leave Jessica alone tonight, and he'd used it to get me to wear a monkey suit.

He lifted a shoulder. "It would be foolish to waste such a perfect opportunity."

Jessica had the same life philosophy, though I liked to think she wasn't as merciless about it as Dean.

My gaze roved the open space beyond the foyer that made up the living room. I found Jessica seated on the sofa. She wore some kind of shapeless sack dress and leggings. Normally I preferred styles that highlighted and hugged curves, but on her, it looked great. Her attention was on her brother, whose hands sliced and diced the air as he related some kind of wild adventure, and a happy smile lit her face. She looked radiant. My breath hitched a bit at the sheer wonder of her beauty.

Dean clapped a hand on my back. "Let's get you something to drink."

The last time I'd been under the influence while pissed at Jessica, I'd said some inadvisable things. Of course, the last time I'd seen her, I'd done the same thing sober. Apparently it didn't take alcohol to turn me into a dick.

55

A good number of people had turned out for the party. I found myself surrounded by friends for most of the evening, playing a slow game of Avoid Jessica as I shifted around David and Brea's exquisite new digs to socialize with different groups of people. Dean was never far from my side. Due to the agreement he'd made with Brea, he was also avoiding Jessica.

"Are you going to drink that wine?" Dean gestured toward the glass I'd been nursing all evening.

"It's almost gone." I had no intention of overindulging. Not that Dean needed to know, but I was gathering my courage to apologize to Jessica. I'd come close to approaching her twice, but both times, visions of her in another man's arms made fury burn in my chest. It was best not to engage when jealousy boiled in my veins.

An hour later, I found myself alone in one of the guest rooms. For people who didn't plan to expand their family anytime soon, a family home like this didn't make sense. This extra room lacked personality. It had basic bedroom furniture and a couple of chairs.

David had told me the unit across the hall was coming on the market in the next couple of months. Perhaps I'd put in an offer. My loft wasn't conducive to having a child running around.

The bed was neatly made. I was about to open a drawer—snooping was an occupational hazard—when the door to the room opened. I paused with my hand on the knob. With the curtains open, city lights streamed into the room. It was enough light to get around, but not enough to read a book. My position put me behind the door, so I wouldn't be immediately seen.

Jessica came in and closed the door. I didn't need light to recognize her shape or the uneven walk she affected when she was tired. Without looking in my direction, she hobbled toward the rear of the room. Next to a closed door that led into a private bathroom, she stopped. She set her palms against the wall next to the door and leaned forward. Then she lifted to the ball of her foot and lowered down slowly.

In the middle of a party, she was taking time to do the exercises she needed to maintain strength in the hip she'd badly injured in a car accident.

I frowned. "Jessica, are you okay?" I knew she wasn't, but since she wasn't aware I was in the room, I needed to reveal my presence.

She froze. "Fine." Her tone was as crisp and rigid as her stance.

If we were on better terms, I would have called her on the lie. Instead I came closer. "Were you sitting for too long?"

"I came in here for privacy." The undercurrent of her statement said this room belonged to her, and I had no right to be there.

I glanced around at the generic space. Sure, it had cozy touches, but it still managed to be austere. "I didn't realize this was your room."

"Because there's not a glittery, wood-carved sign on the door that says, 'Jessica's Room?'"

"Yeah. That'd clear up any doubt."

"I'll make one after I finish the order I'm working on right now." Though she tried to swallow it, a small gasp of pain leaked out. She pressed the heel of her hand into her hip.

We hadn't called a truce, but I was determined not to be a dick. Plus, I hated when she was in pain. The part of me that was still head-over-heels in love with her wanted to take care of her. That need overrode the images of her making out with the guy in the art shop.

I touched her hip tentatively. "Let me help you."

In the half-light, I watched her eyes close and her face scrunch up in a grimace. "It's just a spasm. It'll pass."

She'd once said I had magic hands. Apparently anger won out over pain, otherwise she wouldn't be giving me the brush-off.

Of course, she also knew I was a Dom, and sometimes I couldn't help myself. It was likely she wanted me to take control of the situation. If she didn't, then she could say so. I lifted her in my arms and carried her to the bed.

The fact she didn't protest was telling.

I set her on the plush comforter, and she rolled toward me, exposing the hurt side. "You don't have to do this."

"I know, darlin'." For this, I unleashed my native Georgia drawl. In the past, Jessica had proven especially receptive to it. I used it now to help calm her.

I lifted her dress to expose her hip. Though her leggings preserved her modesty, the thin fabric provided a minimal barrier. I set to massaging the tight muscle. Damn, but it was rock-hard. No wonder she was hurting—and she was hurting more than she let on.

After a time, I paused.

She shifted, ready to sit up, but I stayed her with a hand on her hip.

"Darlin', you're in a bad way right now."

"I know." Her voice, normally strong, came out softly. "Thank you for trying, though."

"I'm not done. Have you used arnica before?"

She shook her head, her short locks catching glimmers of light as it moved. "I'm limited as to what I can take right now."

"I know, but arnica is topical." I tapped her hip. "I know David has some. I'm going to get it, and then I'll rub it into your hip. I'm going to need you to take off the leggings, though."

It didn't take but a minute of rummaging to find a tube of arnica in a drawer in David's bathroom. Given the impact play Brea enjoyed, arnica was a logical thing to have for aftercare.

When I returned, I found Jessica seated on the bed, her feet on the floor. She'd removed the leggings. When I closed the door, I twisted the lock on the handle so nobody could stumble in while Jessica was so vulnerable.

Her gaze lifted, and it met mine. In the silence, I read shades of misery and yearning in the dark flecks of her brilliant eyes. That's when I realized she'd been holding back tears. Damn, but she was a master at hiding her feelings.

I'd always known she was guarded, but in that moment, I realized she'd never quite let down her guard around me. At most, she'd camouflaged it.

"Lay on your stomach."

Her gaze dropped. "I can't get comfortable on my stomach."

The tiny swell I'd seen a week ago hadn't seemed like much, and the dress effectively hid her condition, but I wasn't going to argue. "Okay, then. On your side."

She scooted to the center and positioned herself to expose the area needing attention. Unfortunately it put her in the shadows. Turning on the lights in the room would pop the conciliatory bubble we'd created, so I set the bedside lamp to the lowest level. It cast enough light for me to see her, but not enough to illuminate the harsh realities of our situation.

I warmed the cream up in my hands, and then I massaged it into the muscles around her hip. This meant I touched her hip and thigh, and she didn't protest when I slid her panties out of the way to minister to her luscious ass.

Jessica had a great ass—a heart-shaped curve that never failed to get my blood pumping. My cock noticed what I was doing, and I had to coach it back into subservience. She'd made it clear she did not want a physical relationship with me.

With my mind back on the task at hand, I noted it no longer felt like I was squeezing iron. The spasm was subsiding. I massaged a while longer, grinding three knots into dust, and then I stopped.

A soft sigh sounded from Jessica. Though she faced away from me, I knew her eyes were closed.

"How does it feel now?"

"Much better." She sat up with a groan. "Thank you."

I sat back on my heels and let my gaze roam her body, searching for what had triggered that groan. "Darlin', it sounds like you're still hurting. Tell me where, and I'll take care of it."

"I'm fine, Jesse. Thank you. My hip doesn't hurt at all." She flashed a placating smile, but the expected eye-contact never happened.

Before she could scoot out of reach, I leaned over her, resting my fist on the opposite side of her body. "Darlin', I'm serious. Where else do you need a rubdown?"

She tried to put more distance between us, and her boob brushed against my arm. I enjoyed the contact, but her groan captured my attention. Kneading her ass had always turned her on. It seemed like I truly hadn't lost my touch.

She wrapped her hand around my wrist. "Jesse."

Since she didn't push me away, she didn't quite warn me away, and so I wasn't sure what she wanted. "Yes, darlin'?"

The next thing I knew, her hand cupped the side of my head while her lips ravaged mine. With the swipe of her tongue on my lower lip, she had me opening to let her deepen the kiss. She tasted like a sweet slice of passion, the kind I'd give anything to have again.

The Dom in me wanted to lay her back and take over, hear her sigh and moan as I broke away to trail wet, sucking kisses down her neck.

But for once, I didn't let that inclination drive my actions. Jessica had made it clear she was not a sub, and she didn't want me to be her Dom. That being the situation, I didn't move except to kiss her back. Electricity sizzled between us, a strange heat fraught with all the things we'd left unsaid.

With a groan, she pushed me. The way she swung her leg knocked my weight from where I'd balanced it on my hand, and I tumbled to my back. With lightning quick movements, she straddled me.

Her hands were everywhere, caressing the exposed skin on my neck before traveling south to grip my arms or shoulders. She shoved my shirt up, and those sensual, rough caresses sought out my abs. My cock, which I'd already talked down once, reasserted itself.

Though I touched her back, I assumed a passive role. My caresses remained outside of her clothes until she guided one hand up her thigh and under the hem of her dress.

"Tell me to stop," she breathed in my ear.

"Why?"

"Because nothing's changed. I can't give you what you need."

59

Right then, I needed her. I yearned to feel her skin against mine and the heat of her pussy enveloping my dick. I craved the sound of her moans and the way her breath caught just before she had an orgasm.

I cupped her face and brought her lips back to mine. "I need this, darlin'."

"Just one last time," she agreed before she resumed kissing me.

Her deft pickpocket hands flew down the row of buttons on my shirt, and she had it open faster than should be humanly possible. She broke away from kissing my mouth to nibble and kiss a path down my chest. Everything she did was incredible, and for the first time in my life, I let myself lay back and enjoy it. Normally I'd bide my time while she played, and then I'd take over, but assuming control wasn't in the stars tonight.

The moment I accepted that truth, something curious happened. Everything in the past and my anxiety about the future melted away. I was completely in the moment, my brain blissfully free to enjoy without thought.

She unzipped my pants, and I lifted my ass so she could ease those down my legs. Soon I found myself naked. Jessica discarded her dress, bra, and panties. She knelt next to me, and I drank in the exquisite sight of her singular beauty. Soft light glistened from her skin, highlighting her curves and the gentle swell of her abdomen.

I propped myself up on one elbow and leaned forward. My lips landed on her stomach, and I trailed my fingertips across this slight evidence of our bond.

She ran her fingers through my short hair, ruffling it as she accepted this token of affection. The moment I finished, she straddled me. She positioned my cock at her entrance and sank down slowly. I held her hips, but I didn't seek to guide or control the action. She undulated, and I stroked her body, exploring her sides and kneading her ass. I closed my hands over her breasts and sucked her nipples to sharp points. Everything I did elicited moans and squeaks—the exact same sounds she made when I'd dominated her.

It seemed she was right—it wasn't my dominance she craved.

The sounds of pleasure she made grew louder, moans and soft cries that fed the heat inside me. Her body shivered, and her pussy contracted, squeezing me so hard I had no chance of holding off my climax.

She collapsed on top of me, and I caught her in my arms. I held her, stroking a light caress down her back. After a few minutes, I moved us to cover us with the sheet. She slid to the side, taking her weight off her stomach. She didn't shiver or clutch at me, and for the first time after sex, she didn't seem like she was about to go to pieces.

I didn't know how long we stayed like that before she pulled away and sat up. With her back to me, she whispered, "I'm sorry."

It didn't sound like she was trying to make up with me or get back together, yet hope still surged through my chest. "For what?"

She waved a hand in my general direction as she put her bra and panties back on. "For taking advantage of you."

Reluctantly I abandoned the residual warmth of the bedding to put my pants back on. "You didn't take advantage of me."

"I seduced you." She pulled the sack dress over her head, and it floated down her body. "Right now, you're thinking maybe you can live with a vanilla existence because maybe if you did, we'd have a chance together. Maybe we could be the kind of family you've always wanted, the kind with two parents who love each other raising our kid."

As I buttoned my shirt, I stared at her. We'd just shared something tender and beautiful, and now she was throwing a cold dose of reality on it. "You think you can read my mind?"

"I know you, Jesse. I know what you want." She shimmied into her leggings.

Her cool detachment pissed me off. Maybe this wasn't the start of us healing as a couple, but it hadn't been insignificant. I grabbed her by the upper arms and forced her to face me. "You have no fucking clue what I want."

"You were very clear about what you want." She jerked her arms from my grasp, and I let her go because I didn't want to force her to stay. "You've always been clear about what you want."

I wanted to argue with her, not because she was wrong, but because I no longer had a fucking clue what I wanted.

For the past twenty years since I'd lost my wife, I'd been driven by a need to be in charge, to always be mentally present even when I wasn't physically there. Tonight Jessica had forced me to abandon that mindset, and now I was reeling with the possible implications.

Without saying anything else, I left the room. I found Dean on the balcony regaling a group of women with a tale that ended with him naked and in a hot tub. I motioned that I wanted to leave.

He responded with a small nod, and he graciously extricated himself from his group of admirers.

In the car, he clicked the radio off. "What happened?"

"I'm leaving in the morning, and I was hoping to get an early start. I'm taking some time off, and I'm going to head to Florida to see my mom."

He was quiet for all of thirty seconds, which was a long time for Dean. "Does this have anything to do with the fact you and a certain someone both disappeared from the party at around the same time?"

"No. It has to do with the text I got saying my mom was back in the hospital. Olivia and Mia have their hands full right now, and it's my turn to help her get back on her feet." My mother had been hospitalized on-and-off for the past six months for respiratory reasons. Though she was back in the hospital now, none of my siblings were concerned. Our mother was a chain-smoking hypochondriac, and she'd found a quack with hospital privileges who jumped when she swooned.

I'd known since yesterday she was in the hospital. I'd called her to check up, and she'd said there was no reason for me to come out.

So, yeah—I was running from Jessica and from the way she'd thrown my life into chaos once again. I needed to get my head on straight.

If this came out of left field for Dean, he rolled with it just fine. "You want company?"

"Nah. I'm looking forward to some time alone, and I haven't seen my mom since Christmas." Everybody knew I was in the habit of dropping by one weekend a month to see my mother.

It was a great cover for why I suddenly felt the need to hightail it out of town.

Chapter 6—Jessica

City lights streamed through the window. I didn't bother with turning on a light as I sat on the edge of the mattress and stared at the keys in my hand. Behind me, the covers were mussed, a calling-card of sorts left by Jesse. He was unapologetic about his lack of interest in making a bed. Accepting that side of him meant it didn't irritate me.

Light glinted from the cascade of keys as I turned them over in my hand. I'd picked Jesse's pocket because he'd grabbed me in anger and frustration. This correlation needed no illumination from my therapist because it had a huge neon sign pointing to it. I didn't like feeling like I wasn't in control.

This interlude with Jesse had been unexpected—and it had been wonderful, up until he'd lost his temper. While I didn't mind arguing with Jesse, when he asserted his Dom side to strip me of control, it sent me into a panic.

That's why I had his keys. When I'd emerged from the room and rejoined the party, I'd found Jesse had left. He was going to notice his keys were gone when he got home. I wondered if he'd come back here and yell at me? I definitely deserved it.

We weren't together anymore, which meant I had no right to pick his pockets.

Technically, I guess I had no right to pick anybody's pockets, but I couldn't seem to break this particular habit. I'm not sure it was better than smoking, but it hit the same pleasure centers, so I'd told Nikki I could cut out one or the other, but giving up both vices was going to take more time.

I'm not proud to say, when I went to bed, I snuggled up with the sheet that still held Jesse's scent. However, a bit of my wounded pride combined with guilt over the way I'd used him to make me sleep poorly. I knew he was still in love with me. I knew he was still hurting over our breakup. I shouldn't have slept with him.

In the early morning hours, I ate a breakfast of leftover party food, mostly vegetables and cheese, and I stowed a few lemon bars in my bag. Then I wrote a note letting Brea know where I'd gone, and I left.

Since I didn't have a license or a car, I hopped on a city bus and took it to Jesse's place. I encouraged myself with platitudes about how returning his keys meant I was doing the right thing, and I'd be able to sleep better tonight knowing I'd made amends with Jesse.

And I needed to invite him to the ultrasound, which was the scheduled highlight of my next checkup. I was excited about the prospect of seeing images of our little bean, and I knew he would be as well. No matter what was going on between us, I trusted him to be an involved and enthusiastic father.

I hovered in the parking garage next to his truck, and I realized Dean must have been Jesse's ride last night. Both of them had disappeared at the same time.

With a groan, I leaned against Jesse's truck. Ever since the breakup, Dean had not disguised the depth of his hatred for me. He'd warned me he'd side with Jesse, but I hadn't thought his dislike would be so virulent.

Jesse hadn't been drunk, so it was likely he was upstairs in his loft—he also had some eyeball-scanning device that would unlock his door—but I had no idea if he'd be alone. I really didn't want to run into Dean. He'd avoided me completely last night, most likely because Brea had told him to be nice or stay home. That was how he'd compromised.

A wave of exhaustion overtook me. Now that I was in the second trimester, I wasn't as tired as I'd been early on, but I hadn't slept well the past few nights, and it was catching up with me. The coward part of my brain argued for waiting a few hours before calling Jesse to see if he was okay with me dropping by.

Since I had the keys, I unlocked his truck. The back seat was filled with junk. I organized the tech on the floor with his gym bag, camping equipment, and a bag full of bondage rope. Seeing that made my heart pound painfully. I'd loved being tied up by him. I wished he was the kind of man who didn't also need to dominate me in order to do that, but he wasn't—and only an asshole tried to change someone into who they wanted them to be. Jesse was kind of an asshole in that way, even though he didn't mean to be.

I covered myself with a couple of musty blankets, and I fell asleep as soon as I closed my eyes.

When I woke up, it took a moment to remember where I was. Jesse's voice came from the front seat, and the rhythm of the road hummed underneath. Since he'd taken a few days off—I knew this because Brea had told me that David, Frankie, and Dean had conspired to keep him out of the office for at least a week—I figured he was returning to work today.

I was about to sit up when I heard Dean's voice. Fuck. I did not want to see him, and I especially didn't want to see him by popping up from the back seat. The fact they hadn't awoken me meant they didn't know I was here. How did one go about revealing her presence without freaking out the driver? I wasn't looking to cause an accident, and Jesse's driving already bordered on the edge of insanity.

So I pulled one of the covers up a little higher. Worst-case scenario, they parked at SAFE Security, and I slinked out of the truck after they went inside. I felt better about that plan.

"What the fuck were you thinking?" Dean's voice boomed through the cab, including a speaker near my head, which meant he wasn't in the truck. He was on the phone, and Jesse was piping the feed through his car speakers like he always did.

"Don't judge."

"I'm judging. I have every right to judge. I told you not to sleep with her. You said she's fucking around with some guy who owns an art store." The next part crackled, obscuring whatever Dean was saying to lampoon my character.

I should reveal myself, but I decided that hiding was the best option. This was not a conversation I wanted to overhear, much less participate in.

Dean's voice came back, clearer and stronger. "You deserve better than a woman who can't make up her fucking mind."

"She's made up her mind," Jesse returned. "She just didn't decide in my favor."

"Yet you're still planning ways to get back in her good graces." Dean growled loudly, the sound reverberating through my teeth from the speaker next to my head. "She's a con artist, Jesse. She lied to you all the time about pretty much everything. She led you on. Last night was no different. It didn't mean anything to her."

I couldn't argue with Dean's assertions about me being a liar or a con artist, but I disagreed with him on the implications. I'd openly lied to Jesse, but not because I was conning him. I'd been conning myself. Also, last night had meant something to me—I just didn't quite know what.

"I don't want to talk about this with you," Jesse said. "You're more pissed than I am, and I'm still pretty pissed. The last thing I need is for you to feed the negativity."

"Is that why you're running away?"

"I'm not running, asshole."

65

"Fuck you're not. She's fucked with your head so much that you don't know which end is up. You threw yourself into work, and when we made you take a break, you found your way back into her bed."

"She started it."

"Doesn't fucking matter. You let it happen. You're the Dom, buddy. Nothing happens without your say-so."

"It was vanilla, so there was no D/s, and even if it was, it would be consensual."

"Not what I'm saying. I'm saying you were weak. You let her use you, and now you're running away. She's trash. She's not worth it."

Shock had me holding my breath. I'd never heard Dean talk like this. Even when he was being a dick to me, he'd been solicitous. Last night had been beautiful and bittersweet. Jesse had dropped all the roles, games, and pretenses that went along with his usual power play, and for one night, he'd been exactly what I needed him to be. That did not make him weak.

Or maybe we were both weak. Either way, it was none of Dean's fucking business.

Speaking of Dean, he was on a roll. "She's fucking around, Jesse. You don't want to dine at a buffet where everyone's stuck their fingers in the food. She's damaged goods."

Okay, that was the last straw. Rage had me popping up. I was on my knees and leaning over seat to yell into the speaker on the console before I knew what I was doing. "Fuck you, Dean."

Jesse glanced over his shoulder, shock widening his eyes, and the truck swerved onto the shoulder of the freeway. We were not in Kansas City anymore. I noted this, but I was too focused on putting Dean in his place to care.

"I'm damaged goods because I made out with a guy I've known the whole time I've lived here, a guy who helped me get back my fine motor skills, and Jesse is in pristine condition? Fuck you and your misogynistic double standard. I know he seduces targets on missions—you both do—and when he's not on the road, he has three subs. He was never a one-woman man, and *I'm* the one who's damaged goods?"

"Jessica—" Jesse recovered control of his vehicle, and he slowed his speed.

Dean cut him off. "Jessica? What the fuck? Were you hiding in the back like a psycho ex-girlfriend?"

"Don't fucking evade the question. Explain how what I've done is worse than what Jesse has done."

"He never lied to you, and once he met you, he stopped being the honeypot—not that we employed that tactic more than a handful of times over the years." Dean wasted no time in coming back at me. "He was there for you when you couldn't walk. He was there whenever you needed anything. He gave you everything, and you gave him nothing. You used him, broke him, and discarded him."

Once again, Dean dodged the question. I glared even though he couldn't see it. "That is between Jesse and me, and you still haven't explained how him having three subs while we were together is okay, but me kissing a guy after we broke up makes me damaged goods."

"You're not damaged goods." Jesse growled at both of us. "And you didn't have a problem with me having subs when we were together. Why are you making a big deal out of it now?"

It had always been a big deal, but I'd been loath to bring it up because I knew I couldn't make him give them up if I wasn't willing to replace them.

Shoving all that aside, I turned my vehemence on Jesse. "Dean said I was damaged goods like it somehow means I'm worthless. You spent a whole morning fucking around with Wendy—you even invited me to watch—and then you had the nerve to get pissed at me for kissing Deshaun? You don't have a fucking leg to stand on, Jesse."

Dean cleared his throat, and his acerbic tone neutralized. "You slept with Wendy?"

"No, I didn't sleep with Wendy." He shot me a nasty glare via the rearview mirror.

I responded with a snort and an eye-roll. "He just got off on feeling her up."

"I did not."

"I was fucking there, Jesse. I know what it looks like when you've got an erection."

Though we were on the freeway, he slammed on the brakes. We came to a screeching halt on the shoulder of an exit ramp, and then he whipped. Our glares clashed. "Brat, just as you have no fucking clue what I want, you have no fucking clue what you saw."

What I'd seen had hurt me. Even though I had no right to expect him to sit at home and pine over me, it killed me that I was so easy to get over. He'd professed his love for me, but how much could he really have loved me if I wasn't enough for him?

Every time I thought about how his subs had always been more important to him than me, I died inside a little more. The fact he'd wanted me to witness a demonstration of just how little I mattered to him had seared a fresh wound onto my heart.

67

For the sake of our child, I was trying to put it all behind me, but it was really fucking hard. This was my doing. I'd broken up with him because being with him would have obliterated everything that made up *me*. That didn't mean I'd fallen out of love with him. It didn't mean I wanted to see him with other women.

Arguing with him wasn't going to lead to anything but more heartache. "Then I guess I'm both worthless and stupid."

He glared, the muscle on his jaw ticking with fury.

I climbed over the seat and went out the passenger door. He could fucking live without his keys because he obviously had another set. The steady roar of cars on the freeway calmed my rioting emotions enough to focus on my surroundings. I needed to call someone to come get me, and it was helpful to know exactly where I was before I made that call.

As I stomped down the incline toward the crossroad, I noted the two gas stations and six fast food places. None of it looked immediately familiar, and the warmer air smelled somehow different from the KC area.

A hand on my arm had me wheeling around, and I threw a punch because I knew it was Jesse and I was pissed and I wanted to hurt him for hurting me.

Of course, he easily avoided impact by leaning out of the way. "Brat, where do you think you're going?"

"Home. I'm finished with you." I parked my hands on my hips. There was no way this asshole was getting an invite to my ultrasound. He could wait to see the baby after she was born.

He gestured to our surroundings. "We're in Tennessee. Nobody is going to come this far to get you."

Tennessee? How the hell did we get over five hundred miles away? I looked up to find the sun high in the sky. Half the day was gone. If I was going to give him the satisfaction of hearing me beg, it would be of me begging to differ. Instead I crossed my arms. "It might take a few hours, but there are plenty of people who would come get me."

He closed his eyes, and his lips moved, forming numbers. Bastard was counting because he was pissed at me? Fuck him.

While he was otherwise occupied, I resumed walking away. I didn't get far before he picked me up and flung me over his shoulder.

"Stomach," I yelled. "This hurts."

He set me down, and then he loomed menacingly. "I'm not going to leave you stranded in some random city just because you haven't got the sense you were born with."

I had more sense than most people, and my skill set involved surviving in strange places with little to no money. I shoved at him because no matter how menacing he got, I knew Jesse would never physically hurt me. "Get out of my personal space. I can take care of myself. What the fuck are you doing in Tennessee anyway?"

"What the fuck were you doing in my back seat?"

I set my mouth in a mulish slant because, as I'd said, I was finished with him.

He motioned to the truck we'd abandoned halfway up the ramp. "You can either get in by yourself, or I can help you. I'm not leaving you here."

Arms crossed, I stalked back to the truck and got inside.

Jesse climbed into the driver's seat and put on his seat belt. "Call your parents and tell them you've run away from home again."

I gasped. "I did not run away. You're the one who's running away from the stupid, worthless whore you slept with last night."

He flinched. "Jessica, don't do that. You're not any of those things."

"Whatever. If you actually believed that, you'd also defend me when your friend called me the same things. Instead, you agreed with him."

"I apologized for insinuating you were a whore. I regretted it as soon as I said it, and I don't mind apologizing again. I'm sorry, Jessica. I shouldn't have said that."

The apology mollified me a little, but not enough to salve the sting of being called worthless. "So then I'm just a stupid, worthless woman."

"I'm not playing this game with you." He started the motor and merged into the empty lane. "You're smart enough to not buy into things you shouldn't, and I'm not going to apologize for anything from a conversation you eavesdropped on."

"I didn't mean to." I directed my pout out the window. "This truck was parked in Kansas City when I fell asleep in it."

He waited until traffic cleared from both lanes of the cross street, and then he re-entered the freeway.

"Where are you going? I thought you were taking me home?"

"Destination hasn't changed just because you stowed away in my back seat."

"I can't go to Florida. I have orders to fill, and physical therapy tomorrow." And I was due to meet with my therapist the day after that. I needed those sessions to help me keep my mental house in order. Right now, a tornado had swept through my figurative living room.

"You should have thought about that before you got into my truck."

Eyes wide, I stared at the man who was sometimes familiar and sometimes a stranger. "I was going to invite you to the ultrasound, you asshole. I didn't mean to run away with you."

That got his attention. He glanced over, a frown marring his brow. "You hid out in my truck because you wanted to invite me to our baby's ultrasound?"

"No, I hid out in your truck because I didn't know if Dean was in your apartment, and I didn't want to run into him. I figured I'd wait for you, and then I'd ask you when you came out of your apartment. I didn't plan to fall asleep. I don't know how you didn't notice me."

He was quiet for half a mile. "How did you get into my truck?"

"When you started yelling at me last night, I stole your keys."

With a curt nod, he accepted my explanation. "Back seat is a mess. I didn't notice you because you blended in."

"Because I'm a mess?" Even I found that one a little funny.

He grinned. "If the shoe fits."

"Jesse?"

"What?"

"I don't want to fight with you. With our history, I know it won't be easy at first, but I think if we're both committed, we can do this parenting thing together." My heart beat faster, the start of an anxiety attack. Honesty was difficult for me, and baring my most heartfelt feelings sometimes sent me to a horrible mental place. Nikki and I were working on that.

Chapter 7—Jesse

Her quiet declaration took me by surprise, coming on the heels of her explosive reaction to Dean's comments. I knew Dean was saying those things to help me get over Jessica, but I wished he wouldn't. I'd never had blinders on where Jessica was concerned. I knew she lied, and I knew she was manipulative. I also didn't want anyone maligning the mother of my child. I'd been about to say those things to Dean—again—when Jessica had startled the crap out of me. She'd popped up in my rearview mirror looking like a woman who'd been well-loved.

I'd fallen in love with her because she was a strong woman. Lies and manipulation were coping mechanisms, and she'd never used them with malicious intent against me.

I glanced over to find the color drained from her face. Asking for a truce had taken a lot of courage given the kind of emotional honesty with which she struggled. I reached over and squeezed her hand, and then I let go.

"I'd like that too, and yes, I want to go to the ultrasound. I want to be there every step of the way, and I'm thankful you're still willing to include me."

"Yeah, no problem." Her voice fell flat.

We were still at the part where it wasn't easy. I could make it less uneasy with an explanation about why I wasn't willing to turn back. "My mom is in the hospital. She didn't tell anybody she'd been admitted. I only know because my aunt texted me last night."

"Is she okay?"

I shrugged. With my mom, it could be something or it could be nothing. "She hasn't responded to the voice messages or texts I've left."

She nodded. "Okay, sure. When we get there, you can drop me at an airport. I'll call Warren and ask if he can get me a ticket home."

"I'll get you a ticket after I go see my mom, but you go ahead and let them know where you are."

I listened to her half of the conversation and tried to fill in the blanks. If she were my sub, I'd have her put it on speaker so I could listen in.

As the thought completed, I frowned. Was it really my business? Even if we were together, it seemed invasive to want that much transparency. These were her relationships, separate from the one she had with me.

For the first time, I considered my Dom-ly demands from the point of view of someone who valued her privacy—as Jessica definitely did. She needed to have things that were all her own. So did I. So did everybody, right?

Perhaps my demands had been invasive and selfish. Part of what attracted me to this lifestyle was the focus on considering my sub's needs and putting them first. I'd failed to do that with Jessica.

"Hi, Mom. Guess what? I'm going to Florida...No, I'm not after more paintings...I guess I could...Jesse...Yes, I know...It was an accident. I fell asleep in his truck, and he didn't notice I was there when he left this morning...Yeah, I know. I'll explain when I get home...Maybe tomorrow. Jesse's going to put me on a plane home after he sees his mom...She's in the hospital...I will. Can you call Brea? I left my charger at home. Thanks. I love you. Give Dad a hug from me."

When she ended the call, I dug into the center console and handed her a car charger. "We have the same phone." Technically, her phone belonged to SAFE Security.

"Not anymore. I have a new phone and a new plan."

It took a lot of effort to keep from scowling. "Why? You've had that phone and plan for a long time."

She cleared her throat. "Dean didn't tell you, did he?"

"Tell me what?"

"He cancelled my phone. I kept the number, though. At least he let me have that."

My first inclination was to not believe her. Why would Dean do something like that? Having her on our plan didn't cost extra. We'd agreed—all four of us—to supply her and Brea with phones connected to SAFE Security. It allowed me to install software on them for a variety of purposes—like tracking one of them if they turned up missing, which had happened before.

I tried to call her on it in a nice, non-threatening manner. "You're sure that's what happened?"

She regarded me curiously. "You really are clueless."

"Then explain it to me."

She heaved a sigh. "After we broke up, Dean cancelled my phone and raised the rent on Unexpected Treasures. Then he transferred my physical therapy outside the city and told the state I had a seizure so I can't get my driver's license back for another year."

I felt like someone had sucker-punched me. "That's why you moved out of the building?"

"Yeah. It's a great location, but I can't really afford to pay market rates. I understand it's expensive to throw money down that kind of hole, so I didn't blame him for what he did."

I blamed him. I'd been patient—even slightly gleeful—with him talking shit about Jessica because it did make me feel better to cast her in a negative light even though I knew it was a false light.

But this was just plain old vindictive.

"David, Frankie—*Brea*—didn't do anything to stop him?"

She shrugged. "It makes sense to have PT closer to my parents since they're the ones doing all the driving. I'm okay with paying for my own phone because it stops you from keeping tabs on me. The seizure report and losing the storefront—I'm used to having the rug pulled from under me. I know when to step aside so I don't land on my ass."

I hated that she now put one of my best friends on the same level as every other fucker who'd screwed her over—and she had every reason to do so. "I can't believe you're not livid about this." I rubbed a hand over my head, ruffling the short hairs on top. "I can't believe you haven't blown up his house."

A laugh startled from her, a small gasp that turned to a chuckle. "Dean once told me that he's exactly like me. I can't be mad at him for doing exactly what I would do in his place."

"Yes, you can. And I don't believe you'd be so nasty to someone." I couldn't believe Dean would treat Jessica the same way he'd treat a mark we needed to screw with.

"God, Jesse. You're still wearing rose-colored glasses when you look at me. It's okay to take them off. I'm not sweet or altruistic, and I've done worse to people for less."

"Because BS made you."

"Because I wanted to. Jesse, when I told Marc you and I were mercenary fuck-buddies, I wanted him to stop allowing Wendy to see you. I know you don't go around using that kind of language to describe what you do, and I knew she was a cop before I said anything. Maybe it didn't work, but I gave it my best shot."

It had worked, but I wasn't inclined to share that with her, especially not after what she'd confessed.

"I'm not sure if I should be more pissed at you or Dean."

"You have every right to be pissed at me, but Dean was just doing what he thought a friend should do."

I sidled my gaze over for a brief second. "I don't understand why you're defending him."

"He's your friend. You've lost enough. You don't need to start alienating your friends. Plus, Brea is getting things under control. Last night, she made Dean promise not to be nasty to me."

Her reasoning was more in line with the person I knew than the one she'd described. "He avoided you the whole time."

"It's a start." Sadness flickered across her features when she thought I wasn't looking.

"You miss Dean."

Her fingers smoothed a wrinkle from her black pants. "Doesn't matter. I have my parents and Leon. Sometimes I have Brea."

History was on the side of her having Brea. "You also have David and Frankie."

She made a scoffing sound. "Neither of us has them. They're staying out of it, waiting us out because they think it'll blow over. At least Dean has the balls to really be there for you. Maybe that's why I respect him—he's unapologetically loyal."

Loyal or not, I was going to have words with him about the crap he'd pulled with her. The least he could do was get the report of a seizure taken off her record so she could get her driver's license next month. Thinking back over her confession, I connected what she'd yelled at Dean to our last car trip, when I'd called Wendy, and Jessica had quietly flipped out.

The dots made an ugly picture, and I had to know if I'd drawn it correctly. "Jessica, did you break up with me because I have other subs?"

Her response took long enough for me to realize the answer was in the affirmative. When she spoke, though, she was less clear. "I told you why. Do you really want to rehash that again?"

"I want to know if you broke up with me because you wanted to be my only sub. Maybe you said you weren't submissive because you didn't want to share my attention." Why the fuck hadn't I seen that before? Of course she hadn't wanted to share me. We'd been having an idyllic weekend, almost honeymoon-esque, and then it had gone to shit. When I'd informed her Wendy was coming for a session, I'd known she was upset, but I'd chalked it up to how she claimed she didn't want to be around when I was with my subs.

I hadn't realized the reason she didn't want to be around was because she considered it a lack of fidelity on my part. Pain seared my chest at the realization I'd been the one who'd driven her away.

She'd retreated to Unexpected Treasures that night to give herself time to deal with the emotional blow, and I'd pushed her. At the time I'd been intent on exerting my dominance in order to bring her home—to the home I wanted to share with her. In my relentless pursuit of making her open herself to me, I'd made her vulnerable, and then I'd torn her apart.

I was a fucking bastard.

A glance over showed that even now, four months later, she was having trouble holding it together. For the second time in less than an hour, I squealed to a halt on the shoulder of an exit ramp.

Before she could utter a word, I flung off my seat belt and pulled her into my arms. "I'm so sorry, darlin'. I'm so fucking sorry. I didn't know—I didn't realize—I'm, fuck—I'm sorry." I undid her belt and slid her onto my lap.

"Jesse, it's fine. You didn't do anything wrong. I'm not submissive. I tried to be—for you—but I'm not, and I can't." She stroked her fingertips back from my temple, soothing me as I tried to soothe her.

"It's not fine. I hurt you. That's why you wouldn't move in. That's why you kept leaving." I held her tighter, burying my face in her neck and inhaling her scent. "Why didn't you ever say anything?"

"It's in the past. It doesn't matter."

"It does matter."

She hooked a finger under my chin and guided my face out of her neck until my gaze met hers. Tears shimmered in those deep green depths. "I know you don't like hearing this, but it *doesn't* matter. I ended our relationship because you're a Dom and I'm not a sub. Perhaps I didn't like sharing you, but I knew that I'd never be able to give you what they do, and so I kept my feelings to myself. I knew from the start we were doomed, and I told you that, but you refused to listen. Maybe I liked your optimism or your tenacity. You made me want to think we had a real shot, so I tried. I swear I did, Jesse."

Her lips brushed mine, a tender expression that was over almost before it began—like our relationship.

She rested her fingertips against my cheek. "You once asked me to be honest with you, so here goes: I think I'll love you for the rest of my life, but that doesn't change the fact you and I would be miserable together. Misery would slowly turn to resentment, and I never want to see the day when I resent you."

I wanted to say something clever, to find the words that would negate everything so we could be together, but I couldn't. For the first time, I really listened to her. All those times I explained what it meant to be a sub, she *had* heard me, but she hadn't connected to what I'd been describing.

Like an ornery mule, I'd stuck by the idea she'd come to her senses eventually. If I was in love with her, then she had to be a

75

submissive, right? Because that's how the universe worked, right? David had found his sub, and I'd expected to find mine. Dean wasn't looking, so he didn't count.

Well, it looked like fate had once again intervened to make sure I would walk my path alone.

Jessica framed my face with her hands. "Jesse, how about this? Let's try just being friends."

"Go back to the way things used to be?" Her boob was pressed against my arm, and the pressure and warmth of her body on my lap made me want to propose a different solution, but I knew better than to try that route again.

Her shoulder lifted in a shy shrug. "If you're ready."

It looked like I didn't have another choice. "I'm as ready as I'll ever be."

Chapter 8—Jesse

I had planned to drive through the night, maybe pull over at a rest stop for a few hours if I got too tired, but as the sun set, one glance at Jessica showed purple circles forming under her eyes.

"Do you want to climb in the back and get some sleep?"

Most of the ride through Georgia had been devoid of conversation. We'd both tried to talk about benign topics, but those forays never lasted for long.

When she didn't answer, I glanced over to find her staring out the window, but her eyes were glazed over. I reached over and touched her arm. "Hey, daydreamer, it's okay if you want to climb in the back and lie down, get some rest."

Seconds passed before she blinked. Then she looked down at my hand on her arm. "I'm okay."

Something in her tone made it seem like she wasn't answering the question I'd asked. I tried another strategy. "Do you want to stop at a hotel for the night?"

"How far are we from your mom's?"

"Ten hours."

She glanced over at my speedometer, no doubt noting my excessive speed. "I guess the question is whether you think you can drive for ten more hours. I'm okay with stopping off if you want, and I'm okay with driving through the night. I know you're concerned about—"

She broke off at a weird point. My mom wasn't a touchy subject. "Let me call and see if I can get her on the phone. I'd feel better if I knew what was going on."

I dialed through my dashboard. I knew it drove Jessica crazy when I routed my calls through the tech in my truck, but it was safer than holding a phone to my ear or looking at it to find a button.

Ringing filled the cab. On the third one, it picked up. "Jesse, my loving son, I was just about to call you."

I perked up at that. If she had been about to call me, then she must be feeling better. "How are you doing, Mom? Aunt Gigi told me you were in the hospital."

"Oh, that busybody. She has nothing better to do than poke her nose in my business."

"I'm in Georgia, about ten hours away."

She laughed. "I'm not dying. You worry too much. I'm here for some routine tests, follow-up from the last time."

I wasn't under the impression hospitals kept patients when there was no need. "What kind of tests?"

"There are certain things a mother does not discuss with her son."

A glance at Jessica showed an amused smile.

"So it's gynecological?" Way down there in Naples, Florida, I imagined my mom blushing. Southern women of my mother's generation didn't discuss women's health issues with their sons. If Mia or Olivia had called, there was only a fifty-fifty chance she'd tell them.

"Jesse, it's uncouth for a man to talk about such things."

"Mom, I can handle it."

She huffed. "It's none of your business. It's late, and I hope you're not planning to drive through the night. I have a brunch date tomorrow that I do not want to miss."

Having me there was not a reason to change her plans, but I was pleased by the implication she would be discharged in the morning. "I can pick you up from the hospital, and I'll go to brunch with you."

"You aren't invited."

"Mom?" I scowled. "That's a shot to the heart."

"The last time you went on a brunch date with me, you glared at my date the whole time. Men of my age who are healthy enough to meet my needs are rare, and I don't need you sabotaging my love life."

Jessica snickered and slapped a hand over her mouth.

I spotted a billboard for a hotel at the next exit. "Fine, Mom. I'll be there tomorrow afternoon."

"Bring chocolate. You know what I like."

"Yes, ma'am. I'll see you tomorrow. I love you."

"I love you too." She made a kissing noise before hanging up.

It didn't take long for Jessica to bust up. I shot her a dry look. "We'll stop off at a hotel tonight."

"Your mom has a date."

"I'm aware."

"Did you really scare off her last boyfriend?"

I slid into the parking lot of a large discount store. "Let's get you a toothbrush and whatever else you didn't pack."

She gestured over her shoulder. "I stayed last night at Brea's, so I have toiletries in my bag."

I looked her over, noting her clothes. "Did you pack fresh panties or a change of clothes?" I didn't bother asking if she wanted those things because she'd probably answer in the negative even if she didn't have them on hand.

"I can wash out what I'm wearing and sleep in one of your shirts." She set a hand on my arm. "You're going to put me on a plane tomorrow, so there's no need to buy a bunch of stuff."

That settled it. "Come on." I got out of the truck.

She hurried after me. "Really, Jesse, this isn't necessary."

"Didn't say it was." I kept to myself grumblings about what she considered unnecessary and how her standards were so much lower than mine. She lived every day like she was stuck in a third-world country, and I wanted her to get used to having more than a few of the basics.

At the hotel, I grabbed the clothes she'd been wearing, the panties, two shirts, and the single pair of stretchy pants I'd bought, and took them down to the washing machine while she was in the shower. She could sleep in one of my shirts.

After I loaded everything in, I sat on the single chair in the small laundry room and called Dean.

He picked up immediately. "I'll admit to morbid curiosity regarding how she came to be in your truck."

"She stole my keys at the party, and she came by to return them."

"By hiding out in your truck?"

"She thought you might be in my apartment, which you were, and she wanted to avoid you, so she waited in my truck. While she was waiting, she fell asleep."

"Of course. And she conveniently chose to hide out in the back, where you somehow failed to notice her, and then she fell asleep so she didn't notice you getting in, driving, playing the radio—nothing until our phone call."

I wasn't sure how much of the call she'd heard, and that was not a can of worms I cared to reopen now that we'd called a truce. "Dean, why did you cancel her phone, raise her rent, and move her medical care? I've told you repeatedly to leave her alone."

"She told you all this?"

"Yeah."

"Bitch is looking to drive a wedge between us."

"Not particularly. When I got mad, she defended you. She said you're the only one who had the balls to be unabashedly loyal." It meant a lot to me to have Dean as a friend, only I hadn't wanted him to go after the woman who would always own my heart. "And I'm going to ask you to stop calling her names."

"Did you two make up?" Dean sounded half-suspicious and completely disgusted.

"No. We called a truce because we're having a baby together, and we'd like to have a cordial relationship for the sake of our child."

Dean growled. "Fuck, Jesse. Don't do this to yourself. She's just going to hurt you again. Fine—let's say that she got in your truck by accident. There has to be an airport nearby. Put her on a plane back to KC. I'll pay for her ticket. I'll pick her up and make sure she gets home."

Part of me didn't trust Dean with Jessica. "She's not going to hurt me again. We had a good talk about the past and the future." I'd realized a few things, but I wasn't ready to talk about anything with Dean. He was still too furious with Jessica, and I wasn't too happy with him. "Since we called a truce, and since you're on my side, you're going to be cordial to her from now on."

An aggravated groan was his only response.

"Dean, I mean it. The things you did—taking away her storefront and studio—that's a really low blow. And transferring her to other doctors?" I made a disgusted noise. "That was mean. I'm glad you came to your senses enough to not kick her off SAFE Security's insurance."

Though David was paying the premiums and footing the cost of Jessica's medical care, we'd agreed to have her on our rolls as an employee so she could get insurance.

"Not for lack of trying, and I did it all for you."

"For me?"

"Yeah, dumbass. You refused to come home. You did everything you could to avoid Kansas City. For four months, you've been gone, either on a mission or to visit one of your relatives—like what you're doing right now. I transferred her doctors closer to where she lives because that way you won't have to worry about running into her when you're home. I pushed her out of the building for the same reason."

I scoffed. "You're trying to make yourself sound altruistic, like you did it all to make life easier for me, but you did it to get back at her."

"Is that what you're pissed about? That, in making your life easier, I made hers harder? Wake the fuck up, Jesse. She doesn't care about you. Just because she's knocked up with your kid doesn't make her less of a manipulative bitch. Open your eyes and see her for what she really is—an opportunistic con-artist who is using you and your baby-daddy credit card."

Jessica had never once used me for money. Even tonight, when I'd insisted she buy clothes, she'd gone straight to the clearance rack. "Dean, you gotta get over being mad at her. I'm not innocent. I did things to drive her away, and I fucking ignored her when she told me she didn't want those things. She left because I fucked up." I ran a hand over my hair. "She left because I didn't listen to her."

"She's using you." Dean was also not listening to me.

"No, she's not. This isn't easy for her either."

"Oh, yeah? Why don't you ask her why I couldn't cancel her health insurance even though I took her off our employee rolls?"

I sat up straight. "You fucking did what? Dean, she needs health insurance. Not just for her hip—she's pregnant. It's *my* baby who will suffer."

"Ask her, Jesse. See how she's using you now."

I opened my mouth to yell at him, but the screen showed the call had ended. Fucker had hung up on me. I made my way back to the room, and I found Jessica snuggled under the covers.

She sat up as I came in, revealing that she wore my shirt. "You were gone a long time." Her lips pressed together, probably quelling the urge to ask where I'd been.

"I called Dean."

"Oh." Her gaze flickered away. "I'm finished in the bathroom. I used one of your disposable razors for my legs. I hope you don't mind."

This woman was completely at odds with the portrait Dean had in his head. To reaffirm that idea, I took a chance on Dean's question. If she wasn't on SAFE Security's insurance, I needed to know she was covered somewhere. If she wasn't, I'd change that situation immediately.

"Jessica, Dean said that he tried to cut off your health care by firing you from SAFE Security."

"Let's not talk about any of that unpleasantness. I've landed on my feet, okay?" She rolled to her other side and pulled the covers up, signaling that she was finished with the conversation.

Nothing got to me faster than an uncooperative Jessica. I sat on the edge of her bed and eased the covers from over her face. "Who is paying for your insurance?"

Her chest heaved a sigh. "You are." She didn't meet my gaze.

I was meticulous about my bank accounts. I hadn't seen an increase in money flowing to health insurance. Actually, my monthly premium cost had dropped a few dollars. "How?"

She chewed at her bottom lip in a rare show of nerves. "Maybe you should ask David? It was his idea."

Now my curiosity was piqued. I peeled back the covers and lifted her until she sat up and faced me. "Darlin', I'd like an explanation."

"We're married."

Shock she would marry anyone was superseded only by the fact of who she claimed to have married. How the fuck could she marry David? He was already married. "How? Did he divorce Brea and not tell anyone?"

She winced. "No, I'm married to you."

This didn't make sense. "I would remember a wedding." Especially one I'd dreamed about for over a year.

"David pretended to be you. Brea heard Dean on the phone trying to cancel my health insurance, so she and David hatched a plan. He forges your signature pretty well." She trailed off, her eyes glazing over. This didn't seem like something to cry over, but with pregnancy hormones, I heard that anything was possible.

"Jessica." I waved a hand in front of her eyes. In a few seconds, her eyes focused.

"And so he filled in for you." Her gaze fell. "I'm sorry for lying to you about this, but I was in a desperate position. If it was just me, I'd stop PT and the other stuff because it won't kill me not to have it, but with the baby on the way—I was scared. Brea asked Frankie first, but she refused. She said that you should be the one to marry me."

In her position, I would have been terrified. More than just physical therapy, she needed a battery of regular tests, and she definitely couldn't make it without her therapist.

She grabbed my hand. "I know you're mad. You have every right to be, but I—I didn't see another way. When Dean said he was going to break me, I didn't think he'd be so ruthless about it. But I guess I should have known."

Her lower lip quivered, and I knew she was berating herself for letting down her guard—for letting any of us get close to her.

But I was still reeling from finding out I was married to the woman of my dreams even though she wanted nothing to do with me. I extracted my hand from her grasp and paced the length of the room.

Desperation had accomplished what love couldn't, and I felt like shit about it. I also felt betrayed. One of my closest friends had impersonated me to protect a woman I should have been protecting. No matter what was or wasn't going on between us, I had an obligation to Jessica. David should have told me. I would have stopped Dean.

82

Snatching up my phone, I called David. As soon as he picked up, I laid into him. "You son of a bitch. You pretended to be me instead of telling me what Dean was doing to her?"

"Jesse, I heard you picked up a hitchhiker."

"Don't fucking be pleasant when I'm pissed at you."

David dropped his cheerful demeanor. "Look, I did what you didn't have the courage to do."

If he was next to me, I would have punched him. I had been planning to marry Jessica from the moment we met. Courage wasn't the problem. "You should have told me."

"I tried, but you wouldn't listen to anything having to do with Jessica. You've spent the past four months running from any mention of her."

"When the fuck did you try to tell me what Dean was doing?" I couldn't remember a single time he'd attempted to bring up Jessica's health insurance.

"Thanksgiving. I told you that I wanted to talk to you about Jessica, and you lit out for your sister's house."

I vaguely recalled David bringing her up, but he hadn't said anything about her health. I'd assumed he wanted to talk about the failure of the relationship or urge me to try again. David was big on not giving up. It had worked out for him.

"I always go to Olivia's or Mia's for Thanksgiving."

He sighed. "Jesse, it's been hard for you for a long time. I'm glad you came last night, and I'm kind of glad you got stuck with Jessica because the two of you are overdue for a long talk."

Now that anger was receding—David, the poster-boy for cool, calm, and collected, was great at talking me down—I wondered about the logistics. We looked nothing alike. "How did you get an ID with my name and your picture?"

He laughed. "You're married to an excellent forger."

I looked to where Jessica sat on the bed, staring off into the distance. Melancholy and exhaustion dulled the green of her eyes.

"Just don't do something like this again without asking me first, okay?"

David chuckled. "Here's hoping it won't be necessary."

He ended the call before I could point out that he hadn't promised anything.

Jessica got out of bed, and my gaze fell to caress her bare, shapely legs. My brain went into caveman mode. "As long as you're married to me, you can't screw around with other men."

She paused, her lips pursed. Those shrewd eyes studied my face. "Then you can't screw around with other women."

I lifted a brow. "Can we screw around with each other?"

She twirled a strand of hair around her finger, thinking, not flirting. "That's probably not a good idea."

Chapter 9——Jessica

I couldn't bring myself to say no. An outright refusal wouldn't leap from my tongue.

He came one step closer, but that's all it took to put him within touching distance. He stood there, authority dripping from his shoulders, and yet he somehow managed not to dominate the space. He was adept at making me feel like there was no room when he was around, and I recognized the conscious effort he made not to do it.

After all this time, I finally felt like I had a place in his life. Perhaps if he hadn't made room for me, I would be able to deny his request. That pale blue gaze held me captive. I couldn't move. I could barely breathe.

"If you had told me what Dean was doing, I would have stopped him."

I didn't want to debate the past. I knew David had told him he'd tried to talk to Jesse. When that had failed, Brea had championed a course of action I sincerely hadn't wanted to follow, but I hadn't been able to see another choice. My parents couldn't afford my care, and having me on his plan didn't affect Jesse's premium cost. Ironically, Brea had fixed things so adding me brought down his rate more than enough to pay for mine. I didn't understand how insurance rates were calculated, but apparently a married man was cheaper to insure through their company than a single man—especially after they finished talking to my sister.

A fluttering in my abdomen drew my attention from the matter at hand. I'd been feeling a tickling inside for a couple of months, but lately I'd been able to feel it when I put my hand on my stomach.

I took Jesse's hand and put it where I felt movement. "It's really light, but if you concentrate, I think you'll be able to feel him or her moving around."

We waited in silence, but at last he shook his head. Wordlessly he pulled me closer and brushed his lips against mine. "I noticed you didn't say it was a bad idea."

I wanted to kiss him back. I wanted to throw myself at him and revel in the way it felt to have his arms around me and his cock inside me. The raw hope in his voice jolted me into my right mind, and my tongue stopped holding onto things it shouldn't. I pushed him away, an easy move because he cooperated. "It's a bad idea. We talked about this. You're going to get hurt even more."

He cupped my cheek. "Stop pretending like you aren't just as hurt. I know this is hard for you."

My heart thumped painfully, knots of regret and shards of broken love keeping it from beating normally. I knew where he was heading. "Having sex isn't going to make it hurt less."

He pulled me to him and held me for the longest time. Being in his arms did salve the pain a little, but it was a bitter bandage.

"Tampa has an airport." Jesse threw that out as we passed a sign indicating it was the next exit.

We'd passed airports in many major cities on our journey, but this was the first time he'd offered to stop at one. I eyed him curiously. "I thought you wanted to get to your mom as quickly as possible."

"She said she was okay. Right now, she's finishing up brunch with her date that I'm not ruining."

The tension we'd generated last night with the brief interlude had somehow grown. I was so aware of him that my bra felt like it was smashing my girls and constricting my chest. Hoping a shift in gravity would work, I sat forward. "You want to get rid of me because you don't want me to meet your mom. Okay, drop me in Tampa."

His forehead and chin wrinkled, a sure-fire sign he was going to disagree with me. "I'd love for you to meet my mom. She knows all about you."

That brought me up short. "All about me? What does that mean?"

"She knows you're pregnant, and she knows we broke up. She keeps telling me to get you flowers, although so did your dad."

Now it was my turn to frown. "Warren told you to bring me flowers?"

"He said it wouldn't hurt. Instead I got mad at you for making out with that art guy, and then I said some mean things to you. Flowers probably would've gone over better."

I laughed because I didn't know what else to do. My father was giving Jesse advice for trying to win back my heart? I knew he had good intentions, but he didn't know the details of why Jesse and I weren't compatible.

My brain skipped back to a part I'd glossed over. "Does your mom hate me for breaking your heart?"

"She said she's reserving judgment until she meets you." He glanced over. "I haven't brought a woman to meet my mother since I was fifteen."

I was surprised he'd stopped so young. "Fifteen? Let me guess—no woman is good enough for her perfect son."

"Perfect?" He laughed. "I annoy the shit out of her after about two hours. She makes me stay in a hotel."

"Nice evasion. C'mon—help me prepare. What did the first girl do that was so bad you were too afraid to bring around all the rest of your girlfriends?"

"She was one of those people who was always super happy and upbeat." He shot me a sideways glance. "My mom loved her. They became very close."

This was surprising to me, but it also explained why he hadn't brought around other women. Even after their teen crush had ended, if his mom was still hanging out with Jesse's ex-girlfriend, it would make for awkward social situations. "Is your mom still holding out hope you'll end up together?"

He frowned. "No."

"Are they still friends?"

His lips pressed together, and I deduced I was treading into delicate territory.

"I'm sorry. You don't have to answer. I just want your mom to like me."

"Well, I can't guarantee you'll like her or she'll like you."

"Tell me about her. What does she do with her time? What are her likes and dislikes? Where has she traveled?"

A bark of laughter burst from him. "She's not your next mark."

"I know." I was a little hurt he'd think I had nefarious intent. "But if I know she hates flan, I won't ask her if she wants me to make her flan for dessert." Flan was a fun dessert, and I was kind of craving it right now.

"How about you meet her and see how it goes?" His grin had a devil behind it.

"I like to stack the deck in my favor. If she hates me, she's not going to like our kid."

"She doesn't like Griffin—you remember Mia's husband?—and she loves Harper, Landon, and Lilias just fine."

When we'd visited last fall, Griffin had been nothing but nice to me. He was much more friendly and outgoing than I was. If that was the way Mrs. Foraker rolled, my future prospects didn't look so hot. "Does she know about my past?"

"Does it matter? We're talking about the future."

"Yes, it matters. Did you tell her more or less than what you told your sister Olivia?"

"I didn't tell her you had a fantastic ass, so less."

We argued like that for a half hour before it hit me that we were bantering—flirting—and I fell silent. Nikki and I had discussed what it would be like to have Jesse back in my life, and this kind of scenario hadn't come up. Anger and aloofness, I expected and understood. The kind of playful banter and flirting in which we'd engaged when I was still wheelchair-bound—I'd thought I'd killed it.

I didn't know how I felt about its return, or about the invisible rope that seemed to pull me toward Jesse.

About an hour south of Tampa, he turned off the freeway. He chose roads in a way that let me know he'd driven this path dozens or hundreds of times. At last he pulled into the parking lot of a florist's shop.

I turned to him, mouth agape. "You're not seriously buying me flowers?"

"Hadn't planned on it." He put the transmission into park, but he didn't cut the engine. "Wait here."

While I waited, I used the last of the charge on my phone to call Brea. She picked up right away.

"Jessica, what time is your plane due?"

"I don't know. We stopped off at a hotel for the night, and now he's taking me to meet his mother."

"Oh?" A wealth of questions sprouted from that single syllable.

"What do you know about her? I want her to like me, but Jesse isn't giving me anything to work with."

Brea laughed because she knew exactly what I was doing. "I haven't met her, but from what Frankie and David have said, she's really nice. She's one of those people who hugs everyone and is always trying to make you eat something. Just be yourself, and she'll love you."

I wasn't sure. Now that I was better equipped to think from a mother's perspective, I knew I'd hate anyone who broke my baby's heart, no matter how old they were.

"She knows I broke up with him."

"Yeah, but I don't think she knows why." Water ran, and pots clanged. I gathered she was in the kitchen, though that didn't mean she was cooking. David had some mad skills in the kitchen, and so he often prepared meals for them.

I heard David's voice in the background, and then Brea came back. "Hey, David says he's never brought a woman to meet his mom."

"Yeah, he told me the last one was when he was fifteen."

"Fifteen? I can see why you're nervous."

I loved that I didn't have to explain myself to Brea. She understood how I thought, and she drew the same conclusions.

While love for her welled in my heart, David's voice came through the speaker. "He married that one."

"He—what?"

Brea answered. "David says that Jesse married the girl he brought home when he was fifteen. And now he's bringing you, and you're also married. I'm sensing a pattern."

My lungs didn't want to hold air. "We're not really married."

She shrugged so loud that I heard it in Florida, but before I could reach through the phone and slap her, Jesse returned. He had a bouquet of red roses and calla lilies. Red roses were for romantic love, and calla lilies symbolized marriage.

I hung up on Brea and shut down my phone before he got into the truck. "Those are pretty."

He grunted and set them on the floor of the backseat.

Striving for a casual tone, I said, "Have you ever lived in Florida?" He already knew I'd spent a few years in various locations in the Sunshine State.

"I was stationed outside Jacksonville for a couple years. I had an apartment for when I wasn't deployed."

Jacksonville was on the other side of the state, and we were a few hours north of Naples, where his mother lived. This fishing expedition was getting me nowhere. Never once had Jesse mentioned being divorced or having been married.

I was quiet for a couple blocks, but curiosity was eating me from the inside. "Jesse, have you ever been married before?"

"Have you?" He countered fairly quickly and with a neutral tone.

The first rule in conning information from someone is to keep the conversation going. "I've been engaged as part of a con, but I've never been married. It seems so permanent." Yes, I was leading. Sue me.

"I'm not going to divorce you." During my shocked silence, he turned a corner before glancing over. "That's what you're fishing for, right? You want to know how long after you have the baby am I going to wait until I divorce you. Never. That's the answer. If you want a divorce, you're going to have to do all the work, just like you did for the wedding."

His tone was a little crusty, indicating irritation. "Last night, you didn't seem all that mad about it." Now that he'd slept on it, perhaps he'd changed his mind. "Are you against divorce for some reason?"

He shrugged. "It works for some people."

This was getting me nowhere, but before I could bust out with what I really wanted to know, he turned into a cemetery, the kind with wrought-iron gates and tree-lined drives. It would make a great park.

Back in the day, Brea and I used to hang out in cemeteries a lot because they were peaceful, and often nobody was around to care that two little girls weren't in school. We'd find an older grave, spread a blanket, and spend hours reading, drawing, and talking. BS never thought to look for us in a cemetery.

Jesse navigated the maze of byways until he came to a stop. "Wait here." Without looking at me, he reached in the backseat and got the flowers.

I really wanted to know who he was leaving them for. Geographically it didn't make sense for him to have a dead wife buried so far from where they'd lived, so this had to be someone else.

Wasn't his brother at Arlington? He'd been killed in battle.

Instead of asking, I nodded. "Sure."

He walked a bit, skirting larger headstones, until he was halfway to the next street. Then he squatted down and placed the flowers, carefully arranging them. From my vantage point, I couldn't see the headstone. It was the kind that was a flat stone on the ground.

I got out of the truck to stretch my legs. As long as I kept away from where he was, I didn't think he'd feel like I was invading his privacy. Carrying my cane because I figured I'd need it soon, I walked to the end of this section of paved road, looking to see how the plots and rows were marked.

Before I got too far with my research, a car pulled up behind Jesse's truck. A middle-aged man who looked like an accountant got out. He even had glasses and beige pants. He was around the same height as Jesse, but he was much thinner, and a bit of paunch pushed out his waistline. He held a bouquet of roses.

He crossed the same expanse of grass, heading toward Jesse though he didn't seem to be aware of him until Jesse turned. The two stared, but no lips moved. I had a side view of both of them, but it was enough to know it was a tense exchange. A minute later, the other guy retreated.

Jesse crouched back down and bowed his head. I stood behind the truck and tried not to look like I had been watching.

If ever there was a time for the urge to smoke to strike me, now was not convenient, so that's when it happened. It wasn't a small urge, either. It was powerful, so overwhelming I had to lean against the rear bumper to do my breathing exercises.

"Are you okay, ma'am?"

I looked up to find the accountant regarding me curiously. "I'm okay."

"Pardon me for saying, but you don't seem okay. Usually when a pregnant woman breathes like that, it means she's in labor."

I peered at him curiously. "Are you an obstetrician?"

"Manager at a health services office."

Close enough to make my guess of accountant correct. "Then why would you assume I'm pregnant?"

He glanced down, a brief flicker of the eye.

It was enough. I snapped my fingers in front of his face and, as I gently pushed him back, my light fingers went to work. "Maybe I'm just fat."

His eyes widened. "I'm sorry. I'm—sorry. I just wanted to see if you were okay."

And I wanted to know who had the balls to even start a staring contest with Jesse. Sure, he'd lost, but he'd participated. People didn't usually go up against Jesse like that. I spun away and went to the passenger side of the truck where I could check the wallet I'd stolen for ID.

Darin Pennington had an address for an exit I'd seen in the past hour, so he was local. He also had seven credit cards, two grocery club cards, and a frequent-haircut card. He was two away from a free cut. I counted seventeen dollars and three faded photos of a pretty blonde woman. In one of them, a much-younger and passably handsome Darin had his arms around the woman. They were both beaming.

I pivoted suddenly and went back to where he stood next to his car. "I'm sorry." I reached out to touch his arm, and I managed to stumble at the same time so I could slip his wallet back. "I overreacted. It's these pregnancy hormones, and you were just asking if I was okay. Please accept my apology."

"Oh, it's okay. I understand."

I gave him my best bemused smile. It bordered on flirty, and it maybe wasn't appropriate for a cemetery. I wasn't sure. I'd never tried to use my manipulative gifts in a cemetery before. Lots of firsts for me this week. "You have a wife?"

"No, not anymore, but I remember the hormones." He laughed nervously. "She was pregnant when she passed away. Car accident. She died instantly."

"I'm so sorry." From the periphery of my vision, I saw Jesse approaching.

Darin tensed. "Are you with him?"

I turned. "Yes. That's my husband."

His eyes widened, and he backed away. The next thing I knew, his car cruised past and turned out of view.

Jesse approached, hands in his pockets and his expression aloof. "What are you doing, Brat?"

The nickname, one I'd hated at first but had secretly grown to like, indicated he wasn't fooled by my innocent act. I rubbed my hands together. "I was craving a cigarette, so I stole stuff from that guy."

His incredulous expression had me rethinking my strategy.

"I gave it back. He won't even know it was gone. When I returned his wallet, all seventeen dollars and a free haircut card was still in Darin's wallet."

"Darin? You're friends now?"

"I saw his license."

Before I could say more, Jesse tilted his head. "What's his last name?"

"Pennington."

"Address?"

I shook my head. "No. You're not driving me to his house so I can apologize. I gave it back, Jesse. I could have just asked him for a cigarette. He had a pack in his other pocket."

Just when I thought Jesse would blow up at me, he sat on the bumper of his truck and leaned against the tailgate. An ironic chuckle started in his gut. "Eighteen years, I've been trying to find out that fucker's name. You did it in minutes."

The Jesse Foraker I knew was a formidable man who could track anyone anywhere without knowing their name. I'd seen him identify people from grainy satellite photos. This guy at least had a car with a license plate, and Jesse knew how to use that to dig up anything he wanted about a person.

"Eighteen years? You didn't want to know his name."

"Maybe I didn't." He washed a hand down his face.

"Who is he?"

"Darin Pennington, apparently."

"Jesse, I saw you two have a staring contest."

"Wasn't the first, won't be the last."

Sensing that he was about to spill his guts, I sat next to him and said nothing.

He began with a sigh. "That girl I brought home when I was fifteen? I married her two weeks after we graduated from high school."

I glanced toward the unknown grave, guessing where this story ended.

"She's buried over there. Car accident. She was supposed to have been coming home from her college classes in Tampa. She moved there to be closer to her classes, and when I was stateside, I stayed on the base whenever I had to report. We spent more time apart than together, even when I was home." He paused to kick at invisible gravel on the road. "The night before she died, she'd called me in Afghanistan to ask for a divorce. We argued—you know how pig-headed I can be— and she hung up. That's the last time we ever talked. The next day, I got a call that she'd been in a fatal collision."

I'd already done some math of my own. "She was cheating on you with Darin?" Having seen them both, I didn't see how someone who found Jesse attractive could be happy with the pencil-pusher type. They were diametric opposites. Though I didn't voice those negative, judgmental thoughts, I realized she had probably been looking for the opposite of Jesse. She'd been young and newly married, and he'd shipped out almost immediately. That had to have been really hard.

"I don't know. She never said there was anybody else, but he showed up at the funeral. He was the only other guy there who looked as gobsmacked as I felt. And every year on her birthday, he shows up here. Sometimes I see him, and sometimes I don't, but I see the flowers. He brings white roses, and he's never said a word to me." He rubbed the palms of his hands down his jeans. "Doesn't matter. Let's go."

Before he could get anywhere, I slipped my arms around him. He hugged me to him, burying his face in my hair as he held me tightly. It was more than what I'd give a friend but less than what I'd do for a lover.

I waited until we were on the freeway to say more. "What was her name?"

"Josie."

He certainly had a thing for J-names. I poked fun at him in the hopes of elevating his mood. "Josie and Jesse? And then your second wife's name is Jessica? Am I seeing a type emerge? Was she short, with brown hair and green eyes?"

Though no smile lifted his lips, the frown disappeared. "She was short, only five feet even, but she had blonde hair and brown eyes.

When we get to my mom's place, I'll show you a picture, and you can see how different you are from her."

Having been through Darin's wallet, I knew what I'd find.

Chapter 10—Jesse

My mother's car wasn't in the carport when I parked in the lot near her condo. I looked around, but I didn't see it anywhere else, either. Being a retirement community, the carport was directly in front of the condo, so it didn't make sense for my mom to want to park anywhere else. She was the kind of woman who trolled the rows at the grocery store, waiting until an appropriately close space opened up when she could have been parked and finished with half of her shopping if she'd opted to park a little farther away.

She'd do sixteen miles up and down the aisles, but she wouldn't walk an extra fifty feet to her car.

Jessica watched me quietly. She'd been calm on this trip, which was a nice change from our last road adventure when she'd been a stressball the entire time. After a minute passed, she reached out and touched my wrist. "Did you change your mind about introducing me?"

"No." Truth be told, my mom had been after me to bring Jessica for a visit since before Jessica had moved to Missouri.

"I won't steal anything. I promise."

I looked down at where her fingertips rested on my skin, and I fought a powerful urge to take her in my arms. I wasn't sure if the urge originated from the desire to reassure her or from a need to soothe the ache in my heart.

Being with her was hard, but it was my own fault. I could have turned around the second I found her in my truck, and we'd passed dozens of airports where I could have sent her back. But I'd chosen to keep her with me, most likely out of a morbid streak of self-destructiveness. Maybe I was as much of a masochist as I was a sadist?

Maybe I was punishing myself for losing her. Or maybe I'd meant to punish her?

She wasn't behaving like being with me was a punishment. For the first time since we'd had sex, she was relaxed. The tension and anxiety she always seemed to carry around were gone.

This year, I had every intention of skipping my ritual of putting flowers on Josie's grave because I hadn't wanted to face questions from Jessica. But after our talk yesterday, I didn't think she'd make it awkward or difficult, and my instinct had turned out to be right.

Things were different between us, and the more time I spent with her, the more I realized all the ways in which I'd stifled her. She was definitely not cut out to be a submissive.

And yet, that no longer seemed to matter to me.

I squeezed her hand and set it back on her side of the cab. "If you feel the urge, target me. My mom will definitely not like you if you steal from her or her friends."

"How are you going to introduce me?"

All this time, I'd been mooning over losing Jessica, when in the eyes of the law, she was legally my wife. If that didn't beat all, I didn't know what could.

Though I had every right to be mad, hearing about their scheme had done the opposite. The fury that had driven me for the past four months had evaporated. I was married to the woman I loved. Now I just had to find a way to make it last. I'd fucked up my first marriage by not being there when she needed me; I'd be damned if I was going to fuck up this one.

I grinned at my beautiful bride. "By your name. She's not senile, darlin'. She remembers everything I've told her about you."

"Jesse, I'd feel better if you told me anything about her." Eyes wide, she came as close as she felt comfortable to imploring me for something.

If this marriage was going to have a shot, then I needed to give her what she needed. Information was power, and she needed some right now. "She loves cigarettes, mimosas, and bingo. She has two sisters who live in the next town over, and she's close to my aunt Gigi, short for Georgina, who is my father's sister. Aunt Gigi lives in the same complex, so you'll meet her at some point. You may also meet my mom's sisters, Carol and Cynthia, because once word gets out that you're here, they're all gonna come armed with casseroles."

"Casseroles?"

"Aunt Carol makes good casseroles. Hopefully they'll work together, and Aunt Cynthia will bring cake." I probably should have warned her about all this before now. She'd been under the impression she was only meeting my mom, which was probably stressful enough, and now she was realizing that meeting my mom was the tip of the iceberg. To be fair, I had previously told her about the size of my extended family. "I have a couple of cousins who live around these parts too, so they might come around for a look."

96

She worried her lower lip with her teeth, but after a few seconds, she nodded. "Like ripping off a bandage. Thank you for being open to me picking your pockets. That'll help take the edge off."

Nobody responded when I knocked, so I knocked more insistently and called out, "Mom? It's Jesse." Nothing happened, so I rang the doorbell, which my mom hated. It echoed through the house loud enough to wake the dead.

"Do you have a key?" Jessica asked. "Maybe she needs help."

It was more likely she was out playing bingo. She wasn't one to let my impending arrival change her bingo plans. At any rate, it was unusual for her not to leave the door open or a note taped where I'd find it. I fished a key from my pocket and unlocked the door. The stale smell of cigarette smoke wafted out, and it grew heavier once I stepped through the threshold.

"Mom?" I called for her as I searched the first floor.

Jessica came inside as I mounted the stairs to check the two bedrooms and bathroom on the second floor. They were empty. I returned to the main floor.

"She hasn't been here in a few days." Jessica held up a stack of circulars and junk mail. "I found this in her mailbox outside."

This wasn't adding up. My mom wasn't in the habit of misleading me. If she didn't want me poking my nose into a subject, she told me so the same way she had yesterday. If she was still in the hospital, she would call to tell me she wasn't at home. I shooed Jessica out to the porch because I didn't want her breathing the air in there, and I slid my cell phone from my pocket.

"Hi, Aunt Gigi. Listen, I'm at my mom's. I was supposed to meet her here today."

"Jesse, I'm so glad you came. Sheila is still in the hospital. They did surgery this morning."

I felt like someone had punched me in the gut. "Why didn't you call?"

"Oh, honey, I know what day it is. Sheila didn't want me to call you at all because she thinks you'll do a better job of letting her go if you stopped visiting the cemetery. She knew you'd stop there if you came down now. You did stop there, didn't you?"

"Of course I did." I wiped the back of my hand across my forehead. I visited my father and my brother Bailey every year as well. While I didn't think it was possible to "get over" the death of someone I loved, I didn't see how remembering those I'd loved and lost meant I hadn't moved on with my life.

Gigi cleared her throat. "Anyway, your mother is out of surgery, and she's resting. I'll text you her room number so you can come visit. Are you staying at her place?"

"Hadn't planned on it." I had a reservation at a nearby hotel. "Are you at the hospital with her?"

"Yes."

"Then I'll see you soon." Next, I faced Jessica. "Sorry about this—"

She waved her hand, cutting me off. "Let's get to the hospital. I know you're worried."

"Hey, there." A male voice called from the sidewalk. I looked over to see an older man, still reasonably tall and fit, waving at me. He wore tan slacks and an orange polo shirt. A safari hat shaded his face and neck, but enough hair peeked out to show off a full head of hair—or at least a decent toupee.

"Can I help you?" I took a few steps in his direction, and Jessica fell in behind me.

"I'm looking for Sheila." He indicated the house. "We had plans earlier, but she sent me a text postponing until tomorrow. I wanted to stop by and see if she was okay."

I didn't know this guy, and my first instinct was to chase him away from my mom. However I quelled that urge. My dad had passed away more than a decade ago, and she deserved whatever happiness she could find.

Offering a hand, I introduced myself. "I'm her son, Jesse."

"Ben Sheets. It's nice to meet you, Jesse. Your mother has told me a lot about you."

I glanced over my shoulder to find Jessica melting back like she didn't want to be part of the conversation. In the spirit of my newfound non-Dom role in her life, I let her stay out of the spotlight. "Ben, my mom is in the hospital still. I'll tell her that you stopped by."

His eyes widened. "The hospital? Is she okay?"

I wish I had a fucking clue, but she'd refused to tell me anything. "I'm sure she'll be fine. I'll have her call you when she can."

With that, I guided Jessica to the truck, noting how she kept her face turned away from Ben. This was a curious development, though my priority was getting to my mom. I watched Ben amble down the sidewalk as I drove away.

"What was that about?"

She chewed a cuticle and frowned into the middle distance. "I don't know."

"Darlin', I know what you look like when you're trying to fly under the radar."

98

"I'm not saying I wasn't, just that I don't know what it was about."

I reached over and took her hand away from her mouth. "How about you tell me instead of chewing off your fingers?"

She heaved a sigh. "He looks familiar, but I can't remember from where."

"Bad-familiar?" Otherwise, why would she try to hide from him? "Like from when BS had you?"

"Possibly. It's a feeling more than a memory." She swished her hands in the air like she could maybe catch a fish there. The odd movement conveyed a lot of frustration. After the accident, three years in a coma and several strokes had taken a toll on her memory, among other things. "I'd like to say it'll come to me, but I've been trying to accept what's gone is gone."

"It's okay to be frustrated."

"It's pointless. It's not like I can do anything to bring it back." She ran a hand through her hair, messing it into a tumbling riot of curls. She glanced over. "You're smiling."

I couldn't help it. She was adorable. However, I didn't want her to think I found her damaged brain funny. "Four months ago, you would have turned your life inside-out trying to find out where you might have met him before, and now you're just mildly frustrated. You've come far in a few months."

A small smile curved her lips, a smaller reflection of mine. "I'm trying."

"I know you are, darlin'. I'm proud of you." Yeah, it wasn't my place to be proud of her, but I wasn't going to pretend I didn't care or that I wasn't rooting for her when I wanted nothing more than to be her loudest cheerleader.

A security station at the hospital door gave us visitor badges and pointed us in the right direction. In the elevator, Jessica leaned back and rested her weight on the wall. "When we get out, don't wait for me. I'll only slow you down."

The chivalrous part of my nature rebelled at that idea, but my better sense prevailed. "You're sure?"

"Yeah. You're worried about your mom. Plus, this'll give you a few minutes alone with her. I'll wait outside the room until you're ready for me."

The door opened, and I shot her one last questioning glance.

"Go, Jesse. I'm right behind you."

I smacked a kiss on her cheek and left before she could react.

In my mom's room, I found my aunts Gigi and Cynthia already there. With the vaguest nod to acknowledge their presence, I beelined to my mom's side. My gaze roamed the parts I could see, and I noted a huge bandage wrapped around her torso. "Holy shit, Mom. What happened? Is it your heart?"

As questions sprayed from my mouth, I leaned down to kiss her cheek. Her skin was pale, and she had dark circles under her eyes.

She lifted a hand and patted my cheek weakly. "My heart is fine. I'm fine. It's nothing."

From a chair on the other side of the bed, Aunt Cynthia snorted. Like my mom, she sported short blonde hair, and like my mom's, it used to be light brown. Cynthia was the middle sister, younger than my mom by two years.

"Hi, Aunt Cyn. What's wrong with Mom?" I knew my mom wasn't going to tell me.

"Well—"

"Cynthia, it's none of his business."

Cynthia rolled her eyes. "She came in for a routine checkup, and they found an infection, so they did surgery to remove it. She'll be fine."

The bandage was around her chest. I'd been on the battlefield enough to know that infections in that area were bad news. "What kind of infection?"

"Jesse, I'm fine. They're going to keep me for one more night, and I'll go home in the morning."

I sighed. "Mom, you know if you don't tell me, I'm just gonna hack the hospital and find out for myself."

Her eyes shot daggers, but her mouth spilled the beans. "My implants were leaking, which caused a problem that led to an infection. Two days ago, they removed the implants and drained the infection. Then they put me on antibiotics to clear up the rest of it. This morning, they put new implants in. There—are you happy now that you know my boobs are fake?"

Having never paid attention to my mom's chest, I had no response except to stare like an idiot.

Cynthia, who always managed to find something amusing, laughed.

A flash went off, and I looked over to see Gigi fiddling with her phone. "I'm posting this because nobody will ever believe you had a dumbstruck expression on your face. Oh—I already have sixteen likes. Brady says you look like someone stole your favorite gun. Mia wants to know who stole your cookies and left collard greens in their place."

100

Brady was my cousin via Gigi. He and I liked to spend time at the gun range every now and again, though he really didn't know much about firearms. Mia knew I hated collard greens.

"I—um—so, you're okay now?"

"Yes, Jesse. I'm fine. You'd better sit down, though. You don't look so good."

I pulled a chair closer to her side and sat down. Then I clasped her hand in mine. "I was worried about you."

"I told you not to worry."

"When you skimp on the details, I assume the worst."

She petted my head. "When are you going to let your hair grow? It doesn't look like you're going bald yet."

If I went bald, I wouldn't have to shave my head as often. Rather than answer, I hit on her annoying habit. "When are you going to quit smoking?"

"Never."

"Well, there you go. I'll let my hair grow when you quit smoking."

"Jesse," Aunt Cynthia whispered. "There's a woman leaning against the wall across from this room. She's trying not to look inside. Did you pick up an admirer between the parking lot and here?"

It looked like Jessica had arrived. I smiled at my mom. "Mom, I brought a friend, but I don't know if you're up for meeting her just now."

My mom sat up straighter and touched her hair. She glanced nervously at her support system. "I don't look fit for company, do I?" Without waiting for Cynthia or Gigi to respond, she shook her head. "I'm not wearing makeup, and my hair isn't done."

"Jessica isn't wearing makeup either, and her hair is a mess." As I said it, I winced. The last thing I needed was for Jessica to overhear me saying unflattering things about her again. "You know what? Never mind. I'll see if she'll stay another day. I'm sure she'll also want a chance to freshen up before meeting you."

"Another day? She's leaving?"

"Yeah. Long story, but she was planning to catch a plane home tonight."

"Oh, then you'd better bring her in now. I've been wanting to meet her for a while. I just wanted to look better, you know—make a good first impression."

I smoothed my mom's hair in some spots and fluffed it in others, and then I got her makeup bag from her purse. "How about a little color?"

She sat still while I did her makeup. Growing up with older sisters, I'd learned at a young age to paint a face. When I finished, I handed her the small mirror she kept in the case. She inspected my work, and then she nodded. "I'm as ready as I'll ever be."

"I'll go get her."

In the hall, I found Jessica staring into space. Her hair looked better, which meant she'd probably stopped by a restroom on her way down the hall.

Smiling, I touched her arm. "Daydreaming again?"

She didn't respond.

"Jessica?"

Nothing.

I took her by the shoulders and gave her a little shake. "Jessica?"

After a few seconds, she blinked and smiled. "See? I told you I'd make it."

"What were you daydreaming about?"

She frowned. "When?"

"Just now. I called your name a few times, but you didn't snap out of it until I gave you a shake."

Color drained from her face. "I was staring straight ahead?"

"Yeah." I found her reaction confusing.

"And I didn't respond when you called my name?"

"No." All amusement fled. Something was wrong.

"For how long?"

I shrugged. "I don't know, for like ten seconds."

She closed her eyes and pressed her hands to her heart.

"Darlin', what's wrong?"

Her eyes fluttered open, and a sheen of disappointment wet her eyes. "Absence seizures. I thought I was having them again, but I wasn't sure."

"Absence seizures? What the hell is that?"

"It's a small seizure where my brain takes a vacation. I freeze for around five or ten seconds. When I come back, I don't remember having one, so it's kind of hard to tell."

I thought about the past two days with her, and I realized this wasn't the first one I'd witnessed. "You've had a couple more, I think."

She nodded. "Just when I thought I was over them."

"Can you take anti-seizure meds?"

"They don't mix with pregnancy." She took a deep breath. "It's fine. I can handle these. They're short, little electrical storms in my brain."

Suddenly I was against her flying home alone, but this wasn't the time to bring that up. "My mom is ready to meet you, but if you'd rather postpone it, I can explain to her that you're not feeling well."

"I'm fine. These aren't the kind of seizures that make me curl up and sleep for the rest of the day. Really, I don't remember them." She gave me a brilliant smile. "I guess Dean actually did me a favor by keeping me off the road. Having one of those while driving would be a recipe for disaster."

"You're really dismissive of this." I knew she'd suffered from seizures before—the violent kind where they had to turn her on her side and clear her airway—but I'd never witnessed one.

She set her fingertips on my cheek. "I'm fine. Any seizure where I don't end up on the floor covered in my own urine is a win." Without waiting for me, she went into the room.

I guess enduring my questions was more stressful than a room full of maternal women ready to judge her for her place in my life. I caught up in two strides. Cynthia and Gigi were on their feet, and my mom was sitting up higher. All three sported huge smiles.

My mom held out her hand. "You must be Jessica."

Jessica took my mom's hand and squeezed it. "Good evening, Mrs. Foraker. It's a pleasure to meet the woman who whipped Jesse into shape."

Mom laughed. "Sheila, please, and if I'd done my job correctly, he would have married you by now."

"I did." That tidbit slid from my primal brain and out my mouth without consulting anything in between.

Stunned silence came from three women in the room, and Jessica regarded me curiously.

"For real?" Leave it to Gigi to come to her senses first. "You eloped? I'm guessing, because I don't remember getting an invitation to the wedding."

Cynthia motioned to Jessica's hand. "I don't see a ring."

"It was a quick thing, paperwork, mostly, for the insurance." Jessica shoved her hands behind her back, stealing my wallet in the process. "We don't live together."

"Oh." Mom sat back, disappointment dripping from the utterance. "I see. At least you're providing for them as a father should."

"Why aren't you living together?" Cynthia asked. "Even if it's a marriage of convenience, it seems like it would be easier if you lived together."

103

Jessica pressed her lips together and shot me a dark look, which was okay because it was my place to endure this inquisition. It was my fault for opening my giant mouth.

"She lives with her parents for health reasons." I nodded to Mom. "I've told you about her mobility issues."

Cynthia frowned. "You could help her with that stuff."

I prayed for a greater power to save me from this henhouse.

Jessica sat down on the chair I'd vacated, and she sighed. "Sheila, I can't believe how beautiful you look so soon after surgery. I've been in a car all day, and I know I don't look half as good as you right now."

Impressed she'd been able to read my mom so well, I leaned against the wall behind Jessica and let her get to know the other women in my life.

Mom beamed. "You're sweet. Tell me about yourself, Jessica. How did you meet my son?"

"When I came out of my coma, he was standing watch over me with one of his friends. Since I had a tube down my throat, he did all the talking. I found out a ton about him before I was able to get a word in edgewise."

Mom, Cynthia, and Gigi peered at me curiously.

Jessica caught the drift of their question and laughed. "It was quite a while before I found out he's the strong, silent type."

"Which friend?" Gigi asked.

"Dean." The way she said his name left no doubt that their estrangement was a sore spot for her.

I chimed in. "Her life had been threatened, so Dean and I were guarding her while the rest of our team aided law enforcement to apprehend the target."

My aunts knew enough about what I did not to ask more questions.

"That's when you first mentioned her to me," Mom said. "And now, here you are. Tell me one thing, Jessica—do you play bingo?"

Jessica thought about that one, and after a few moments, she shrugged. "Not that I remember, but I'm willing to learn."

Mom's shining eyes met mine. "She'll do."

Chapter 11—Jesse

Back at yet another hotel, I threw my suitcase on the end of the bed and opened it up. The inside contained my clothes and the ones I'd purchased for Jessica the day before. I liked seeing her things mixed in with mine.

"My mom really liked you." I wasn't surprised at this development, but I was pleased nonetheless.

"She was hopped up on painkillers. It was the perfect time to introduce me." Jessica's voice floated out of the bathroom.

"Don't sell yourself short, Brat. You had your charm powers dialed up to eleven."

She emerged from the bathroom with damp hair. On her body, she wore one of my shirts and nothing else. The large, shapeless shirt fell to mid-thigh and floated around her hips, obscuring the curves and bumps I longed to see.

"Did she tell you why she was there?"

I lifted my brows. "Woman problems."

She sat on the bed with her knees tucked underneath. "That's terribly not specific."

"Apparently, I never noticed my mom had breast implants. Hers got infected, so she had to get them removed, and then she got them put back in." There was a limit to what I wanted to know about my mother, but the idea of breast augmentation mystified me. "I wonder when she had it done?"

Amusement sparkled in those captivating green eyes. "Probably fifteen or twenty years ago. Implants don't last forever. They need to be updated every other decade."

I had trouble keeping my gaze from her bare legs, so I busied myself with selecting my next black-on-denim outfit. "Seems like something she wouldn't need at her age."

Jessica wrinkled her nose. "I'd imagine, after breast-feeding four kids, time and tide took their toll. Maybe she got tired of tucking them into her pants."

Throwing my suitcase to the floor, I turned my back to her. "I'm tired of this conversation. I wish I could tuck it into a deep, dark hole and forget about it."

She laughed. "Did you get my plane ticket?"

I hadn't, because I was afraid for her to fly alone. What if she had another seizure? I'd used the time she was in the bathroom to research absence seizures, and I'd found they were common in children or people with brain injuries, but they weren't the kind that necessitated a trip to the ER for a pregnant woman. Still, I worried. As I imagined worst-case scenarios, I felt her hands on my shoulders.

"You're tense. Today was hard for you." Her fingers dug into the muscles there, revealing soreness where I hadn't known it resided.

I exhaled as she found a particularly large knot. "My mom's okay, so I can relax now."

"Not just that."

Without naming names, she brought up my wife. First wife. I guess I needed to change the way I thought about Josie because Jessica was currently my wife.

"Come, sit down and let me work on your back."

I let her guide me back to the bed, and I helped her remove my shirt. Not having anticipated her presence on this trip, I'd booked a room with one bed. Falling asleep with her so close while I didn't have the right to touch her—that was going to be a difficult feat. Hopefully she could help me relax this way, and then I'd take care of my wood in the shower.

As she worked through the worst of my stress, it became difficult not to lean against her. After the tenth time I apologized for sagging back, she pushed me onto my back. Kneeling at my side, she worked on my pectorals.

I liked this view. The look of determination and concentration on her face was cute and familiar. I think watching her relaxed me even more than the massage. There came a point when the visual and the tactile stimulation began to negate the softening of my muscles.

"Close your eyes."

"Why?"

"Because you're tensing up again. You need to concentrate on relaxing."

"Darlin', I'm as relaxed as I'm gonna get." I sat up, moving out of her reach.

"Oh. I'm sorry. I'm not as good at this as you are."

I twisted around to assuage her ego. "You did great, but if you keep touching me, I'm going to want to start touching you, and we already said that was a bad idea."

Her gaze fell to below my waist, where my jeans didn't do a great job of hiding my budding erection. "Yeah," she said, biting her lower lip savagely. "I have trouble controlling myself around you as well."

The next thing I knew, she was on my lap, straddling me, and her mouth devoured mine. One hand roamed my chest while the other held the back of my neck to keep me from moving out of reach.

It took all my willpower to push her away. Even then, I only got her to stop kissing me and lay her forehead against my shoulder.

I stroked her back. "Jessica, you said this was a mistake."

"It is." Her whisper-soft affirmation tore at my heart, and the anguish beneath kept the wound from closing. "It's just—I miss you, Jesse. I miss being in your arms. I miss the way you make me feel when you look into my eyes right before you kiss me."

I missed those things too.

Gently, I urged her to lift her face and look at me. When her eyes met mine, I read the misery there, and every piece of me wanted to make it go away.

"Tonight." I brushed a curl back from her face. "Just one night, okay?"

Her gaze roamed my face, searching for something, but I didn't know what.

"It's okay to say no."

"I don't want to say no." Her gaze didn't waver from mine, but the way she clutched at my shoulders betrayed her anxiety. "But I know this isn't just one night. You're not that kind of man."

"I can be."

She laughed, a melancholy sound. "Jesse, it's already more than one night. You aren't mad I married you without your consent, and you introduced me to your mother as your wife. I'm not stupid. I know you're playing the long game."

I wrapped my arms around her bottom and scooted us both so my back rested against the pillows. If she wanted to have this talk, then we were going to have it. I affirmed her guess. "I didn't buy you a plane ticket."

Since my hands were already in the region, I ran them up her thighs and over her hips. She wasn't wearing panties.

Pressing her forehead to mine, she gave a shaky exhale. The fact that I cupped and kneaded her breast may have contributed to her breathing problem. "Nothing's changed. You're a Dom, and I'm not a sub."

To prove her point, she undid my jeans and slid them down my legs. I helped by lifting up. It wasn't chivalrous to expect her to do all the heavy lifting. As we resettled into negotiating position, I captured her lips for a hungry kiss. She moaned, leaning into it while her hands roamed my flesh.

Though it broke our kiss, I lifted her shirt over her head to reveal those luscious curves. "I don't have to be a Dom all the time."

"That's not what you said when we talked about this before." Her hand wrapped around my cock and pumped it slowly.

"I was an ass before. I was listening, but I wasn't hearing you." I closed my eyes to savor heat rising in my veins. "Darlin', I didn't dominate you last time, and I'm not doing it this time either."

Her ministrations paused. I opened my eyes to find her regarding me with tear-bright eyes. "This isn't the kind of sex you want to have."

I cradled her face in my hand. "Sex with you is the kind of sex I want to have." I kissed her cheeks and the tip of her nose before feathering light brushes over her eyelids and along her temple. "Jessica, I love you. That's never going to change."

I lifted her and lined my cock with her opening. As she sank down, her body shuddered with passion, and a delicate breath exhaled on a sigh. I thought she might get a rhythm going, but she stilled. Her eyes opened. "I don't want you to hold back this time."

This was a test, and I wasn't sure I'd studied the right material.

Thinking back over everything we'd talked about didn't illuminate any correct answers. "Are you sure?"

"Yes. I'm sure. Did you need clearer consent? Like I'm okay with you pulling my hair or smacking my ass?"

"I would appreciate it."

Her grin turned wicked. She licked a swath up my neck and blew cool air across it, leaving me shivering with chills. "How about you do what you feel the need to do, and I'll make liberal use of my safewords?"

That didn't make it easier for me to decide on a course of action. The scenes we'd done before were ones I'd meticulously planned. Tonight wasn't planned, but maybe that's what she liked about it. She wanted me to improvise, to follow my natural inclinations.

First thing, I flipped us over so she was beneath me, and then I captured her lips for the kind of searing kiss I'd been craving for months. She slid her foot down the back of my thigh and tickled along my calf. Her hands explored my upper body, light caresses that turned into scratches and sent shivers through my body.

Without having her tied up, I had no real control over what she did, and I was finding I liked having her touch me. I felt connected to her in a way I hadn't before, and it made being inside her that much sweeter. I thrust slowly, unhurried movements designed to draw this out for as long as possible.

I kissed her lips, and then I explored her neck and throat with light brushes and sucking kisses. I palmed her breasts and squeezed her nipples. She squeaked at the pain, but her breaths came quicker, and a pre-orgasmic blush stained her chest.

Feeling emboldened, I spent some time torturing her breasts with my fingers and my lips. She writhed under me, wild and out of control. Moans and gasps that sounded a lot like my name whispered from between her lovely, kiss-swollen lips. I loved driving her to this point, and I hadn't needed to overtly dominate her to do it.

Then I felt her hand close around my balls. With a gentle pressure, she fondled and pulled. A sharp pleasure-pain combination had me crying out and increasing my pace. I was close, and my Dom-brain took over. I hiked up one of her legs to let me deeper inside. My other hand tangled in her hair and pulled in time to my frenzied thrusts. Her body arched into mine, and her nails dug into my shoulders.

"Jesse, oh, Jesse."

My name became her mantra, and it drove me wild. I pounded into her hot and tender pussy until it convulsed around my shaft. In that moment, I belonged to her and she belonged to me, and all was right with the world. With one last thrust, I cried out my climax and collapsed on top of her.

She held me tightly until the pulsing in her pussy had subsided. As her grip loosened, she pushed lightly at my side. "You're crushing the baby."

Nothing she said could have made me move faster than that. I'd completely forgotten about what the swell in her tummy area meant. "Sorry."

I rolled to the side, taking her with me. Right now, any distance between us was too much. Our legs were twined, and I held her in my arms. This was nirvana.

We stayed that way, stroking light caresses over each other's bodies, until we cooled, and then I pulled the covers over us. A million random thoughts circled my mind, and I opened the gate for the main one to present itself.

"Darlin', what does your therapist say about me?"

Interestingly, something different came out than what I'd expected.

Her gaze, which had been on my chest where her finger was drawing patterns, lifted. "Conversations with Nikki are confidential."

"I know. I'm not asking for what you say about me. I'm asking if she had any insights into what makes me tick." It seemed like that would be a therapist's job, right?

A sly smile curved her lips and invited another kiss. Afterward, she still regarded me with amusement. "Are you asking for secondhand psychotherapy? You know, she has partners in her practice if you need someone to talk to."

I kind of was asking for exactly that. "I don't have enough issues to talk to a shrink."

"There's not a minimum requirement. You have an issue or two—that's all you need."

I really didn't think I had any emotional problems that required talk therapy, but I was interested in hearing Jessica's perspective. "What are my issues?"

"You recently broke up with someone you care about."

"Love," I clarified. "I was recently dumped by the woman I love, but it turns out she conspired with my friends and married me anyway."

"It's a complicated situation," she agreed. "You might want to talk to someone who can help you navigate how to be in a doomed relationship that isn't really a relationship."

Lying with her like this, naked limbs entwined with mine, I had a hard time with her assertion that we weren't in a relationship or that we were doomed. "I think we turned a corner tonight."

"A corner?" She studied me, guilt staining her eyes a darker shade of green.

Before she could launch into some kind of apology where she called our coming together a mistake, I started talking. "Darlin', tonight was incredible. I felt like we connected in a way we never have before. Yeah, I did dominant things to you, but I didn't force your submission—and it worked out really well."

"It was one night." Leave it to my Brat to work her counterargument into my perfectly good reason why we should give it another try.

"It doesn't have to be. You said it yourself—I'm not a one-night kind of man, especially not with you."

She rested her fingertips on my cheek and traced my lips with her thumb. "I'm still not a sub, Jesse. I don't want to give you the kind of control over me that you want to have. It's just not who I am. I wasn't happy before. Nothing's changed—not the circumstances or our feelings for each other. I kind of hoped that you had taken this time to fall out of love with me."

That was never going to happen, and we both knew it. "Well, I didn't, and neither did you."

Her stomach, which was against mine, pressed suddenly harder in one spot. I looked down.

"You felt that?" She grinned.

"I felt that." A tiny, rectangular piece of her abdomen pressed again. Wonder surged through me, and my grin matched Jessica's. "I felt that too. Wow—somebody's awake and has already learned to interrupt Mommy and Daddy when they're having a serious conversation."

"Distraction must be a hereditary skill for the offspring of a commando and a con artist."

The fetus pushed again, and I chuckled. "Persistence. Definitely my kid."

Jessica laughed, and then she sobered. "Jesse, I wish I had answers that were different from before, but I don't. I only know I'm not what you need, and that's eventually going to make us both miserable."

It struck me that she kept saying she wasn't what I needed. "But you're not bothered by me being I'm a Dom?"

"I've never known you as anything else."

"Yet it bothers you that I have other subs."

"I never said that."

Point of fact, she had done everything to indicate it, but she'd never come out with a simple declarative statement. "But it does. I've been doing some thinking, and you left some fairly large clues. You considered it emotional infidelity."

She shifted, pulling away from me physically so that she could protect herself emotionally. "I never said that. I know you need them."

"Wendy is gone. Your ploy worked. It seemed she'd kept the true nature of my work from Marc, and he objected once he found out. I'll call Damon and Belinda tomorrow to release them."

Sitting up she found a shirt I'd discarded and put it on. "Don't do that."

"Is it too little, too late?" I watched her closely, looking for evidence she was pleased more than she was freaked out.

"No. It's not fair." She combed frantic fingers through her hair. "I'm never going to be what you need, Jesse, and if you let them go, then you're going to have nothing."

I sat up and watched her engage in calming behaviors—petting her hair and smoothing the shirt over her hip—and I decided it was time to act. I got out of bed and went to her. I took her in my arms and pushed her cheek onto my shoulder. I stroked her hair and her back, and she snuggled closer.

"Darlin', I've had a lot of time to think. Those relationships are empty. Not one of my subs really knows or cares about me, and for the longest time, I was fine with that arrangement. But then you came into my life, and it suddenly wasn't enough. As you came to occupy a larger and larger place in my heart, it turned into just another responsibility. For a long time, I've been going through the motions, meeting an obligation because I'd agreed to do it."

Music came through the walls from the room next door, a slow song, and our bodies swayed in time to it. I'm not sure Jessica even realized what was happening.

"It doesn't fulfill me anymore. Since you came into my life, I'm not the same man I used to be. I hope I'm a better version, someone worthy of loving you, darlin', because that's who I want to be."

"You enjoyed your scene with Wendy." Her muffled argument heated my neck.

"I enjoyed you watching that scene because in my head, I had you in the ropes. It's no longer about flogging someone or dominating them or tying them up. It's about being with you, sharing experiences with you. Jessica, maybe dating didn't work out so well for us because we weren't committed enough. How about we give marriage a shot?"

Hot tears scalded my skin, and I held her closer because I knew she was pulling away. I'd bared my soul, and she was still running away.

Chapter 12—Jessica

I woke up to find Jesse clear on the other side of the bed. He'd messed up the covers so badly my feet were exposed to the cool air in the room. As I was overly hot, it felt good. With a groan, I stretched and pushed the blanket off my sweaty torso.

"Wow." His scratchy voice let me know he'd just woken up. "You're throwing off some majorly high temperatures, darlin'."

"Hormones. I'm glad I won't be pregnant in the summer. You sleep okay?"

"Yeah. You?"

This was the kind of banal morning conversation two people had after one of them caved to temptation and selfishly let the other one believe they had a chance together. Jesse was mine for the taking, but only if I wanted to set him up for a lifetime of disappointment and resentment.

I loved him too much for that, and I owed it to myself not to live that kind of life.

"I'm going to rinse off in the shower before we get breakfast. Are you going to take me to the airport?"

"Holy cow."

I turned to find out what had triggered that exclamation, but I found him staring at me. "What?"

"Not cow. Bad choice of words. I'm just—you—wow." He scrubbed a hand over his eyes like he couldn't believe what he was seeing.

I looked down to find my stomach twice the size it had been the day before. The gentle swell had popped out overnight, and now I looked like I had a small basketball under my shirt. I sat down and felt it with my hands. "I'm huge."

"Naw." His Georgia drawl came out in full force. "You're pregnant. It's beautiful."

I lifted my shirt to assess the damage. "Says the guy not wearing stretch marks."

"There's a cream pregnant women rub on their bellies that's supposed to help. I'll get you some today."

"At the airport?" I was dedicated to leaving as soon as possible. Jesse had come here to get away from me, and I'd only made things worse.

"Probably the grocery store."

I dug into his suitcase for a pair of pants. He'd bought a larger size, but as I held it up to me, I realized I'd passed that size up overnight. "Damn. I should've got ones with a stretchy panel in front."

He came over and surveyed the situation. In seconds, he pulled on jeans. "I'll go down and get you some breakfast, and then I'll go out and get you something to wear. You go ahead and have a lazy morning."

Two hours later, he returned with many bags.

Freshly showered and wearing another of his shirts—mine were too tight—I was in bed watching a real estate show.

He set the bags on the foot of the bed and opened up one. "I found a maternity resale shop. I wasn't sure what you'd like, so I got a bunch of different things."

Over the next five minutes, he presented me with dresses, leggings with belly panels, shirts with lots of room for growth, and fashionable maternity pants. There were even a couple of sturdy bras in the mix and a package of huge underwear. Given the quality and style of the garments, it looked like he'd visited an upscale boutique. Part of me wanted to admonish him for spending so much money, but most of me was inordinately happy to have these nice things. In one morning, he'd doubled my entire wardrobe—including non-pregnancy clothes. I'd never been spoiled before, and it felt nice.

He'd also happened upon a couple of hats and sunglasses—because we were in southern Florida—and some sandals he'd thought I'd like.

The last bag was smaller. It held cocoa butter lotion, disposable razors, a hairbrush, and the same shampoo brand I used at home.

My jaw wouldn't close to form words until I saw the shampoo. "You bought all of this to take with me to the airport?"

He began folding the clothes he'd stacked on the bed. "I'm not putting you on a plane, not after the seizures you've been having. You'll stay here with me for a few days, and then I'll take you home. I don't want you left alone."

"Absence seizures aren't bad."

"Oh—and I got you this." He fished a plastic package from a bag and tossed it to me.

"A charger for my phone?"

"Yes. I know you want to call Brea and your parents, and you have an appointment today with Nikki that you can keep by phone." He tucked some of the garments into his suitcase, and he tossed one to me.

It was a pretty dress, the kind that would hug my breasts and fall in loose waves down my body. It had short sleeves and a pattern of lemons and sunbursts in the fabric, meaning it was not at all the type of thing I usually wore.

I turned my back to Jesse and tried out the new bra first. My original one was a little tight, and it was very old. The new one fit perfectly, so I tried the dress next. The soft cotton caressed my skin, and the dress fit pretty well. It was tighter in the back and on the sides, but it was loose around my belly. The style managed to be flattering even though it highlighted the bowling ball my abdomen had become.

He whistled appreciatively. "I have not lost my touch."

"Your touch?"

"I'm freaking awesome at picking out women's clothes."

As I surveyed myself in the mirror pinned to the wall, I had to agree. "That's an interesting skill."

"You're welcome."

"Jesse, I have to get on a plane today. I have orders to fill. My business is actually doing better ever since I put it completely online."

"Your business?"

I shrugged. "Repurposing furniture. I've found people don't care that I'm making something I've seen somewhere else. They just want conversation pieces. Last week, I cut a door in half, glued it at right angles, and added triangle shelves to make a corner shelving unit. I found the door in someone's trash, and I sold it for almost three hundred dollars, and I have orders for six more."

"I'm happy for you," he said. "But I'm not putting you on a plane."

"Jesse, you're not my Dom." Last night, I'd talked him down to the point where he'd agreed to be just friends.

"I know." He spread his hands wide, and his mouth curved with a smile. "We're friends. I'm treating you the same way I'd treat Dean, David, Frankie, or Brea if they were having seizures. I'm looking out for you. I've got your back."

I indicated his overflowing suitcase. "You bought me a whole new wardrobe."

He picked up my cane and tossed it from one hand to the other. "I had this special-made for Frankie. I've bought expensive Scotch for Dean and a tux for David. I got Brea a whole set of baking pans for no particular reason."

115

"You wanted cake."

"It's a gift with many benefits," he agreed. "The point is I'm generous to my friends, and you're my friend." He handed the cane to me. "Additionally, you're the mother of my child. That, more than any other factor, means I will always be here for you."

I studied the cane Frankie had given to me. It was extraordinarily beautiful and it fit my hand comfortably. Jesse had given me gifts today, and I had two choices—I could be a petulant brat, or I could accept them gracefully. I cleared my throat from the sudden rush of emotion. "Nikki said I needed to temper this fierce need I have to be independent with a thoughtful acceptance of help from people who care about me."

He chuckled. "If you've come that far, then I guess you're really not spending your time talking about me."

"Oh, we talk about you." I flashed my best con-artist smile. "We talk about you a lot. I've even showed her pictures."

He held up his phone and blinded me with the flash. "Send her this one of you accepting the gift of necessary clothing from the guy who knocked you up."

I realized that he was nervous about how I'd presented him to Nikki. Sure, we'd fought, and we'd both said mean things, but he wasn't any better or worse of a person than I was. However I couldn't recall a single time Nikki had analyzed Jesse's personality.

"She doesn't say anything about you, if that's what you're wondering. My therapy is centered around me—my feelings, thoughts, and actions. She doesn't judge me or you or anyone else I talk about. That's one of the reasons I like her."

His gaze searched my face. "You do seem happier and healthier than you've ever been. I'm glad you have her."

"Are you going to leave me alone so I can talk to her? My session starts in four hours."

He shook his head. "I'm not leaving you alone, but I'll make sure you have privacy. We're going to pick up my mom. She's being discharged this afternoon. Then we'll take her home and get her settled."

I didn't see where that would afford me any kind of privacy, but I knew when nothing was going to change Jesse's mind. He was hell-bent on making sure I wasn't alone. Truthfully, I didn't want to be alone. Having seizures I wasn't aware of and retained no memory of—that scared me.

While plugging my phone in, I turned it on. The thing pinged to life with messages. I looked them over to find the expected ones from

Brea teasing me for the predicament in which I found myself. Sylvia and Warren had both left messages asking me to call them as soon as I had any flight information, so I called them first to let them know about Jesse's change in plans and the reason behind it. They agreed with his decision.

At the hospital, I gave Jesse some time with his mom, and I went to a designated area to call Brea.

"How is day three of your trip?"

I sighed. "I slept with him."

A woman about twenty years older than me pressed her lips together and threw a disapproving look in my direction. Rather than flip her off, I moved farther away and lowered my volume.

"With Jesse?"

"No, with The Rock." I huffed out a low growl. "Of course with Jesse. And—I'm huge. This thing doubled in size overnight."

"Well, you *have* been on the small side for a while. It was bound to happen. I can't wait to rub your tummy. When are you coming home?"

While I didn't like most people touching my stomach, I was fine with Brea doing it. She talked to it and blew it kisses as well. "Jesse won't take me to the airport because I keep having absence seizures. I told him they were no big deal, but he disagrees." It wasn't fair to say he hadn't listened. He'd researched them, and he knew their reappearance meant I needed to be watched. It was the whole reason I was living with my parents in the first place—I required babysitting.

"Are you two getting along any better?"

I laughed. "I told you we had sex."

"That could just be hormones."

"It was more than hormones. He's a drug I can't quit. I'm telling you, if he were cigarettes, I'd still be smoking." Speaking of the little cancer sticks, I wanted one so badly right now.

I settled for stealing mints from the judgmental lady's purse.

"Well, then I'm happy for you—if you're happy. I mean, nothing's really changed."

"I know, but Brea, he was perfect—a little bit alpha, but not over-the-top Dominant."

"Wow. Maybe he's willing to change to win you back?"

"That's not fair to him. He shouldn't have to change to be in a relationship."

Brea's huff of air was the kind that came with one of her patented eye-rolls. I didn't need to see it to know it was there. "You know what? He hasn't been in a relationship in eighteen years. What he's been

117

doing isn't working for him, so it makes sense for him to change if he wants to be happy."

I thought about how he'd told me his wife had been cheating and she'd asked for a divorce. Had he been an alpha-hole with her? Somehow, I didn't want to share that with Brea after he'd confided in me what he'd never confessed to anyone else.

"He asked me to give the marriage a chance."

Silence came from the other end as Brea processed this new twist. "Okay, and you said no?"

"I said we were better off as friends."

"Was this before or after you slept with him?"

"After." It was also after he'd confessed to still being in love with me and I'd told him I'd always love him.

"Jessica, he's not going to give up."

I sighed. Honestly, I wasn't sure how I felt about it. She was right—nothing had changed, including my feelings for him. "I know. This morning, he bought me all sorts of really nice maternity clothes, cocoa butter lotion for my tummy, and a charger for my phone."

"Yeah, well he chose this course of action the moment he realized you were in his truck and he refused to bring you back. Look—go with it for now, okay? You know you want to, so stop fighting against happiness and start fighting *for* it. Be honest. Tell him to let go of his subs."

"He did already."

"Great. And he already knows you don't want a D/s relationship."

"Yeah, he does."

"And last night he was perfect—those were your words."

"He was." Damn, but she was building a strong case for him. "Is he paying you for this?"

"Funny. I just want you to be happy, big sister, and if he's the one who makes you happy, then I want you to have him."

"Brea, I don't think I can make him happy. I mean, I can't give up picking pockets, and he has to give up his subs?" I popped a purloined mint into my mouth. "It doesn't seem fair."

"Relationships aren't about fairness. If you look at me and David, or even at Warren and Sylvia, you can point out hundreds of things that aren't fair. Right now, I have a vibrator strapped to my leg and David has the remote. That's not fair, but it works for us."

"You—I called at a bad time."

"Nah, you're doing a great job of distracting me. If I orgasm, David has something more nefarious planned."

"None of that appeals to me." While I wasn't against sex toys, I was against the mind games and the torture aspects.

"Doesn't have to. You're not me. Maybe you and Jesse should talk about what does appeal to you. Jessica—don't pretend that not one part of the lifestyle appeals to you. You told me what bondage was like. I'd give my left tit to get to deep subspace that quickly."

I didn't promise anything but that I'd think about it.

The passage of a few hours found me on the back patio of Sheila Foraker's condo. She wore a baggy white shirt over her bandages, and Jesse served us tea and sandwiches.

"Jessica, I want to get to know you better. Jesse said you were raised by your kidnapper?"

It seemed Jesse's mom was the juicy-gossip kind of southern woman.

"Mom, that's not a first-date question."

The look Sheila leveled at her son was equally as firm as the one he leveled at her. I could see where he got his authoritative personality. I didn't want to talk about my childhood, so I sipped tea and waited for one of them to break.

Sheila gave in first. "Fine. Sorry. I didn't mean to be intrusive. I just want to know what experiences shaped you into the person you are today."

"I think reconnecting with my parents has gone a long way toward shaping who I've become since I woke up from the coma. I've learned to let people in and how to build solid relationships with those I love." I passed a hand over my abdomen. "Of course, my experiences from before the coma taught me to be resourceful and independent."

She studied me, pursing her lips. "Okay, so you can handle Jesse. That's good. He's sometimes too assertive. He gets that from being in the Special Forces."

"Leadership is an occupational hazard," Jesse muttered.

"You won't respect a woman who lets you call the shots and walk all over her."

I could see why Jesse and his mother only spent a few hours together at a time. The pair of them were too much alike in some ways, and they rubbed each other wrong in other ways. Yet the fact they loved each other couldn't be missed.

"Sheila, when we stopped by yesterday, we met a man named Ben Sheets. He was sorry that you missed brunch."

She waved her hand and a blush stole up her neck. "Oh, him. We go out a few times a week. He's a nice man."

Jesse looked like he was biting his tongue.

119

I touched her wrist. "We should all have dinner together, if you're up for it."

Sheila beamed. "We should. Oh, Jesse, I think you'll like Ben. He was in the military too, but Air Force, I think."

"Sure, Mom. How about tomorrow? I can fire up the grill. You want salmon or steak?" He did not look all that enthused about meeting the man who might one day be his step-father, but he managed to muster up some sense of acceptance, if not actual excitement.

"Salmon. I've been on a Mediterranean diet lately—more fish, less red meat." She rubbed her hands together. "I'll make baba ganoush and corn-on-the-cob."

Turning toward me, she added, "Do you have any special dishes you'd like to contribute?"

Jesse nearly fell out of his chair laughing.

I almost pushed him to complete the job. "What Jesse is trying to say is you don't want me in the kitchen unless it's to clean up."

Sheila didn't seem impressed by my admission. "I guess it's good I taught him how to cook."

"Yes," I said. "I appreciate that. He's a pro at ordering takeout."

She gestured toward my belly. "Have you started thinking of names?"

Jesse and I had not discussed names or anything else, but I'd settled on one months ago. I smiled. "Bailey."

Sheila and Jesse both stared, eyes wide as I uttered the name of Jesse's younger brother who'd given his life for our country. Choked with emotion, Jesse glanced away.

Sheila wiped away a tear. "It's a boy?"

"Bailey works either way."

The next thing I knew, Sheila swept me up in a tight hug. From here on out, I didn't think there was anything I could do to lose her favor.

Chapter 13—Jesse

I cornered Jessica after my mom went inside to fix her makeup, which was code for "have a cigarette." When she came back, she'd smell like mouthwash, air freshener, and nicotine—and her makeup would be perfect.

Jessica and I were on a patch of grass that led to a canal full of alligators. I wasn't sure if I was in position to wrestle on her behalf, or if she'd splatter it verbally before I got anywhere near it. God, but I'd really missed having conversations with her. Nothing and nobody kept me on my toes like she did.

The afternoon sun glinted from her dark hair, revealing reddish highlights. The dress I'd selected fell to her knees. It emphasized her full breasts, the curves of her ass and hips, and the swell of her abdomen. She looked like a sexy fertility goddess, and I wanted to take her in my arms.

"Are you serious about naming the baby Bailey?"

"Yes. I told you I liked that name." Then her eyes grew wide as she gasped. "Are you mad?"

"No. I'm speechless. You'd do that for me?"

"Yes. Bailey Zinn has a nice ring to it."

There was no way in the world my child wouldn't have my last name. "Bailey Foraker."

She pursed her lips, considering what I was asking. "Foraker-Zinn."

I called bullshit. "You've had the name for a little over a year. You can't be that attached to it."

Her spine straightened, and she poked her finger into my chest hard. "Nobody is taking that name from me, Jesse. Nobody."

"Brea changed to Eastridge when she married David."

"That's her. I'm going to be a Zinn until the day I die, and my kid is going to have my name as well."

Recognizing her resolve and understanding the reasoning behind it, I backed off. Sometimes it was good strategy to lose the battle to win the war. "Why Foraker-Zinn, but not Zinn-Foraker?"

"I figured it would make you happier that way."

She was right—it did. And I realized she was meeting me halfway. I gave a curt nod. "Thank you."

I couldn't help it; I parked my hands on her hips and brushed a kiss across her lips. She rested her hands on my arms and kissed me back, deepening it with the sweep of her tongue on my bottom lip.

Before things got indecent—we were on a public walkway behind dozens of condos full of retirees—I brought the kiss to a close.

"That was unexpected."

She shrugged. "I talked to Brea."

"Yeah?"

"Yeah. She said I should give us another chance." Jessica's gaze slid away.

"You don't sound overly excited about the idea." It was better to acknowledge the truth than to pretend she was all-in. I'd made that mistake last time, and it hadn't eradicated her reservations.

"I'm scared it won't work out. I'm scared I can't make you happy. I'm scared one day you'll hate me because I'm not right for you."

"So—same objections as before." I traced a caress along her face with the side of my thumb. "What made you change your mind?"

"You." She swallowed, and when her gaze met mine, I recognized her vulnerability. "Jesse, you're still dominant, but you're not demanding my submission. The past couple of days... I like your dominant side. I just can't handle being submissive. It sounds like a recipe for disaster. But this—being with you—" She closed her eyes. "If you're willing to accept me as I am, then I'm willing to take this chance with you."

I was more than fucking willing to accept her the way she was—knowing full well she didn't want to be my sub. I lifted her up and spun her around, shouting joyous whoops at the top of my lungs.

When I brought her down, I kissed her with all the love in my heart.

Dazed and bemused, she stared up at me. "You didn't say you accept my terms."

Ahh—she knew me so well. I snaked an arm around her waist and pressed her stomach to mine. "What about bondage? That doesn't have to be a D/s thing."

"One step at a time, Jesse." She waited patiently for me to get the point.

"I accept your terms, darlin'."

122

Jessica handed me a sheet pan with salmon steaks marinating in a special sauce I'd whipped up from ingredients in my mom's kitchen. I'd wrapped them in foil so I could throw them directly onto the grill.

As I slid them, one at a time, onto the grill, I ran an idea past her. "How about you change your last name to Foraker-Zinn?"

"Only if you do it too." Not only didn't she miss a beat, but she injected a hint of irony into her tone.

"That's a woman-thing, not a man-thing."

"It's a sexist construct."

"It's tradition, not sexism."

"Not arguing with you." She squeezed a handful of my ass. "Because you'll realize you're wrong after you've thought it over."

She knew me too well. I couldn't keep the grin from my face.

Today she wore a blue striped shirt with matching leggings, and she once again looked absolutely ravishing. Unfortunately I had to spend the next few hours with Ben, the guy I'd overheard my mom tell Jessica was great at the horizontal mambo. That was something I didn't want to know about my mother, even if she'd been talking about my father.

"Has Ben said anything to you?" I hadn't forgotten Jessica's instinct that had kept her from wanting Ben to notice her.

"He keeps asking about where I've lived. I hope I shut him down by telling him I had a traumatic childhood, and I'm not in a place where talking about those memories makes for light conversation." She turned her back to the grill I'd closed and looked out over the canal. "You weren't kidding about your mom being a chain smoker."

"Nope. Stay out here as much as possible. I don't want you near the secondhand smoke."

A brief frown marred her brow before disappearing.

"What's wrong?"

She shook her head. "You give orders all the time. I'm reminding myself that just because you give one doesn't mean I have to follow it, and then I'm arguing with myself about whether I should do something just because you said not to."

"I see. You're struggling with your bratty side. Nothing new there. How did you decide on the issue of avoiding being near my mom while she's smoking?"

"I'm okay with it. I want to keep the baby away from it, but for my own sake, I need to stay away. I've been having some powerful cravings lately." She rubbed her hands on her arms. "I thought pregnancy cravings would be for pickles and ice cream, not for cigarettes."

Before I could analyze whether her craving was related more to pregnancy or stress, the screen door slid open, and Mom came outside. "Did I hear you say you're craving cigarettes?"

A flush crept up Jessica's neck, and she stole my car keys from my pocket as she turned to face my mom and Ben. "Yeah. I stopped smoking almost five years ago." She didn't have pockets to stow her bounty, so she kept them palmed and out of sight.

I made a mental note to make sure any other clothes I bought for her had pockets because I knew how badly she needed an outlet for stress, and I'd rather have her do this than resume smoking.

Mom patted Jessica's shoulder and led her to the patio set under an umbrella. "Honey, you have my sympathies. I tried to stop once, but I was never able to do it. At my age, I figure there's no point. I'll be dead soon anyway."

Ben joined me at the grill. "Need any help? I'm a champion griller."

I had it under control. "Later, when everything gets done at the same time, I'd appreciate the assistance."

He chuckled and handed me a beer. "Your mom tells me that you were in the Army for most of your life."

"Twelve years. Now I co-own a private security company."

"Your mom told me about that. It's one of those companies that does black-ops work for different governments and organizations?"

"No." I wasn't going to elaborate. Ben seemed like a nice guy, and he really seemed to like my mom, but his background check was still a work in progress. I had Dean looking into it between his other duties. David had texted me that Brea was cracking the whip about Dean not doing his share of the paperwork, which made me happy since I didn't have to be the one to get on him for once.

He laughed nervously at my short response. "Bodyguards?"

"Sometimes." I softened my non-answer with a smile.

"I served a stint in the Navy during Vietnam. I remember guys like you—they all went on to become SEALS or some kind of Special Forces. They did some scary shit back then, let me tell you."

I didn't need for him to tell me the kinds of missions those guys went on because I'd spent years carrying out covert missions. Unlike this guy, I knew anything he heard was just a rumor. Real missions were kept quiet to minimize endangering our lives or the mission's success.

Flashing another smile, I twisted the cap off my beer and said, "How did you and my mom meet?"

He got the hint that I wasn't going to talk about my service or my job. "My sister-in-law dragged me to a bingo game, and when I went

124

out to have a smoke, I ran into this gorgeous woman. We started talking, and we hit it off."

"Where are you originally from, Ben?" Most people in this place were transplants from other states, retirees who liked the warm weather, especially when it was cold and wintry elsewhere.

"Actually, I live in the Fort Myers area. I raised four kids there, and now I live with my youngest. I have a suite with my own kitchen and my own entrance."

I shot a glance toward where my mom and Jessica were chatting. They both wore real smiles. It made my heart happy to see them getting along so well. With my volatile ladies, this mix was either going to work or explode.

"My sister keeps trying to get Mom to move in with her, but Mom's happy here. It's hard when she gets sick, though, because we're all so far away."

"Yeah." Ben nodded. "It's good to have family around when things go bad."

I really didn't want to talk tragedy with Ben, so I steered him back toward his relationship with my mom. "Did you drive all the way down here the other day just to see my mom?"

"Yes." He shook his head and chuckled. "I thought I'd come on the wrong day. Sheila has never stood me up before. I'm glad everything worked out okay with her surgery. We have plans to go dancing as soon as she gets out of the bandages."

"My mom loves to dance," I observed.

"I'm guessing your gal doesn't dance much because of her leg problem?"

"She doesn't let that keep her from doing whatever she wants to do. Maybe it takes her longer or she has to work harder, but she accomplishes whatever she sets her mind to."

He lifted his beer in a toast. "Here's to strong, determined women."

"I'll drink to that."

After we both sated a bit of thirst, he said, "Where did you meet your lady? Is she from around here?"

I saw what she meant about Ben fishing for background on her. "She's originally from Minnesota, outside of St. Paul, but I met her in Michigan, and now she lives outside of KC."

"So she moves around?"

Giving nothing, I shrugged. "I grew up in the Atlanta area, lived in Florida for a few years, and now I'm in KC. I guess she moves as much as anybody."

By the time we sat down for dinner, Ben had given up trying to pump me for information. We ate on the patio. I made sure Jessica's plate was filled while seeing to my own. I didn't think it was too overt of a Dom move, but when I told her to take another section of salmon, she narrowed her eyes in warning.

Figuring out how much was too much was definitely going to depend on her mood. I predicted some spectacular fights in our future, and I looked forward to lots of makeup sex.

"I'm so glad you decided to stay for a few days," Mom said as she squeezed Jessica's wrist. "I never thought I'd see the day when Jesse got married again, and I'm so excited for another grandbaby."

Ben grinned. "This is number six for you, Sheila?"

"Yes. Olivia has two, and Mia has three."

Jessica turned the full blast of her charm on Ben. "How many do you have?"

"Four, with one on the way. My oldest two have two each, my third one doesn't want kids, and my youngest daughter's wife is expecting a baby in a few months." Suddenly, his demeanor darkened. "I finally remembered where I know you from. You're Sadie Adams, and your father destroyed my life."

I glanced at Jessica because I wanted to give her a chance to respond if that's what she wanted to do. Ben's accusation was not far-fetched, given her past, but I was ready to spring to her defense if she needed me.

She stared at him, her tight expression revealing nothing except that she was uncomfortable, as anyone would be in this situation.

Mom looked from Ben to Jessica before setting a hand on Ben's shoulder. "Her name is Jessica. Perhaps you're confusing her with someone else?"

"No. It's been about fifteen years, but I'm sure. I mostly dealt with her father, but I met her and her sister a few times. I'll never forget him—Brian Adams, he called himself, though the police said it was an alias. He said he represented a local manufacturer who wanted to use my shipping company to boost distribution. I was doing well, really well. I had a big house, college funds for all my kids, and a vacation home in Colorado. It turned out that he was using my company to ship stolen merchandise. When the FBI busted in, he was long gone." Ben's eyes flashed, and the artery in his neck throbbed angrily.

Jessica finished off her row of corn on the cob, and then she wiped her hands on her napkin. "It sounds like you have every reason to be mad at this guy, but I'm not him."

"No—you were part of the sell. He trotted out his two, sweet-natured daughters to charm me into believing he was a legitimate businessman." Ben rose to his feet, towering over Jessica.

I stood as well, and I moved to stand between Ben and Jessica. "Ben, why don't you have a seat?" Ben might be taller than me, but he would present no real obstacle in a fight.

He pointed past me. "He took everything from me—my wife died after we lost the house and our savings. I'm living with my son because my business is gone. My retirement is gone. It's all gone because of this—this *hussy*—and her father."

Jessica shoved me out of the way and faced Ben with her hands on her hips. "He wasn't my father—he was my kidnapper. He stole me and my sister from our parents' backyard when we were very young. He told me that my parents were dead and he was all we had. Maybe he stole your money, but he stole twenty-seven years *of my life*. The only escape I had from him is when he died in the same accident that put me in a coma for three years. My *father* is the man who spent twenty-seven years looking for me, not the man who terrorized me and my sister, so don't fucking preach to me about how he ruined your life. What he did to you isn't nearly as insidious as what he did to me."

She stormed out, but not before lifting my mom's cigarette pack.

Hand on heart, Mom regarded me with wide eyes. Her mouth opened and closed a few times.

With a firm hand on Ben's shoulder, I sat him back down. "I know you're upset, but you're mad at the wrong person."

I didn't want to say she had nothing to do with it. Though she'd been brainwashed and controlled by a very bad man for most of her life, once she'd reached her teen years, she'd helped Brian Sullivan plan and carry out many of his schemes. No doubt she'd played an active part in destroying Ben's life.

Right now, I couldn't imagine what she was feeling, but I knew a pack of cigarettes in her hands wasn't going to lead anywhere good. I shot my mom an apologetic look and took off after my wife.

"Jessica." I called to her as soon as I made it to the front walk. She hobbled along at a fast clip on the sidewalk. I knew she heard me, but she didn't stop.

It was a good thing I could outrun her. I jogged to her side and studied her tight expression.

"Jessica, let's go back to the hotel."

"You don't have to come after me every time I walk away." She did not slow down.

When something went wrong, her first inclination was to flee. "I'm not sure you'll come back."

She stopped and faced me, her eyes puffy though she hadn't yet cried. "I'm not running from you."

"Not this time."

"Jesse, when I walk away, I'm always running from myself. It's never been about you or anyone else." She gestured in the direction of my mom's condo. "I don't remember that guy, but I don't doubt his story. You know what else I don't doubt? That Brea and I helped sell it. That's one of the things we use to do because how can BS possibly be a shady character when he has two charming daughters? You wouldn't believe the number of people who fall for that kind of scam. You just— you make someone feel good about themselves, flatter them, flash a few real pieces of merch, and then you've got the groundwork for a re-shipping scheme."

The Dom part of me wanted to take her in my arms and urge her to lay her burden at my feet, but the logic piece of my brain knew she needed to deal with this herself, otherwise she'd never feel in control of her life. "Okay, so you ripped him off. That's not who you are now, Jessica. You made a conscious effort to not be that kind of person even before you knew he wasn't your father. You have to give yourself a break. You can't possibly make amends to every person you fucked with."

She considered that. "If only because I don't remember them."

"There is that."

"I'm looking forward." She swallowed down some tears. "Because looking back too long will suck me into a vortex of painful things I can't change."

I held out a hand. "Speaking of not looking back, how about you give up the cigarettes? You're only supposed to steal from me."

She looked down at the half-empty pack hiding in her palm. "You don't smoke. You can't steal something from someone if they don't have that thing."

Easing the pack from her grasp, I shoved it into the back pocket on my jeans. "You don't smoke either, so you don't need these."

"I kind of do, Jesse. I need something." She ran a shaking hand through her hair, mussing the curls into a wild riot.

"Sure, but pick something else."

Chewing her lower lip, she thought. "Bondage. Shibari."

That's the last thing I'd expected her to ask for, especially since she'd so recently refused to discuss it. "You're sure?"

"My brain is going at a million miles an hour right now. I need to slow it down. In the past, when you've tied me up, it clears my mind. It calms everything down, and I go to a mental place that's really nice." She crossed her arms over her chest, a defensive pose that left her looking exposed and vulnerable, two things I knew she hated being. "You have rope in your truck."

I knew exactly what was in my truck even though I'd tossed it in the back without apparent care about where it landed. It looked like she was going to test me on my assertion that bondage could be outside the D/s dynamic. I'd never done it that way, so this was going to be new for me.

Slinging an arm around her shoulders, I steered her back the way we'd come. "Let's go, darlin'. In the morning, I'll take us back home."

"You don't have to cut your visit short. You can still put me on a plane."

"My reasons for not doing that haven't changed."

"I could put myself on a plane."

"You could," I acknowledged, "but I'd prefer if you didn't."

"You can leave me at the hotel."

"Nope, for the same reasons I won't put you on a plane." I noticed she wasn't pushing very hard on this front, and I realized this was what she'd wanted all along—for me to be dominant while she maintained control of her life. Seeing her reaction tonight and listening to her words drove home just how important it was for her to feel like she was in control of her life. At the same time, she needed me to be strong enough to support and catch her if she stumbled.

It threw into sharp relief how I'd tried to thrust my expectations for submission onto her instead of giving her the time and guidance to find her own way. Yeah, I knew I wasn't supposed to think of her as submissive because she'd rejected that title, but I couldn't pretend that at least a third of her behaviors and reactions weren't those of a submissive.

And for the first time in my life, I was actively thinking about what had driven me to become the type of Dom I'd become. Did I really want total control over another person, or had that come as a knee-jerk reaction to the situation surrounding the loss of my first wife?

Maybe Jessica and I both needed time to ease into this. If we did this right, we'd have the rest of our lives to find our way together.

Chapter 14—Jesse

I loaded Jessica into my truck, and then I went back inside my mom's condo to say goodbye.

Mom waited for me at the door. "Jesse, is she okay?"

"No, she's not." Lying to my mom wasn't something I did. If I couldn't tell her something because it was confidential, I just told her it was confidential. "But she will be."

"That poor woman. I can't imagine living through a life like hers." Mom sighed. "Ben is taking a walk out back. I don't know what to say to him about all of this. Losing his business was hard, and he blames the loss of his wife on those hard times. I understand why he's upset."

"So do I." Letting myself inside, I slipped her cigarette pack onto a table near the door. When she came inside, I hugged her. "Look, Mom, I'm not asking you to take sides, but be clear that I am and will always be on Jessica's side. Since she woke up from that coma, I've watched her piece together a life and try to put the past behind her. Ben is allowed to be angry, but I'm not going to let her be around him when he's in this state."

She hugged me back. "He won't be here tomorrow, okay? How about we go out to the pier, just you, me, and Jessica? I'd hate if she kept the baby away from me because she didn't like my boyfriend."

Did it matter if I assured my mom Jessica wasn't that kind of person? Because I sure as hell was. Unless Ben had a huge change of heart in the way he planned to treat my wife, I wasn't going to let her or my child anywhere near him. If my mom got serious with him, that would necessarily limit my visits here. It didn't matter if Jessica was the forgiving kind or not—I wasn't willing to put her in that situation.

"Mom, it's not her you have to worry about."

I'd never expressed a sentiment like that to my mom before, and she pressed her hands to her heart. "Jesse Lee Foraker, are you giving me an ultimatum?"

"It hasn't come to that. I'm just letting you know where I stand. Jessica has had a hard life, and it's going to take years for her to fully come to terms with it all. I'm not going to put her in a position for a setback when I don't have to."

The sparkle left my mom's blue eyes. "She broke up with you a few months ago. Women like that—they aren't stable."

Stability was overrated. I shrugged. "And now, she's my wife."

"I just don't want you to get hurt. Josie was a sweet girl. She came from a good home, and she was a good wife. There are more women like her out there."

I'd never mentioned Josie's infidelity to anyone. She was dead, and I hadn't seen the point in maligning her memory. "Mom, I love Jessica. I don't care whether she's sweet or salty, stable or crazy—I love her." I hugged my mom again. "I love you too. We'll wait and see how the situation with Ben plays out, okay?"

Back in the truck, I found Jessica with a kitten. It had a black-and-white tuxedo look, and it was curled up on her lap.

"Where the hell did that come from?" Seeing as how it was a nice evening, there were a lot of people out for an evening stroll, but I couldn't see how she could pickpocket a kitten without being noticed.

"I was sitting here, waiting for you, and I heard something crying. It sounded like a baby, so I looked around and I called out, and this thing came climbing out of the engine of the car next to yours." She stroked the fur, a look of wonder on her face. "I've never held a kitten before."

Fuck. I was not a cat person. Dogs were more my speed—big, tough, guard dogs like a Doberman or a Dalmatian or a Rottweiler, maybe a Great Dane or a German Shepherd. Definitely not a fucking cat.

"We should find the owner."

She lifted her gaze to meet mine. "I was thinking that if you lose a kitten, it's because you want it gone, and then I wondered if maybe it was playing in its yard and its mom stepped away for a potty break, and then I realized that I was reading too much into this."

By the time she got to the end, tears streamed down her cheeks. I scooped up the kitten. "I'll be right back."

"Where are you going?"

"I'm going to give it to my mom. She can take a picture and put it up on the social media site for the condo association. By morning, she'll have found the owner, and the kitten will be reunited with its family. Okay?"

She nodded.

Back at the hotel, she carried my bag of ropes inside.

"Do you want me to teach you how to check the ropes?"

"Sure. What do you check them for?"

131

"Weak points, frayed ends, rough spots—anything that could be uncomfortable or a safety hazard." By this point, we'd made it to the room. I unlocked the door and let her inside.

"Sure. Okay."

"You don't sound sure." I secured the door and searched the room. My counter-surveillance habits did not go away just because I was on vacation.

"Did you want me to do some landscaping and put on sexy lingerie?"

I didn't care about landscaping. I knew women were all about shaving and waxing, but I liked the natural look. As I searched for the correct response, Jessica laughed.

"God, Jesse. The look on your face is priceless." She picked up some toiletries and headed toward the bathroom. "Give me ten minutes."

I didn't know what look I had on my face, but I wasn't going to get between a woman and her razor. "Sure."

When she emerged, she wore a plain bra and a pair of fuzzy gray short shorts with the waist rolled down so that it curved under her belly. She'd put her hair into a ponytail, and a bunch of wisps had escaped to frame her face. "I didn't know if you wanted to have sex before, during, or after."

With her looking sexy as hell and wearing evidence she belonged to me front and center, I wanted to opt for all three, but I cleared my throat instead of blurting that out. "When checking the rope, I like to run it through my hands to feel for rough or weak spots."

With a knowing smile, she let it go that I hadn't answered her question. I walked her through my process. She was an apt pupil, eagerly putting her skills to use to check the lengths I'd chosen with her in mind. By the time we finished prepping the rope, she was already calmer, and so I addressed her initial concern.

"Sex is off the table right now. You asked me to do this to send you to subspace, and I'd like to be able to enjoy the Zen side of the experience as well."

Her face fell. "No sex?"

"I'm not saying no sex ever, just not with the bondage. When I've tied you up in the past, it was to dominate you as part of a scene where ultimately we would have sex. Practicing Shibari on you outside of a scene, with no D/s—that's new for me, and so I don't want to complicate it with sex."

She gaped at me. "You got aroused tying up Wendy."

"Because you were there," I reminded her. "I'm not saying I won't find this arousing—you, in that outfit, are an erotic sight—only that I won't be acting on it. Maybe later, after we're finished, if you're awake and in the mood, we can explore that option. Okay?"

"Okay. Do you want me naked?"

"Also barefoot and pregnant."

As she shimmied out of her scant clothing, she took a second to groan at my sense of humor. "I see you're already practicing to medal in the Neanderthal joke category."

I guided her to stand next to the bed. "It was that bad? Darn, I was hoping to try out some dad jokes."

She snorted. "Good thing you have a few months to practice."

"Widen your stance a little."

It amazed me how quickly and easily we'd fallen back into familiarity. As if we'd never been apart, she stood before me, naked and comfortable. She seemed more relaxed than she'd ever been, which I figured was due to the absence of the D/s dynamic. I missed it a little, but the benefits definitely outweighed the loss.

I had the woman I loved here with me, patiently awaiting the application of my ropes. She had put herself completely in my hands. More than submission, this was the level of trust I craved having with my life partner. For the first time, I realized Josie and I had never been this comfortable with each other, and there had always been a slight unease—words unspoken, a chink in the bond of trust between us.

Jessica gazed at me, a question in her eyes, and I realized my thoughts had taken a dark turn away from this room. I shook away images and memories of my first wife so I could be wholly present in this moment.

I brushed a kiss across her lips, and then I stayed to deepen it. Jessica was my drug, an addiction I would never quit.

Then I knelt at her feet. The pattern I wanted binding her legs would look like a mermaid's tail once I finished, but I needed her to stand until I had her thighs bound. "You'll stand for a bit, and then I'll lay you down once I get past your knees. Color?"

"Green." Already a note of peace had crept into her voice.

On her legs, I used a simple design that looped around each leg, knotted down the outside, and created a series of criss-crosses between her thighs. Unlike with any other sub, I allowed myself the freedom to caress her skin and heighten the sensuality of the experience. By the time I made it to her knees, I was falling into Domspace. I shook myself out of it, and checked in with my wife.

Yeah, I was really liking that word a lot more than 'submissive.' It had taken on a more meaningful connotation in my head. Submissives had come and gone from my life, but I planned to keep my wife forever.

I stood up and brushed a curly lock from her face. "How you doing, darlin'?"

The glaze melted from her stare, and she smiled. "Green."

I ran my hands down her arms, over her shoulders, and along her back. I let myself enjoy the soft, silky feel of her skin, and I pressed a series of kisses along her collar bone. A soft sigh fell from her lips and landed on my soul.

I lifted her easily, cradling her in my arms before laying her on the bed. Though her hip could stand up under what I had planned, my wife tended to hit subspace the moment I had her arms bound. I wanted her secured before her mind went on the requested vacation.

Tying the rest of her legs didn't take long, and I wove the remainder of the rope into a triangle shape for the fin part of her tail.

I sat her up at the edge of the bed with her feet on the floor so I could work on her upper body.

"Color?"

"Green. I'm amazed I'm still with you."

"I did your lower half first. I'm working with the theory that you fall into subspace when your arms are bound."

"Oh." She surveyed the work I'd done so far. "You always amaze me. A mermaid's tail? This is beautiful. Are you going to make a seashell bra?"

"No, but I am going to bind your breasts."

I wove a web design that went over her shoulders and incorporated her stomach, but I kept it loose because I'd read that pregnant woman didn't like tight things over their bellies. Around her breasts, I tied a modified corselet that emphasized her swollen boobs.

She watched my progress with a serene expression. The turmoil that had made her eyes a little crazy before was gone. I kissed her forehead.

"Jesse?"

She'd been quiet for most of the time, which was another marked difference from before—the nervous chatter was gone.

I smiled. "Yeah, darlin'?"

"I love you."

"I love you too."

"I never stopped."

"Neither did I."

"I'm still afraid that one day you'll hate me."

"Never, darlin'." I kissed her forehead again. Even when we'd been apart, I'd been angry and resentful. Not for one moment had I hated her—not even when I'd thrown those exact words at her. I'd been angry, and when my emotions had turned in that direction, I'd ended up aching with loss.

I tied a sleeve down her right arm, and before I made it to her elbow, her mind took flight, confirming my theory that binding her arms sent her to subspace. On her left hand, I tied a webbed-glove design. Then I wrapped her right arm so it cradled her belly, and I bound it in place. Her left hand, I cupped to the side of her head, and I bound it there.

Then I laid her back and watched her while she flew.

I might have arranged the tail and fanned out her hair before snapping a few pictures, but otherwise I sat back and admired my handiwork. It was, hands-down, one of my best designs. I'd combined bits and pieces of things I'd learned over the years to make a bondage mermaid celebrating her pregnancy.

After twenty minutes, she showed signs of rousing from her stupor. I stretched out next to her and touched her, following the lines with my fingertips. Small sighs issued from her, and when her eyes opened, she inhaled sharply.

"Color?"

She let the air out slowly. "Green. I—I forgot where I was." The fingers on her left hand, pressed against her face, flexed. "You tied my hand to my head?"

"Yep." I held up my phone so she could see the images of her bondage.

"God, Jesse. That's beautiful. You're an artist at heart."

"And you, my goddess, are my inspiration and my canvas. How are you feeling?"

"Peaceful. Safe. Loved."

"Great. Then you got what you needed?"

"Yes. Thank you." She turned toward me as best she could in her condition. "Before you untie me, can I give you a blowjob?"

My dick jumped for joy, but my better sense prevailed. "You don't have to do that."

"I want to." She turned those large, pleading eyes on me. "Please, Jesse? I want to give that to you."

I kissed her tenderly because the pleading note in her voice and the fact she was begging to serve me activated my Dominant side. If she kept that up, I'd fuck her face.

As soon as she kissed me back, she ramped up the passion involved. Tenderness hardened to lust, and begging mews vibrated in the back of her throat. This genuine, unlabeled, unasked-for submission enveloped and stroked my alpha-ness.

My hands roamed her body, firm caresses that pressed rope harder into her skin. She moaned, and when I brushed the back of my finger across her mound, she whimpered.

"Do you want my touch there, darlin'? You're so very wet."

"Yes, Jesse. Please touch me." Her soft plea washed through me.

"Are you sure, darlin'? You're kind of in a submissive headspace right now, and you're asking me to be Dominant." It was better to put the labels on and bring what we were doing into the cold light of day than to break her open and leave her in a vulnerable state she couldn't handle. I knew she didn't want me to take her to the point where she found herself shaking and sobbing in my arms.

"I'm sure, Jesse. I want you to touch me, and I want to suck your cock."

Though I'd told her before that the submissive was always in charge, she hadn't believed me. Perhaps by heeding her requests, I could show her that, all along, she was the one who held all the power. I was nothing without her.

"All right, darlin'. We're going to do this slowly, and you'll call yellow or red if you need to."

Eyes fever-bright with desire, she nodded. "Green. Bright, neon green."

I petted her labia gently before sliding my fingers into her slit. With her legs tied together, the space I had to play was limited, but that was okay. The second my fingertip came into contact with her clit, she hissed and thrust her pelvis toward me. It was swollen, and it throbbed when I pressed harder. I played for a bit, and then I delved into her dripping vagina with two fingers. Her walls clamped down on me as she came in a flood of moisture. She cried out, and her upper body thrashed as she tried to free her arms. I knew she wanted to grab my arms or hang onto me, but part of the bondage experience meant she lost that privilege.

My cock was so hard it ached.

Slipping my fingers from her warmth, I licked them clean. Then I moved her to lay diagonally across the bed with her knees bent. This allowed me to turn her on her side so that she didn't choke on my dick. I thrust into her mouth shallowly, letting her wet it with her saliva.

She moaned and sucked me deeper. I surged forward, burying my cock to the hilt. I waited two seconds, watching for any sign she was choking, but I found none. Easing back, I let her breathe. She peered up at me, satisfaction and hunger blazing in those emerald depths. I thrust again. In no time, we established a rhythm that let my cock deep into her throat and also let her have oxygen breaks.

This didn't last long. The sight of my wife in my ropes, sucking down the whole length of my cock, sent me over the edge. With one last thrust, I cried out and came in her mouth.

I fell backward, dizzy with pleasure, all my desires sated. When I glanced over at Jessica, I saw her watching me with a dreamy smile.

I untied her slowly, running my hands over the marks left on her skin. I'd never taken these liberties before, and I did so now because she was thoroughly and completely mine.

Afterward, I held her in my arms, and we talked about the future.

Chapter 15—Jessica

I didn't move in with Jesse. I knew he was angling for that, since we were married and all, but I was more worried about the absence seizures I kept having than I'd let on. He traveled for work—he was in Las Vegas right now—and I couldn't be left alone. Also, my studio was at my parents' house. Warren had spent a lot of time transforming the garage into a workspace for me.

For eleven months, I had been seizure free. When I'd awakened from my coma, I'd experienced tonic-clonic seizures for the first four months, and then they'd stopped. It had taken me a long time to accept I didn't have to walk around being afraid my body would flip out while my brain hosted an electrical storm. While I'd never had an absence seizure, I knew what they were because I'd read everything there was to read about all the damages done to my body by that accident. I'd known brain damage could lead to absence seizures.

I'd first suspected I'd been having them at my Aunt Mona's Christmas Party. She'd been celebrating the end of chemotherapy, and my parents had driven Leon and me all the way to Minnesota, where they had lots of memories, and I had none. They'd tried to jog whatever might be left of a 6-year-old's memories locked inside my brain, but nothing had happened. When they drove somewhere and talked about "remember when," I'd zoned out.

Only later did I realize I hadn't been zoning out on purpose.

We'd returned from Florida a week ago, and I was nearly caught up on fulfilling my internet orders. I wore a mask while sanding the door I'd cut in half vertically.

"How are you doing out here?"

I looked up to see Warren with a water bottle and Midge, the kitten. Jesse's mom hadn't been able to find the owner of the black-and-white kitten, so I'd adopted him, and Jesse had named him after an annoying fly. Just like the fly, the kitten always seemed to swarm around Jesse. Midge loved to snuggle with me, but he always meowed at Jesse, demanding he play. He liked to claim he wasn't a cat person, but I caught him smiling and laughing as he played with Midge, and he could be found petting her often.

Warren offered the water to me, and I accepted it with a smile. "Good. I'm turning this into a corner shelf. I can't believe how popular that is right now. I'm going to need more doors."

Warren smiled and pulled over a stool. "I have a buddy who is into remodeling, and he said he has a bunch of old doors he's trying to get rid of. We can take a ride over and look through his stash if you want."

"Sure. I want to finish this first and get a coat of stain on it."

He absently scratched his chest as he looked over my work. "You are an amazing artisan, sweetheart." Beaming with pride, he ran a hand over a sunflower-shaped cutout I'd put above the top shelf.

This wasn't the kind of art I wanted to do, but as I stepped back and looked over my creation through my father's eyes, I saw for the first time that it wasn't an exact copy of something I'd seen before. The beveling was mine, as was the sunflower. I planned to finish the wood elegantly at the bottom and gradually distress it as it went up.

A million artists painted landscapes or people, but that didn't make them copies. Each brought a piece of themselves to the product.

This was art—*my* art, *my* creation.

"I didn't mean to make you cry." Warren's arms came around me.

I hadn't realized tears tracked down my cheeks. "Happy tears. It does look good, doesn't it?"

He kissed my forehead. "It's fantastic. How about you come inside for some lunch?"

As I munched on leftover lasagna and discussed ideas for turning my small living room into the baby's room with Sylvia, someone knocked on the front door. I looked up to see the dark outline of a large man on the other side of the frosted glass.

Sylvia looked over, a frown on her face. "I wasn't expecting anybody today."

In response to our bafflement and lack of movement, Warren answered the door. "Dean." His surprised exclamation carried across the open space that encompassed the kitchen, living room, and dining room.

"Hi, Warren. How are you?" Dean's warm greeting was at odds with my father's tight utterance.

"We didn't expect you today."

Dean gestured behind Warren. "I was hoping to have the element of surprise on my side. If I'd called Jessica before coming by, I'm sure she would have found a way to not be available."

Warren didn't fall for Dean's redirection. "I'll see if she wants to talk to you."

I'd spoken to Dean three times since I'd broken up with Jesse and zero times in the week we'd been back together. I'd known this reckoning was imminent. I finished my last bite of lasagna and stood. "I'll talk to him."

Warren stepped aside, and Dean entered the room.

If there was ever someone gifted at making an entrance, it was Dean. He was a big guy, with bulky muscles like Jesse's, only he was much taller—6'1 to Jesse's 5'8. Like me, he had brown hair and green eyes. In addition to his physical presence, he was handsome and well-dressed. No matter where Dean turned up—even in the mud of a Mexican jungle—he managed to make it seem like someone had set a model down for a photo shoot in the midst of all the chaos.

Before I'd broken Jesse's heart, Dean had been my friend. Sort-of. We'd talked a lot and flirted a ton, and he hadn't hesitated to put his life on the line for me. For all of that, he was still a stranger. He'd let me know the pieces of him he'd wanted me to see, but that was all.

And yet, Dean Alloway wasn't a mystery to me. I recognized in him a person who sought to control every interaction to ensure that he came out on top. He'd once told me that he and I were similar because we shut everybody out, but he was wrong. I'd been hurt in my life. Rather than use that as an excuse to lock people out—because that would have been far easier than opening myself to new sources of pain—I'd worked to heal my scars.

I wasn't sure Dean had actual scars. He might just be a control-freak and kind of an alpha-hole.

I jerked a thumb over my shoulder, indicating he should follow me into my suite. Off of the main living area of my parents' house was a mother-in-law's quarters, a suite with a living room, bedroom, and bathroom separated from the main house by a door.

It wasn't much, but it was my home.

As I sat on the sofa Jesse had bought me for a housewarming gift, Midge rushed in and Dean closed the door. I waited for him to either join me or loom over me, either of which would set the tone for our meeting.

He draped his jacket over the arm of the sofa, revealing a red-patterned sweater vest over a collared shirt that went nicely with his dark gray pants. He sat on the other end of the sofa and folded his hands in his lap.

It looked like he'd come to apologize, but Dean was also very good at throwing his opponent off-guard. I leaned forward. "Is this conversation going to be pleasant, unpleasant, or mildly threatening?"

He chuckled, a sound that showed he wasn't amused. "I'd like to know what game you're playing."

I didn't owe him an explanation, and his tone made me want to throw something at him, but I strove to remind myself he was Jesse's friend and his entire reason for visiting stemmed from his love for Jesse.

"I'm not playing a game."

"You broke up with him because you aren't submissive." He grimaced. "Or so that was your story."

"Don't be an ass."

"Jessica, you'd better not be jerking him around. I was nice last time. This time, I won't be."

"Nice? You took everything away from me you could, and you consider that *nice*?"

He regarded me dispassionately. "One might consider how I helped you achieve the independence you professed to want."

In stripping me of my studio, he'd forced me to create one closer to home, where I could access it whenever a creative whim struck me. Transferring my care was convenient for my parents. Taking away my phone meant that Jesse could no longer track me, which meant I had nobody looking over my shoulder. If he'd done these things for me, I could see where he might have a point—but he hadn't.

"Or," he continued, "one might look at the fact you never once came to me to complain or yell or offer any sort of protest. You wanted me to do what I did."

I got to my feet, not at all a graceful feat, so I infused some extra attitude into the act. "If you didn't come to apologize, why are you here?"

He watched me, a spark leaping to his eyes. "You don't want me to apologize."

"I don't *care* if you apologize. There's a difference. Did you come here to debate with me, or did you have something real to say?"

A smirk lifted the corners of his mouth. He was enjoying our exchange. "Brat, I want to know what's changed. Why are you willing to be Jesse's submissive now when you weren't before?"

I set my mouth in a mulish slant.

"You're going to say it's none of my business, but I'm making it my business. I warned you once that Jesse was my friend, and I told you I understood what kinds of games you play."

I huffed a sigh. "I told you I wasn't playing a game. I love him. He's my husband, and we're having a baby together."

141

He looked around at my Spartan digs. "You're not together. You're still here, and he's still there."

"When he's home, I stay with him. When he's not, I stay here." If I could live with Jesse full time, I think I was at the point where I would give it a shot. These past couple weeks, we'd both been happier than we'd ever been.

Dean wrinkled his nose in disgust and rose. He took a step toward me, establishing that maybe he was leaning toward alpha-hole. "That's not a relationship. You're not building a life with him. You're biding your time to keep your health insurance."

Dean's punches would hurt if I didn't think they were coming from a place of love. Even so, I enjoyed putting him in his place. "I'm having seizures again. I have five or six every day. I can't be left alone. I can't live with Jesse because when he goes away, I have to go away too."

Fucking pregnancy hormones made tears leak from my eyes and clog my sinuses.

"Maybe you did help me stand on my own, Dean, and maybe that's one of the reasons I didn't get mad at you and why I defended you to Jesse when he found out what you'd done. But the sad truth is I'm stuck here because it's the only place where I have the stable support I need."

He grabbed my arms and, given the way his body vibrated with fury, controlled his temper enough to refrain from shaking me. "Excuses—all of these are excuses. If you asked him, Jesse would quit traveling. Or he would hire someone to look after you and to help with the baby. He would buy any house, apartment, or condo you wanted and build you a fucking workshop so you can keep rehabbing furniture or whatever the fuck else you want to do—and you know it."

I hadn't asked Jesse for those things because I wanted him to offer them. He loved his job, and just like with his subs, I didn't want to be the reason he gave up something he loved. It wasn't fair to him.

Shoving all of my selfish reasoning aside, I pushed against Dean's sweater vest. "You don't know any of that."

"I know that if you submit to him, he'll move the stars to make sure you have what you need."

"I'm not submissive. Jesse and I are working around that." I struggled against his hold. "Dean, what's really going on? Things are going well between Jesse and me. I just talked to him an hour ago." He was looking forward to being at the ultrasound in two days. "Something else has you worked up."

He released me so suddenly that I sat heavily on the sofa. His big body came down next to mine. He rocked forward and put his face in his hands.

Now I was concerned. Not once in the whole time I'd known Dean had I seen him anything other than calm, composed, and in control.

I put my hand on his shoulder. "Dean? What's wrong? I know you don't like me anymore, but I was hoping one day you might come to your senses and realize I'm not that bad." I strove for a light, teasing tone because that's the way we'd always talked to each other.

"You're wrong, Jessica."

Stung, I lifted my hand away. I'd meant to soothe him, not fuel his quest to lash out at me.

He sat back, and when he looked at me, a hint of recklessness darkened his eyes. "The problem is I do like you. I've always liked you. I was waiting for you to be in a place where you might reciprocate the feeling, but Jesse didn't wait. He didn't play fair. I've been unconscionably hard on you because I'm trying to compensate for the rage I feel toward Jesse because he won. He got you first."

Stunned, I waited for my mind to comprehend the joke that surely had to be hidden in there somewhere.

Dean's green eyes glittered hard with something soft. "I wanted to drive you to me. I wanted my chance with you. I've never coveted a woman before. I've never been the kind of person who betrays a friend. I've never had to grapple with feeling such intense and opposite emotions about the people I'd give my life for."

Still waiting for the punch line, I gaped at Dean.

He cupped my face, and before I could process the action, his lips were on mine. Strong and skilled, they moved over mine and generated chemical reactions straight down to my toes. But these lips were not Jesse's, and no matter how well they kissed, I didn't want them near mine.

I pushed at his chest, and he broke away. Midge meowed wildly, almost yowling at us.

Before I could lay into him, my vision blurred, and I heard a bell ringing as if from the other side of a tunnel. Then my limbs stiffened as the world went silent.

When I regained awareness, I was on the floor, lying on my side. Dean rubbed circles on my back and whispered, "I'm here, Jessica. I'm here. You're not alone."

"Ambulance is on its way." Sylvia's voice sounded muffled.

"Mom?"

"She's saying something." Dean's voice sounded clearer. "Jessica, you had a seizure. We've called an ambulance."

I knew I'd had a seizure, and it was the bad kind. "The baby?"

"The baby is okay. I made sure you didn't hit your head or choke." Dean stroked my hair away from my face.

My limbs felt heavy, and I was exhausted, but I had pressing concerns. "Mom?"

"I'm here, baby." Sylvia replaced Dean. "Why don't you two go out front so the ambulance can find the house easier?"

I heard the footsteps of Dean and Warren leaving, and I knew they went reluctantly. "Mom? Did I pee?"

"No, you didn't." She wiped a cool cloth over my cheek. "You sweated a lot, which is new for you, but you maintained control of bladder and bowel."

Relieved, I closed my eyes. "So tired. Will you bring a change of clothes? I feel wet all over."

"That's the sweat, and yes, I'll bring clothes and your overnight bag. I don't know if they'll keep you because of the baby."

I was vaguely aware of paramedics asking me questions about my address and who was the president, but I wasn't sure I answered them. Then they lifted me onto the stretcher and loaded me into the ambulance, where I promptly fell asleep.

"Jessica? Wake up, Jessica."

I opened my eyes to find myself surrounded by bright lights and hospital sounds. A pretty, dark-haired woman in a colorful lab coat stood next to the bed. I noted the IV in my arm and the blood-pressure cuff on my other arm. "I'm in the ER?"

"You are." She smiled brightly. "I'm Doctor Revelli. Can you tell me when you first noticed symptoms?"

Struggling against the fog in my brain, I told her about the absence seizures. "This is the first tonic-clonic I've had in over a year. I have a brain injury."

"Well, I'm going to do some tests anyway, just to be safe."

"What kind of tests?" I had regular brain scans, so I wasn't sure I needed another one of those.

"Urine and blood." She wrote something on my chart, and then smiled again. "I'll be back with the results in a few hours. Until then, you have some visitors who'd like to see you."

"My parents."

"Yes, and your husband."

Jesse couldn't possibly have returned by now, so I knew Dean was out there. "Tall, brown hair, green eyes, sweater vest?"

"That's the handsome devil."

I remembered being upset with him. "Not my husband. He can stay in the waiting room."

My parents rushed into the curtained cubicle, one on each side of my bed, and they grabbed my hands. Warren had tears in his eyes.

Sylvia sniffled and brushed hair off my forehead. "Oh, baby. I'm glad you're okay."

"Yeah," Warren said, his voice rough with emotion. "It's been a while since you've had one like that. You scared the pants off Dean."

I chuckled until I remembered what he'd confessed to just before he'd kissed me. Oh, shit. I had no idea how to handle him. Maybe I'd pretend I didn't remember the moments before the seizure? It would be easier for all involved, a do-over for Dean where he didn't have to face his best friend after what he'd done.

It was the least I could do.

Six hours later, protein markers in my urine caused my doctor to admit me to the high-risk pregnancy ward where I had a room to myself. Sylvia unpacked a suitcase into drawers.

"Mom, I'm not planning to be here long enough to unpack."

She sniffled. "Then I'll pack it all up tomorrow. This way, you have all your things where you can get to them easily."

I wished she'd stop crying. "Mom, seriously. I'm not in a coma. Every day I get to wake up is a bonus. This is just because I'm pregnant, and the doctors want to err on the safe side."

"Protein in your urine is a sign of preeclampsia, Jessica. This isn't a small bump in the road. This is a major problem."

I didn't know what that illness meant, only that it was something pregnant women got. "Did the doctor say I had preeclampsia?"

"No, but they admitted you. They're just waiting for the other tests to confirm it." Sylvia sat on one of the chairs in the room and wiped tears from her face.

"Sylvia, I'm okay. Except that I'm tired from the seizure, I feel fine. If I was at home, I'd be in my workshop finishing that piece. I'm so close to being done."

With that statement of bravado, a strange feeling overtook me, and my vision blurred. I meant to say, "Oh, fuck," but I think I screamed instead. That was the last thing I remembered as I had another seizure.

Chapter 16—Jesse

My flight took forever. I know it took the normal amount of time, but even Superman couldn't fly me home fast enough. The moment my plane landed, I found Dean waiting to pick me up. He loaded me into his SUV and drove to the hospital.

"I went over to talk to her, and—it's my fault. I upset her. We were arguing."

Right now, I didn't care if they had argued. "Dean, you didn't do this. She's been having seizures. That's why I had her stay with Warren and Sylvia while I was gone."

"I thought you guys were still playing games, you know how she didn't move in with you before—"

"Dean, I can't right now, okay? I know you're not on board with Jessica being back in my life, but I don't have the capacity to reason with you right now."

He pressed his lips together and exhaled hard. He wove around slower traffic. "I talked to Brea right before I picked you up. She said they diagnosed Jessica with preeclampsia. I looked it up, and it's not good."

I shot him a look. "Define 'not good.'"

"Bad." He gripped the wheel so hard his fingers turned white. Dean never showed fear, so the fact he was losing it now did not bode well.

"Like she could die?"

"Yes. Or the baby. Or both of them. From what I looked up, I think they'll try to manage it through magnesium injections or blood pressure medication and bed rest. It's likely she'll have to deliver early. The only cure for preeclampsia is giving birth. Either way, there's risk to her and the baby."

Liquid hot fear ran through my veins. More than any situation I'd faced in the field, this terrified me. Out there, I could fight, shoot, or run when my life was threatened. Now that Jessica's life and that of our baby—Bailey—were on the line, I couldn't do any of those things. I hated this feeling of helplessness.

Dean dropped me at the door, shouting the room number to me as I sprinted into the hospital. When I got off the elevator, I found a quiet ward with nobody in the halls. I followed the line to a nurse's station.

"Can I help you?" A man who couldn't be more than twenty-five smiled at me. He wore scrubs that looked like they'd been painted with crayons.

"Jessica Zinn—my wife—was brought in yesterday. She's in 3850."

He pointed behind me. "Down there, third door on your left."

I ran, busting through the closed door. "Jessica?"

I came up short when a nurse stepped in front of me with a stern expression of disapproval on her face. Behind her, Jessica lay in bed. She was pale, her dark hair spread around her head like a halo.

"Jesse." She smiled. "It's okay. He's my husband."

The nurse stepped aside.

I went to my wife and kissed her lips. "Dean told me Brea said you had preeclampsia?"

"Looks like." She wrapped her hand around mine. "I'm glad you're here. You're just in time for the ultrasound. It's just a couple days earlier than we'd planned."

"Sure. Okay." I looked to the nurse. "What the hell is preeclampsia?"

"It's when the placenta isn't quite working correctly. It can cause high blood pressure, retention of fluids, and sometimes seizures in mom. We've run a number of tests, and we're going to monitor mom for the time being."

The nurse exposed Jessica's belly.

"The gel is warm." She squirted some kind of gel onto Jessica's skin. Then she put the business end of the ultrasound over Jessica's belly.

Swishing sounds filled the room.

"That's the baby's heartbeat," Jessica said.

My knees went weak. I'd never heard a lovelier sound than my baby's heart amplified by a machine. I looked at the screen and tried to make sense from the static-filled, black-and-white image.

"It's a strong, steady heartbeat. Head." The nurse hovered over a round lump and clicked a picture. "Arm. Hand. Other arm. Fingers. Stomach. Oh—do you want to know gender?"

"Yes." No hesitation on my part. I didn't have a preference either way, but I wanted to start using 'son' or 'daughter' instead of 'baby' to refer to my child.

The nurse looked to Jessica for confirmation. She smiled and squeezed my hand. "Sure."

I did a double take. "You already know."

She only grinned.

The nurse—I guess she was a technician, not a nurse—moved the wand around, clicking images while she poked around. "It looks like you have a shy one. They are not giving us a good shot. I'm going to get some images of the placenta, and then I'll come back and see if this little one is going to cooperate."

"Stubborn," I said. "Just like his or her mother."

Jessica snorted. "Her father, you mean."

"Yeah. Both of us. She had no chance." I stopped short, realizing what she'd said. "She? It's a girl?"

Jessica grimaced. "They did an ultrasound at sixteen weeks. I found out then, but I haven't told anyone. I was doing so well until today."

I pressed a hard kiss to her lips. "You're still doing well, darlin'."

"Yep. There it is." The technician—her badge said Rayah Johnson—pointed to the screen. "See those lines there? That's your little girl."

"Bailey," I said. Elation made me feel a hundred pounds lighter. I wanted to lift Jessica into the air and whirl her around. I wanted to jump up and down and shout at the top of my lungs. But I managed to contain myself. Barely. Okay not at all. I fist pumped the air, jumped up, and *whooped* at the top of my lungs.

Rayah laughed, and the grin on Jessica's face stretched from ear to ear. Not caring if I messed up the ultrasound, I hugged the mother of my daughter.

"My little girl. My brother would be tickled, darlin'. Thank you for this." I kissed her again.

Once I settled down, Rayah got back to work. With a businesslike manner, she snapped more photos. Then she printed out a few and handed them to us. "Here are some lovely pictures of your little girl. Congratulations. The doctor will be by as soon as she's looked at the images."

Alone with my wife, I perched on the edge of her bed. "How are you feeling?"

"Tired." Her smile was wan. "They gave me magnesium to stop the seizures, so that's helped."

I waited for her to continue because I knew she would.

"I was so scared, Jesse. One minute, I was arguing with Dean because he doesn't think I'm right for you, and the next thing I know,

148

I'm on the floor, and he's rubbing my back and trying to say comforting things. He was freaked out, and so was I. That wasn't my first tonic-clonic seizure, but I'd gotten so used to not having them." She paused to catch her breath.

"I'm glad Dean was there."

"If he hadn't been, my mom would have." She frowned. "Jesse, they're putting me on bed rest and keeping me here until I have the baby. My dad said he would try to fill my orders, but—" She shook her head. "He's not an artist. Can you maybe bring my laptop here so I can email my clients and give them the option of waiting three months or canceling their orders? I also have to talk to Nikki and postpone my PT—"

Before she got too far down her list of chores, I cut her off. "I'll take care of everything, darlin'."

She blinked uncomprehendingly. "You can't, Jesse. You're only supposed to be back for two days. You have work of your own to do, and then you're leaving on Friday."

"No, I'm not. I'm on leave, starting now. My only job is to be by your side."

Her blinking came faster and faster, and she smacked her lips in a weird way. It wasn't until the monitors started going haywire and nurses rushed in, pushing me out of the way, that I realized she was having another seizure.

"Sir, I'm going to have to ask you to step out into the hall."

I didn't want to go, but I also didn't want to get in the way of people who knew what they were doing when I didn't have one fucking clue how to help her. I'd never felt so frustrated and helpless in my life. I wanted to fix it by punching someone or writing a computer code that would rewire her brain so it stopped torturing her.

In the hall, I found Dean sitting on a bench. He looked up when I came out.

I sat down beside him. "You didn't have to stay."

"Five medical people just rushed in there. What happened?"

"Another seizure." I leaned my head against the wall and blinked against the stinging in my eyes. "They're keeping her here until she has the baby. A girl. Bailey."

I lost the battle to keep the tears at bay. Dean threw an arm around me and pulled me into him.

When I got myself under control, I said, "I'm going to take an indefinite leave."

"Sure," he said. "You have plenty of time saved up. We'll cover you. We can bring in Malcolm more often, and I have a buddy from way back who might be able to help out. He's flying choppers out of Denver right now."

"Thanks." I looked up and down the hall. "Where is everybody? I thought Sylvia, Warren, and Brea would all be here."

"She kicked them out. She sent Sylvia and Warren home to rest. They were here all night. Then she made David take Brea to eat. She said she wanted to get some sleep." Dean bit his lower lip. "She won't let me into the room."

I didn't have much sympathy for him. "Maybe if you'd gone to make amends instead of to fight with her, she would."

"I meant to," he grumbled.

"By telling her she wasn't right for me?" With everything else going on right now, I didn't have patience for Dean's insistence that Jessica and I weren't meant to be together. Rather than idyllic, these last couple weeks with Jessica had been real—we'd spent time together and apart, and the stress of having to be in Dom mode all the time was gone. We were relaxed as a couple—laughing and talking and being more playful than we ever had before.

"I meant to challenge her, to get her to either commit fully to you by moving in with you or to realize she was yanking your chain." He ran a hand through his hair. "I don't want to see you get hurt again."

I heard Jessica's voice in my head, reminding me Dean was the only person who'd openly and vehemently taken my side. He'd stuck by me, and in doing so, he'd done some things I wished he hadn't.

"You owe her an apology for raising her rent, canceling her phone plan, messing with her doctor stuff, and trying to eliminate her health coverage." While I was happy Jessica was my wife, I would have preferred to have been there for the wedding. I'd originally planned for a romantic proposal and a church wedding.

Dean sighed. "There's no good way or right time to say this, so here goes: I kissed her."

There was no way I'd heard him correctly. "You did what?"

"That's why she won't let me in there. When I went to see her, I kissed her. Then she had a seizure."

My fist connected with his jaw before I could process the fury or find joy in the fact I finally had something to punch. Rage clouded my vision, and I went after him with everything I had.

Dean blocked as best he could, but I was fueled by powerful emotions. On top of worrying about my wife and unborn daughter, one of my best friends had betrayed me. I pummeled him, driving him back against the wall.

"Security!"

At the shriek, I backed off and got myself under control. Breathing hard, I raised my hands to show I didn't have a weapon.

Dean straightened up and brushed lint or something from his damn sweater vest. "It's fine, nurse. Just a friendly disagreement."

I snarled. "Friendly, my ass. Get out."

He nodded. As he passed me, he paused. "I could have lied to you. I'm sure she will."

If Jessica lied, it would be to spare my feelings or because she didn't want me to end my friendship with Dean. While I would prefer she was honest, I could understand what might motivate her to keep it from me.

The door opened, and a doctor stopped in front of me. "Are you Mr. Foraker?"

"Jesse, yes."

She smiled. "I'm Doctor Revelli."

"Is Jessica okay?" I wanted the answer to be, 'Yes. We made a mistake. Machines malfunctioned. Nothing actually happened to Jessica.'

Doctor Revelli didn't oblige. "This was a small seizure. We'd like to see them disappear, of course, but with the complication of her brain injury, it's impossible to tell whether they're completely pregnancy-related or if her previous injuries are contributing to the problem."

That told me nothing. I affected an effective interrogation stance—stern expression, arms crossed. "So the plan hasn't changed—keep her here indefinitely, monitor her and the baby?"

"Yes. The wide chair in there folds out into a bed. We know spouses prefer to stay when they can."

Sleeping arrangements were not at the top of my list of concerns. Bed or no, I wasn't fucking leaving her side. "Is there anything I can do?"

"Just keep her company. Her sister mentioned bringing up some drawing supplies. We're hoping the next few months are very boring for Jessica." Doctor Revelli flashed a cool smile that wasn't at all welcoming or nurturing. "Boring means you'll need to keep your disagreements with your friends outside of the hospital, otherwise you won't be allowed to be here."

"Yes, ma'am." I looked down toward the nurses' station to find Dean casually leaning against the counter. "That'll be easier if you ban him."

She didn't look impressed by my suggestion. "Or you could grow up. He's been here since yesterday, providing support for everyone who has visited. Whatever he did to make you mad—maybe that doesn't make him a bad person."

With that nugget, she walked away. I didn't wait to see where she was going; I went into Jessica's room, passing a passel of nurses on their way out.

"Darlin'?"

"I'm here." She sounded tired. "Jesse, if you don't mind, I really need to take a nap."

I settled onto the wide chair that pulled out into a bed. "Go ahead, darlin'. I'm not going anywhere."

She sighed. "You're going home to take a shower. I texted Dean, and he said he'll take you home, make sure you eat dinner, and then he'll bring you back tonight. I know you'll want to stay the night."

"I don't want to leave you alone."

"Jesse, I want to be left alone. I haven't been alone since yesterday morning, and I'm exhausted. I just want to sleep."

I didn't want to, but I honored her request.

At the end of the hall, Dean waited for me. "I was going to leave, but then I got a text."

"Yeah, yeah. Take me home, you fucking bastard."

Dean didn't say a word until we got to my loft. Though I didn't invite him, he followed me inside. "I know you're upset, but I think we should talk about this."

"I don't want to fucking talk to you about anything. I'm trying very hard not to rearrange that pretty face of yours."

He draped his jacket over the back of my sofa and set a bag down on the floor—my travel bag I'd forgotten in his SUV because I had more important things on my mind. He faced me, hands on hips. "I'm more than willing to spar with you if it'll help you process some of the things you're feeling, but I think talking will accomplish more."

Talk? I didn't want him anywhere near me. I wanted to change my clothes and go back to the hospital. I'd sneak in and resume my bedside vigil. "Get out of here."

"I'm not leaving until I've made sure you eat dinner, and then I'll take you back to the hospital so you can stay with Jessica. Or, if you want to stay here, I'll stay with her."

"You'll stay the fuck away from her."

"Why? Did she tell you she enjoyed the kiss? Do you doubt her fidelity and commitment?"

It wasn't Jessica I doubted, and until today I'd never once questioned Dean's loyalty. Away from the hospital and the specter of immediate danger, the pain of his betrayal stung bitterly. "You used to be my friend."

"I'm still your friend, even though you fucking screwed me over."

I didn't want to have this out with him right now—possibly ever—but he knew how to push my buttons. "I screwed *you* over? Oh, I'm sorry—I didn't recall hitting on your wife."

"She shouldn't *be* your wife. You're wrong for her, Jesse. You only got her because you don't fucking play fair." Dean's eyes glowed menacingly. For someone who had only shown strong emotion a handful of times since I'd met him, Dean sure was obliterating that number.

If we hadn't been discussing Jessica, I might have cared about his crisis. "What the fuck are you talking about? If you're so upset about the way we ended up married, then maybe you shouldn't have gone after her so ruthlessly. You're the one who drove her to do something desperate."

"So, you admit it was a mistake?"

"No." Perhaps we hadn't arrived at this point quite the way I'd envisioned it, but we were here, and that was the only factor of consequence. "Nothing you're saying makes sense."

He stabbed his finger in the air with such a violent jab that if it had been a knife, he'd have skewered me. "We met her together—at the same time. She smiled at me first. She flirted with me first. She barely noticed you for months."

My recollection was very different. Those first few months after the coma, Jessica hadn't paid much attention to either of us because she was overwhelmed by all the changes in her life. Dean's cold assessment triggered one of my own. "She was playing you. It was her default setting. Once she was learning how to have real relationships, she sailed straight into my arms."

Crimson stained Dean's neck and face. "That's because you went after her before she was ready. I *waited*, you fucking bastard. I waited for her to be ready, and you didn't. You moved on her before she was ready, which is why she keeps running from you. I was fucking waiting for her to be in a place where she could accept love and embrace her submission."

From all the mistakes I'd made with Jessica, I'd learned she wasn't a submissive. While she wanted to please me—and she definitely had a kinky side—she didn't feel a soul-deep need to serve or submit. I had accepted this fact, and I was learning to redefine my role as a Dom accordingly. "You don't know her at all."

"I know her better than you'd like. She's the female version of me, the yin to my yang."

His analogy sucked. I could admit Jessica was a lot like Dean, but she wasn't his complement—she was mine. Dean and I had always worked well together, and similarly, Jessica and I were compatible. They weren't compatible opposites at all. They were more like a yang and yang.

"You were never in love with her." I called his bullshit. "You're just mad because I'm married. David has Brea, and I have Jessica. Even Frankie has been dating Jonathan for over six months, and I wouldn't be surprised if they get engaged soon. You not only have no one, but you can't even last with a woman for more than a few dates. You don't want Jessica—you want me."

Dean looked me up and down. "I can't say I've never considered you that way, but I didn't think your bread was buttered on both sides. I'm willing to accept both of you, if that's what it takes."

For years, we'd all speculated about Dean's sexuality because he was consistently enigmatic. Right now I couldn't tell if he was yanking my chain because he was being a dick or if he was honestly desperate enough to pursue a triad if it would bring him closer to the woman he professed to covet.

One thing was for certain—I knew he didn't have a thing for me. "You're full of shit. You weren't waiting for Jessica. You've never been in love with her. If you had been, you wouldn't have spent all that time regaling her with tales of your sexual conquests."

He scoffed. "Advertising. She deserved to know what she was getting herself into. All of my stories were delivered flirtatiously. Besides, you told her stories as well."

Point of fact: I had not voluntarily brought up my sex life to her at all. I rejected his claim. "You brought up stories of my sex life. I downplayed them and changed the subject. A woman doesn't want to hear about your past peccadilloes. She needs to know she's all you're thinking about. You've never once indicated, by look or deed, that Jessica was a target of your affection."

Dean blew up. He threw the first punch this time. I dodged it, stepping closer to deliver an effective elbow jab. When we sparred, we didn't pull our punches, but we did wear protective gear. This time, nothing protected him from my jab. Though Dean was almost half a foot taller than me, we were evenly matched. Back and forth, we traded vicious kicks and brutal punches.

"I courted her slowly." Dean's chest heaved with exertion as he tried to disengage from a headlock that could render him unconscious.

"I honored her delicate mental state by cultivating a friendship first." He broke my hold and slammed the heel of his palm into my groin.

Ignoring the pain that would be debilitating under other circumstances, I whirled out of reach to recalibrate my attack strategy. "So did I, you misogynistic fuckwad. Only my friendship with her wasn't superficial. We talked about real things—hopes and dreams and aspirations."

"Like the time she told you about her lost artistic ability? Oh, wait. She didn't tell you. She fucked you and took off." With that verbal blow, Dean landed a kick to my left side.

I countered by trapping his leg to keep him in hitting distance. Then I lashed out with kicks and punches of my own. "She was in pain emotionally, and I wasn't there for her." If I was being honest with myself, I'd ripped her open and left her alone when she was exposed and vulnerable. Perhaps her quest hadn't been about me, but I'd facilitated it by leaving her when she'd needed me. I would not make that mistake again.

Somehow Dean got the upper hand. I found myself face-down on the floor. His heavy body pinned mine in place, and he'd secured my arms so I couldn't move.

"You jumped the gun and went after her before she was ready. I know we were both in love with her—you wear your fucking emotions on your sleeve—but I wasn't going to put a burden like that on her. She didn't need that kind of pressure when she was trying to figure out who she was and what she wanted. With your rash and reckless pursuit, you hurt her. You stalled her progress, and somehow she still chose you."

I struggled against the hold, but he had size on his side. Whenever we sparred, I knew once I got in this position, I was toast. Frankie and I were going to hit the fucking gym again real soon.

"Watching you with her has sucked for me, but you know what the worst part of all this has been? I wanted to be happy for you. You're one of my best friends, and I've watched you beat yourself up the entire time I've known you because your first wife died in an accident you couldn't have prevented. You've never been able to accept that it wasn't your fault. And Jessica—she's had a shit hand dealt to her, but she hasn't given up. She wakes up every day and fights for something better. I love you both, and watching you two make a mess of this is tearing me apart."

He released his hold slowly, backing off and out of my reach.

I turned and sat up, rubbing my shoulder where he'd hyperextended it. "Maybe it hasn't been perfect, but it's not a mess."

He gestured to my wide open loft. "She doesn't live here."

"No, she doesn't." I limped to the freezer and got an ice pack for my shoulder, and I tossed one to Dean. I'd hit him in a lot of places, so he had a lot of choices for where to stick it. "But that's not because she doesn't want to. I was selfish before when I insisted she move in with me, but I'm learning to look past my wants so I can meet her needs."

Dean pressed the pack to his jaw. "She's rejected you as her Dom."

I lifted a shoulder. "She's rejected the role of submissive, not me as a Dom. It's a different dynamic than I'd envisioned, but we're making it work."

"You can't possibly be happy."

"No, Dean—that's you. I'm deliriously happy with Jessica. She's so much more than I ever dared imagine, and the fact you can't see past some of the technical difficulties means you would've never been happy with her. She would've rejected your dominance the same way she rejected mine, only you would've punished her for it instead of finding common ground." Exhausted from worry, the mission I'd just completed, and possibly losing one of my closest friends, I closed my eyes and leaned against the refrigerator. "You don't know what love is. You only want her because I have her."

He threw his ice pack on the island counter separating us. "When you fuck up again, and she comes running to me, I'm not going to turn her away."

I gaped, incredulous. I didn't know why I was shocked—he'd just confessed to being in love with Jessica, to being pissed at me for jumping the gun on the imaginary contest for her affection, and he'd brawled with me over her. Somehow, I hadn't thought the unwritten rules of our friendship had changed. Perhaps that was why he was informing me, in no uncertain terms, that they didn't apply.

I couldn't believe he'd sacrifice our friendship over this. I'd thought we'd settled this like warriors. After our fight to blow off steam, he should have admitted he was wrong—or an asshole, or something—and vowed to be always faithful to our friendship. Semper Fi, and all that.

So I hit back. "She didn't come running to you this time. If I recall, her method of dealing with the nasty turn you dealt her was to marry me. If that was your way of trying to get her to come to you, it not only backfired, but it confirmed that she was always—and will always be—mine."

Wearing a disgusted look and a burgeoning bruise on his cheek, Dean walked out of my loft, and possibly out of my life.

Never in a million years would I have guessed a woman could come between us. My heart ached for the loss of my friend.

Chapter 17—Jesse

The contents of my travel bag lay scattered over the foot of my bed—which was neatly made, courtesy of my wife who made the bed every morning after we both got up. She never made a big deal out of it, and she never seemed annoyed that I showed no inclination toward helping with that particular task. If I were to be honest, I liked when she made the bed because it was evidence she felt more and more like this was her home. She was leaving her touch on the place.

Of course, this bed had been made days ago, and she'd been sleeping in another one for the past several nights. And now she was in the hospital.

I'd make a million fucking beds if it meant she could be out of danger.

With Dean gone, I'd eaten a quick meal, and now I was packing to move into a hospital room to be with my wife.

I threw the dirty laundry onto the floor, restocked my toiletries, and loaded it with several days worth of clothes. Then I packed up all of Jessica's portable art supplies I could find. Since our failed quest to find her lost painting skill, she'd been slowly filling up sketch pads, practicing techniques more than trying to create a cohesive piece. I found three that were not full, and I threw in her charcoal pencils and her oil pastels. Then I packed her scented soap and cleaning cloths.

Jessica had moved more of her stuff to my place—our place—in the past week than she had in all the times I'd asked her to move in with me. She had clothes hanging in the closet and underwear in the laundry basket. Foods she liked were in the refrigerator, and she'd hung curtains in the bedroom. It was a small touch, but every time I saw them, my heart swelled with love for my remarkable wife.

A knock at the door had me groaning. It better not fucking be Dean, back for round two. I didn't know if he was in love with her for real, or if he'd idealized her in his head because I'd fallen in love with her and he thought he'd lose me the way we'd all lost David.

Not that David was completely gone—but things were different. Our relationships with him had changed because his life centered around Brea. While we all understood why he'd do that, we still missed having him as a more complete part of our lives.

Maybe Dean was just trying to hold onto the past too hard? I should probably cut him some slack. It's not like Jessica had ever looked at him lustfully. Yeah, she'd flirted, but it had been the harmless kind.

Once she was in a better place, I was going to ask her about that kiss. I wanted to share with her the details of my heated discussion with Dean and see if she had insight. Or maybe I wouldn't do that. Maybe it was selfish to put her in the middle of our situation.

I rubbed the side of my head to urge these thoughts to go away. Jessica needed me to be there for her, not to dump a bunch of emotional crap on her.

On the other side of the door, I found Warren and Sylvia. My heart stopped, and I could only get one word out. "Jessica?"

Sylvia grabbed my arms. "She's okay. We came over to talk to you before you went back to the hospital."

I stepped back to let my in-laws pass.

"Can I offer you something? I have water and juice. I could make coffee or tea."

"Tea sounds great." Sylvia took off her coat and looked for a place to put it.

"Here." I held out my hands for both their jackets, which I spread over a table in the workspace I was turning back into a dining room. The table was clear because I'd been cleaning out my stuff to make room for Jessica to have studio space. "The place is a bit of a mess. We're packing stuff up, trying to figure out what should go where."

We weren't sure where to put the baby. Jessica felt strongly that she needed her own space, but I was fine with having her bassinet next to our bed for the first few months.

"Actually, we're going to move." I'd planned to start looking for places this weekend. It didn't change the where-should-the-baby-sleep discussion one bit. "A loft isn't really family-friendly."

"I know," Warren said. "She's been looking at real estate online, but she's not sure about the price range or location."

"Okay. Good." I put two mugs of water in the microwave while waving them toward my sofa. "What kind of tea do you want? We've got peach, lemon, green, and cinnamon-vanilla."

Once I had Sylvia and Warren situated with tea, Warren brought up the reason for the visit. "Jesse, we're glad you and Jessica have patched things up."

So was I, but I didn't comment. That wasn't why they were here.

"But we feel that having her move out of our house is a mistake." Warren cleared his throat. "We've converted the garage to a workshop for her, and she has us nearby at all times. If she moved here, she'd have to work inside, which isn't good for anyone's health, and she would lose the support system she needs. We know you love her, but she needs more supervision than you can provide, especially after the baby comes."

Warren Zinn was still a formidable man. He'd never been a fighter the way I was, but he'd been a steelworker, and he'd stayed in shape through retirement. He was taller than me by a few inches, and he had broad shoulders. In his face, I saw Jessica's round eyes and high cheekbones. This man cared about Jessica as much as I did.

What's more, I agreed with everything he said. "I agree. Are you thinking I should hire a full time nurse, or did you want me to buy the house next to yours?"

Sylvia's quick intake of breath communicated surprise. "You'd be willing to move to the suburbs?"

It struck me that they might be angling for help moving to the city. Their retirement income wouldn't come close to being able to afford my loft. "Or did you want to move to the city?" I rubbed my hand roughly on the back of my neck as my thoughts raced. "I can look for something large enough for all of us, or maybe a pair of houses so you guys can have some privacy. I'll go wherever Jessica wants, as long as it has good schools." I chuckled because that criterion just occurred to me.

They looked at each other. Sylvia set down her teacup. "We don't care where we go. We just want to be able to be there for her, especially when you're gone."

I nodded, my mind racing with various scenarios. I could even build something if we weren't able to find exactly what we needed. "Let me talk to Jessica, see what she wants, and then we'll make it happen. When she gets out of the hospital, she'll be going to her permanent home."

"I've got a surprise for you, darlin'."

I entered the room that had been Jessica's temporary quarters for the past five weeks. I stayed here most nights, but every few days, she kicked me out so she and Brea could have a sleepover. Though she was generally bored, she was being a great sport about having to lie down on her left side for the majority of every day. Her respite came whenever she ate a meal or took a shower because that was the only time she was allowed to sit up.

Her seizures were not gone, but the episodes came farther apart thanks to the magnesium injections and the blood pressure medication.

In the past five weeks, we'd talked a lot about what our living situation would be like once she was sprung. I felt strongly that my baby should live under my roof—and not just because my mom had let me know repeatedly it was my job to provide for my wife and child—and Jessica felt like she was ready to take the plunge into married life. More than anything, she'd always wanted a close-knit family, and now she had one. She didn't care to be in the hospital all the time, but she almost always had a smile on her face now. For the first time in her life, she was genuinely happy, and having me around went a long way toward keeping her in that state.

She looked up when I came into the room, but she didn't otherwise move. The sounds of two heartbeats filled the room with a gently lullaby. "I'm wearing a fetal heart monitor, but it picks up my heartbeat too."

Due to increasing concerns about Bailey, we got daily ultrasounds. I listened to the rhythm. "Sounds good to me."

"It does. Nice and strong. We made it to twenty-nine weeks."

Every week she could stay pregnant was another milestone. I'd bookmarked some great websites about fetal development, and we pored over the next section every time she hit another week.

"Awesome. Do you want your surprise?"

She lifted her head and looked me up and down. "Jesse, don't tease. I've been horny for weeks." Then she lowered her voice to a whisper. "If you want to masturbate while I watch, close the door."

"None of that, darlin'. We can't do anything that would raise your blood pressure." I kissed her lips. "I miss you too, but I'm keeping in mind the greater good."

She sighed. "What's my surprise?"

I handed her my phone. "Swipe left."

As she did, I watched her expression change from curious to puzzled to incredulous. "This house is amazing. Where is it?"

"Midtown, the Country Club district."

She swiped through a few more photos, and then she handed the phone back to me. "Jesse, please don't take this the wrong way because in so many ways, this is my dream house, but I want to be close to my parents."

We'd talked about her specifications and needs many times.

I grinned. "I know, darlin'. This house is a little old and rambling, but it has some built-in benefits. On the other side of that turret-looking thing is what used to be servant's quarters. They've been remodeled to be a luxurious set of bedrooms, living room, kitchen, and even a private patio. That's where your parents are going to live. They're the ones who found this place. Their part is actually bigger than their current house."

Her mouth opened, but no sound came out.

A little thrill ran through me at the fact I'd been able to render her speechless. "Please tell me you love it."

She looked up at me, worry and reservation etched in the tiny lines around her mouth. "Jesse, it's a beautiful house. Are you sure about this? You're not working right now, and neither am I, not that I'll ever make enough repurposing furniture to afford something like that."

I might not be working, but I'd saved enough, and I enjoyed residuals on a few programs I'd written. We were fine for a couple of years, and given the orders that kept coming into her online business even though she'd posted that she was on leave, her business was doing a lot better than she'd ever imagined. "Darlin', this house isn't even at the top end of my price range. It's big, but not too big."

"I love it, Jesse. Are my parents okay with moving to the city?"

"Yes. They went with me for a viewing. They love it, and they love the idea of being closer to Brea and Leon as well. Plus there's a ton to do downtown, and your mom loves shows."

She touched my face. "I'm looking forward to us all being under one roof. Thank you, Jesse. I'm so very lucky to have you."

I kissed her again. "No, darlin', I'm the lucky one."

The alarm on her heart monitor sounded, so I backed off. Damn, even an innocent kiss got her going.

The nurse, Henry, came in, and I moved aside to let him do his thing. In the first week, I'd freaked out every time one of her alarms went off. Now I just sat back and let the medical staff get her straightened out. Except for the occasional seizure, nothing worrying had happened.

Henry pushed some buttons and adjusted some things, and his frown deepened.

I looked at Jessica to find she'd fainted.

Now, I panicked.

More medical staff came in, two more nurses and Doctor Revelli. The head of Jessica's bed had been propped up, and they laid it flat. Then they turned her onto her back and checked vital signs.

The ultrasound machine was wheeled in, and they got that going as well. As long as I stayed out of the way, they wouldn't kick me out.

Suddenly, Doctor Revelli looked at me. "She has to deliver the baby today."

Bailey wasn't supposed to arrive for eleven more weeks. More alarms sounded, and they put an oxygen mask on her face.

"Jesse—I need your consent. If we don't take the baby now, they both will die."

I didn't need anything more to spur me into action. I nodded. "Yes. Save them."

Just like that, my wife and unborn child were wheeled out of the room. I stood in that empty space, holding the phone with the image of the house I'd already bought. I'd planned to wait until after she fell in love with it to tell her it was hers. Right now, her parents, Brea, David, and Frankie were prepping the house to move in.

Her parents.

Fuck.

I called them. "Warren, they're delivering the baby now. They— they took her to the operating room."

"Sit tight. We'll be there as soon as we can get there."

An orderly came into the room. He was a big man, built like a linebacker, but where you'd expect a fierce expression, his was soft and understanding. "Mr. Foraker?"

"Yes?" It was too soon to know anything, so there was no way he was here to deliver bad news.

"I hear you're about to be a father. Let's get you suited up."

I got all the way to the operating room, but a nurse stopped us. "You can't go in there." Beyond her and through the OR doors, it looked like pandemonium had broken loose. There were far too many people in there to handle one little C-section.

My stomach dropped. "That's my wife."

The nurse turned to me, her eyes wide with sympathy. "I'm sorry. You can wait out here, as long as you stay out of the way, or you can go to the waiting room."

As she went into the operating room, I caught a glimpse of Jessica. They'd covered her legs, but her belly was exposed. I couldn't see her face, but I heard the beeping of machines and the call of her oxygen stats.

Then the door closed, and I was alone in the silent hallway. It wasn't quiet for long. People rushed out and in, and I fought the urge to barrel in after them. But what could I do? There was no one to fight, nothing to steal, no tech to hack. All my life, I'd been preparing to fight the good fight, but nothing I'd learned could save the woman I loved and our little girl.

Minutes passed, but they felt like hours. I'd been pinned down, shot at, and forced to lay low for days. At the time, I'd thought the moments had stretched to infinity, but it was nothing compared to the agony of watching that door. I willed it to open, and it did, but each time it burst toward me, it was just a nurse or a resident or someone rushing somewhere.

Where were they going—and why? Wasn't each operating room equipped with what was needed for every eventuality? What was so different about Jessica's situation that they needed so many people?

The next time the door opened, I noted that the medical staff seemed to have broken into two distinct groups. That meant Bailey had been born, and one group attended to her while the other worked on Jessica.

Giving birth was the cure for preeclampsia, so was her condition improving?

Long after I'd gone out of my mind, Doctor Revelli emerged. She wasn't wearing the sterile uniform over her clothes anymore, and I stepped forward.

She smiled, which meant good things, and so even before I heard the news, relief flowed through me.

"How are they, Doctor Revelli?"

"Jessica is much better. Her blood pressure is normal. We're still going to have to monitor her for seizures to make sure they were pregnancy-related and not a return of her post-accident disorder. Baby is experiencing some problems, all things we expected. She has respiratory distress syndrome because she hasn't developed elasticity in her lungs yet, so when you see her, she'll have breathing tubes in her nose. She's jaundiced, so she's going to spend some time in an incubator. The ophthalmologist will screen her for retinopathy—we talked about that, remember?"

I remembered. I remembered every single thing that could possibly go wrong at this stage of development. I knew there was a good chance Bailey would have long-term effects as well, with her vision, breathing, and possibly learning.

Doctor Revelli put her hand on my shoulder. "Breathe, Jesse. She's strong, and we're going to take excellent care of her."

"She'll be in the NICU." I knew this was likely, but somehow I'd clung to the hope that she'd surprise us all and skip that step.

"Yes, until she's breathing on her own, digesting food, and gaining weight steadily. She's just under four pounds."

In order to graduate from NICU, she had to be over four pounds. Given how early she'd been born, she was doing well.

"Can I see her?"

"Yes." Doctor Revelli smiled. "She'll be out in a moment, on her way to the NICU."

"Will I be able to hold her?"

"In the NICU, you will."

"Jessica?"

"She's on her way to post-op now. Once you see the baby, we'll bring you back here so you can be by her side when she wakes up."

If I knew anything, it was that Jessica was going to want to hold her baby. "When will she get to see Bailey?"

Doctor Revelli smiled. "As soon as she can get into a wheelchair. It's likely they'll try to get her to express some milk first. Breast milk is what's best for Bailey right now."

The OR doors opened, and out came a plastic box on wheels. Inside was a baby wrapped in a blanket. She was tiny and delicate, her pink face all scrunched up and kind of swollen-looking. Her eyes were greasy and squished shut. She had one of those breathing tubes, like for sleep apnea, that shot oxygen up nostrils that were barely large enough for the tubes.

On top of her head, she had a thick patch of black hair.

I knew I'd be one of those fathers who thought my daughter was the smartest and best-looking, but I didn't realize I'd think those things while also acknowledging she resembled a wrinkly old lady. I guess that meant she was going to be pretty her whole life.

There was a big, stupid grin on my face that wasn't going away anytime soon.

They stopped in front of me. The nurse smiled, "Do you want to meet your daughter?"

"Bailey," I said. "Her name is Bailey."

The nurse handed her to me. Her little body fit in my hands. I held her head with one and her bottom with the other. My heart burst with a love unlike anything I'd ever felt before, and I snuggled her to my chest.

"Hi, little girl. I'm your Daddy."

Her eyes opened for a second, like she recognized my voice or something, and then she went back to sleep.

I followed them to the NICU, where they put her in an isolette under a light for her jaundice. Then they attached different lines—an IV through her umbilical cord, a feeding tube through her nose, and they hooked her up to machines to monitor her heart and lungs. The neonatologist explained why it all was necessary. While I understood, it was still scary to see her little body hooked up to all those tubes and wires.

Somehow they led me to Jessica's side, so I was there when she emerged from the anesthesia.

Her eyes opened, and she immediately felt her stomach. It was still about the same size.

"Darlin', be careful. You don't want to pull your stitches." Before she could freak out, I continued. "We have a three-pound, two-ounce baby girl. She's in the NICU. She's breathing on her own, but they're giving her some oxygen. She's got your hair, and though she only opened her eyes for a moment, I'm pretty sure she's got your attitude too. So, she's going to be fine."

Jessica smiled, and her eyes filled with tears. "I'm sorry, Jesse. I tried to hold out for longer."

These past five weeks had been a rollercoaster of emotions, and though I was worried about Bailey coming so early, I was relieved Jessica's life was no longer in danger. I smoothed her hair back from her face and kissed her forehead. "None of that, now. You did great."

A nurse came in. There were so many different nurses, and I was too focused on Jessica and Bailey to care if I didn't learn their names.

She smiled brightly. "Hi, Jessica. How are you feeling?"

Jessica tried to sit up.

The nurse set a restraining hand on her shoulder. "Don't get up yet. I'm going to check your vitals and do a blood draw. We have some tests scheduled for you as well."

Jessica's brows drew together, and she frowned. "I want to see my baby."

"I know you do." The nurse squeezed Jessica's hand sympathetically. "But first we need to make sure you're all right."

I knew the moment Jessica's mouth set in a stubborn line that she wasn't going to cooperate. "Nurse, get a wheelchair so I can take her to see Bailey."

The nurse took blood and left, and Jessica grinned at me. "Your Dominant personality comes in handy in situations like this."

"After you see Bailey, you're going to do whatever the doctor tells you to do."

The doctor, it turned out, wanted Jessica to get up and walk around—but not too much. She wanted Jessica to prove that her digestive system was functioning. And she wanted her to pump breast milk as often as she could. That's mostly what she wanted Bailey to eat through the feeding tube.

Four days later, I'd become proficient at operating a breast pump, and Jessica was discharged from the hospital. The fact that I could use the pump meant almost nothing, except I got to play with Jessica's boobs. Of course, she wasn't in the mood for playing around, but it was hard to keep my excitement under wraps. I hadn't been able to touch her in far too long, and it was going to be another eight weeks before she was supposed to be fully recovered from the C-section.

Due to her having been on bed rest and the injury she was already dealing with, I knew it would take longer. As soon as they'd put her on bed rest, I'd scheduled her some PT at her old place with Malik, a guy she knew and trusted. In a lot of ways, she would be starting over, and I wanted her to be with someone who understood her strength of will.

I drove her home, a bit nervous about whether she'd like the house as much in person as she had in pictures. The driveway was in the shape of a crescent moon, and I stopped the car at the walk leading to the front door.

She stared, her mouth agape. "It's beautiful."

Pleased that it stood up to scrutiny, I said, "Stay put." Then I scurried around the truck to her side and opened the door so I could help her out.

She leaned on me instead of using her cane, which I liked, and she let me escort her up the walk. "It's huge, Jesse. It'll take days to clean."

"I've hired a housekeeper." I expected Jessica to spend her time mothering our daughter and working in the studio I hadn't yet showed her. Sylvia and Warren also had enough to deal with, and I wanted them to enjoy their retirement as much as possible.

"It might take a little while before it feels like home," I added.

Pausing halfway up the walk, she put her hand on my arm. "Jesse, wherever you are, that's where I'll make my home."

My heart filled with tender and sappy feelings, just like whenever I looked at or held my daughter.

The door opened before we got there, and Warren came out, a huge smile on his face. "Welcome home, sweetheart." He hugged her tightly and kissed her forehead. "Your mom is making scrambled eggs for lunch because she said the eggs in the hospital were kind of gross."

Jessica laughed, but it was kind of tired and overwhelmed. "It was definitely not Mom's cooking."

We'd all brought outside food in for her, so she hadn't eaten too much hospital fare.

We went inside, and she looked around the foyer. The rich woods gave it a homey feel, as did the regular ceilings. I was used to sixteen feet in my loft, so this was an adjustment for me, not for her.

"It's nice," she said.

"I haven't done anything with it," I said. "I thought maybe we'd live here for a while and change things as we went. I know you'll have definite ideas about what you want." I knew a lot about decorating and furnishing a home—another benefit of having two sisters and a mom who was adamant I know these things so I wouldn't be useless as a husband—but I wanted us to make this our home together. I looked forward to having many discussions about paint color and furniture.

"Sure." She bit her lip and furrowed her brow. Then it smoothed out. "Are you going to show me around?"

"Absolutely." I wasn't sure if she'd want to see the house or just eat, shower, and go back to be with Bailey.

Warren motioned behind him. "End up in the kitchen. I'm going to go help Sylvia while you two get settled."

I appreciated that he was willing to let this be an experience Jessica shared with just me. I showed her the downstairs first.

She surveyed the cavernous living room that featured my leather sofa.

"I know," I said. "It doesn't work in this room. I just love that sofa, though. It's comfortable."

"It's your house." She shrugged as if she didn't have a vote in the matter.

Setting my hands on her shoulders, I stopped her before she could continue on. "It's *our* house. I told you I didn't want to buy furniture until you could come shopping with me."

We'd discussed buying online, and she'd been in favor of that idea, but I felt furniture needed to be sat in and tried out before committing to it. Plus, I thought it could be one of those fun, bonding experiences.

She spread a hand toward the room. "Where would you put it?"

I bit my lip to but some time. "Well, I would move it to another room—we have four bedrooms on our end upstairs, and there's some room in the basement next to the wine cellar, which I've stocked with some excellent varieties of beer."

She snorted at that. "What about the carriage house?"

I grinned. "The carriage house is yours, darlin'. I've already set up your workshop, and there's studio space if you ever decide to take on another medium."

She blinked quickly, and I was immediately on alert for a seizure. But she wiped a hand across her eyes. "God, Jesse. This is almost too much to take in. I've never imagined I'd live anywhere so large. What are we going to do with all this space?"

"Make it ours." I hugged her to me. While it was a large house, it was about average size for the area. "This is our home. This is where we're going to raise our daughter and grow old together."

With a sigh, she turned away from the sofa. "I like that thing as well. Maybe I'll put it at the carriage house so I have a place to relax."

I wasn't against it, particularly since it meant I'd have a spot to hang out while she worked.

Upstairs, I showed her the master bedroom where I had my bed—with the headboard suitable for bondage—and the living room group that had been in the bedroom half of my loft. It was a long room with a slider in the middle of the living room and bedroom halves that led to a balcony.

"Your furniture fits in here much better than at your loft," she said. "I always felt like you had too much room in there."

I knew she wanted to know, so I came clean. "I got rid of the bondage frame."

She'd been taking in the original moldings and the way I'd set up the room. Now her gaze found mine. "Why? I like bondage."

"It wasn't right for you." The frame had been suitable for suspended poses, and she couldn't do anything like that. "You can help me pick out something that fits what we want to do with it. Until then, I don't need a frame to tie you up."

She glanced away, blinking back more tears.

I scrambled into action. "We have our own closets, and there are two sinks in the bathroom, so I can be a slob on my side and you won't have to sigh every time you don't like what I've done with the toothpaste. And I know how you liked that shower I had in my old place, so I made sure this one had something similar. It's not the same, but we can always remodel."

She checked out our private bath. "This is incredible." Then she went back into the bedroom, sat on the bed, and cried.

I was next to her in an instant. "Darlin', what's wrong?"

"I miss my baby. I wish Bailey was here."

I gathered her in my arms. "She will be."

"And we don't have wedding rings."

Having lamented privately about that fact, it perked me up to hear she was upset we didn't have rings as well. "I can fix that. We'll stop by a jeweler tomorrow."

Because it was nice to hold my wife in our bedroom, I held her for a while longer.

We checked out the nursery next, which I thought might elicit more waterworks, but she brightened up. "Oh, Jesse. I hope she likes it."

Then I paused in front of the room next to Bailey's. "I know a lot has changed for you in the past few weeks. I feel like we've become a lot closer, but you've been through a lot physically and emotionally. Add to that the fact you're coming back to a new place—I know it's a lot."

I opened the door so she could see inside. This was where I'd put the bedroom set from her suite at her parents' place, as well as the sofa I'd bought for her. It was large enough to need sitting furniture.

She blocked the doorway, her head moving as she took in the sight. "You don't want to share a room with me?"

"Oh, darlin', I want to share everything with you. But I don't want to push you to do anything you're not ready to do."

Turning around, she looked at me like I'd lost my mind. "Jesse, I want to make this marriage work. I told you I wanted to live with you, and you made it happen. I love this house, and I love you, and I love that you've given me everything I've ever wanted. It's a little surreal because part of me can't quite believe it, and part of me is still in the NICU."

Folding her into my embrace, I said, "I know, darlin'. I've felt like that for the past little while since you've been in the hospital. We'll find a new normal together."

She squeezed me tighter. "I'm excited about that."

For the next month, the pattern of our lives became breakfast with Sylvia and Warren, most of the day spent at the hospital, leaving for meals, and returning for the evening. Friends and family stopped by, but they weren't allowed inside the NICU.

Except Brea. Somehow she got past all the security, and she spent many an afternoon holding Bailey and keeping us company.

One month before her due date, we brought her home. She was tiny, still wearing clothes made for premature babies, but she'd more than doubled her weight. Her eyes were crossed, due to her being born early, and the ophthalmologist had scheduled surgery to correct it.

My mom and sisters all came out to meet my new baby, which meant Jessica and I went out and bought furniture for the guest bedroom, but pretty soon, things settled down into a normal routine.

Chapter 18—Jessica

I picked up the baby monitor, intending to turn it on, but Jesse took it from me.

"She's staying with your parents tonight, darlin'."

This was not news to me. In a theoretical sense, we'd planned for tonight for a long time. I had a clean bill of health. I'd been seizure free since Bailey was born, and my incision had healed. We had the green light from the doctor to resume sexual activity, and Jesse was excited about it. He'd lit a fire in the fireplace in our bedroom, chilled some wine, and cleaned off some sex toys I was sure we wouldn't need. My vagina was out of practice, probably only good for one round.

I'd been very nice to Jesse, waking him up with blowjobs a few mornings each week even though my libido was entirely absent.

Somehow, I'd avoided letting him see me naked for the past seven weeks. I tightened my robe around me. "Habit."

"I know." He chuckled as he set the monitor back on the night stand. "I've already turned it on and off twice."

He held out his arms, and I snuggled into his embrace. With a single, insistent finger under my chin, he urged my face up. The kiss was tender, full of love and affection. He'd done this a lot in the past few months, but this time, I knew he expected it to lead somewhere.

He lifted me in his arms and carried me across the room. Our bedroom was furnished from his loft, complete with the living room group that had been situated in front of the windows there. Here they gave us a view of the fireplace. Jesse had asked if I wanted to buy new furniture, but seeing his things in our private space made me feel giddy inside.

However, the sheer size of this place overwhelmed me. I'd thought Sylvia and Warren's house was huge, but it was nothing compared to this house, which was over a century old.

I put all of that out of my head as I basked in everything that was Jesse. "We've come so far," I said. "A year ago, you were helping me move into my parents' house, and I teased you for being shocked when you found my vibrator."

His grin was the smug kind a man gave when he knew he had the upper hand. "And now I buy them for you." He sat down on the sofa with me on his lap. "I don't know why you're nervous."

I'd gone to great lengths to keep my anxiety under wraps. We'd been through so much in the past year—emotionally, physically, and sexually. Tracing my finger over his wedding ring—we'd both opted for a plain band—I looked over at the items he'd laid out on a towel on the coffee table.

"I guess I'm not sure what your expectations are tonight."

"I want to make love to you," he said. "I want to rediscover all my favorite places on your body."

Tightening my robe even though it didn't need it, I sighed. "Jesse, your favorite places might not be in the same location as before."

"You say that like it matters. Darlin'—you're even more beautiful and sexy today than you've ever been. I like the changes in your body." He slid his hand through the opening in the front of my robe near my knee. "I'm looking forward to rediscovering you all over again."

With that, he closed his mouth over mine in a searing kiss, reminding me that he was a Dom, and even though I wasn't a sub, he wasn't going to stop being himself. It calmed my anxiety far better than his claim that twenty-five extra pounds increased my sexiness.

In moments, I forgot about any of those thoughts.

Jesse's hands, always magical, roamed my body underneath the bulky robe. Before I knew it, he'd opened it up and slid it from my shoulders. He pulled a handful of my hair to urge my head back, and he trailed wet, sucking kisses down my neck. His hands roamed my body, grasping and caressing.

With a groan, he eased me onto my back. I grasped at his shirt, pulling it over his head to force him to take it off. If I was naked, then he needed to be naked too. He obliged, sitting back on his heels so my eyes could feast on his thick, corded muscles.

Then he leaned over me and resumed kissing. His kisses moved down my body and over my breasts. He teased my nipple with his palm, a move I saw, but didn't feel.

"They're calloused," I reminded him. "You're going to have to be a lot rougher if you want me to feel anything."

He pinched it hard, and milk shot out in a stream. It hit his shoulder, and it also leaked from both my breasts.

I looked down. "I swear—I just pumped." Jesse had bought a small refrigerator for our bedroom so I could pump and store without having to leave the room.

Laughing softly, he reached to the floor and got the shirt he'd just discarded, which he used to wipe us both clean. "This came up in my research, but I got overeager in the face of how luscious they are, and I forgot to leave them alone. Do you want to wear a bra for this?"

Looking down, I noted how my milk sacks were lumpy and deflated. It was not sexy. "I probably should."

He put a hand on my shoulder, preventing me from getting up. "Darlin', I'm not asking for me. I love looking at your breasts. Even if I can't touch them, I love the visual. I'm asking for you. I want you to be comfortable."

I wore a bra all the time—even to sleep. This one night, I was luxuriating in how free my girls felt. I knew it wouldn't last for very long, but I wanted to enjoy it while it did. "I'd rather not right now."

The sly grin on his face grew. After a quick trip to the linen closet for a towel, he resumed kissing, revisiting all the places that made me gasp and moan. It took more time than usual, but eventually my pussy responded. Yeah, girl—we were back in the game.

He spread my legs open and parted my pussy lips. He licked from hole to clit, a tentative foray that he repeated twice more. Then, with a shuddering groan, he threw himself into licking and sucking. His tongue swirled, his lips clamped onto my clit, and his fingers joined the mix.

Tendrils of pleasure unfurled in my core, and I gasped. It felt so very good, but I knew I wasn't going to climax this way. Jesse figured it out as well, and he kissed his way back up my body.

"Sorry," I said.

"Darlin', your hormones are different. I expected it to take longer, and I knew I was going to work harder for it. But don't you worry—there's nothing else I'd rather be doing. Kissing you, feasting on you, making love to you—we have all night." With that heartfelt declaration, he kissed me soundly.

Then he grabbed a vibrator. Kneeling between my legs, he drizzled some lube on the vibrator, and he smeared the extra on my pussy. Immediately, heat rushed to my delicate tissues. I gasped.

His grin only grew. "You're going to come for me, darlin'. So, lay back and relax. Let me do all the work."

He turned the vibrator on a pulse setting, and he pressed it to my clit. I didn't know how long he played, but by the time he inserted it into my vagina, I was gasping and writhing. I lifted my hips, helping him fuck me with it. The powerful vibrations took me up the side of the cliff. Molten heat suffused my core, sending signals to the rest of my body. I climaxed, crying out and arching my back as I did.

Jesse spread a towel over my chest, tucking it in under me. The same chemical generated by an orgasm also triggered my breasts to let down. Thankfully, I'd already pumped, so there wasn't much left.

Without missing a beat, he shimmied out of his pants and covered his cock with a condom. Then he positioned it at my entrance.

"Jesse—wait. I want to be on top."

I watched him wage an internal war with his Dom side, and at the end, I won. He lifted me to straddle him. I finished wiping down my chest and discarded the towel. Then I guided him into me. As I sank down, we both exhaled hard.

"You feel so fucking good," he breathed. "I've missed you so much."

"Me too," I said. "I love the way you feel inside me."

With that, I rocked on him. He let me go for all of two seconds before he took over, holding onto my hips as he thrust into me and stole control. He smacked my ass, each stinging slap reigniting the fire he'd just quenched. I rode him faster, and our cries filled the room. When I was so close that I couldn't keep the rhythm going, he twisted his fist in my hair and pulled hard.

My orgasm detonated, and he cried out as he climaxed.

I collapsed against him, and he held me until we both came down.

He stroked my hair and pressed kisses to my temple. "I want to tie you up. I want to watch you fly."

I smiled as exhaustion claimed me. "How about next time? I'm tuckered out."

That was the last thing I remembered saying that night.

Over the next few weeks, Jesse and I worked on my sexual stamina, though we found that with a new baby and the demands on my body, my endurance had taken quite a hit. And so Jesse adapted, making strategic plans for sexual activities.

"Jessica, can we talk?" Jesse came into the living room where my dad sat on the floor putting together a colorful contraption that would dangle toys over Bailey's face. Jesse flashed a grin at my dad. "Hi, Warren. Do you mind watching Bailey for a few minutes?"

"Not at all." Warren held out his arms, and I handed over my baby.

Jesse liked to talk to me all the time, though he usually waited until we were in our bedroom in the evening to bring up private things. He held out his hand, and he led me to his office.

His office was on the main level. The people before us had used it as a gaming room, which meant it had lots of wires and extra outlets. That made it perfect for housing Jesse's tech. He spent more and more time in there every day. I knew he was doing things for SAFE Security. They depended on him to keep their tech working and to develop new tech when needed.

It was like he'd gone back to work, only he hadn't left home.

He closed the door, and motioned to an office chair. "Have a seat."

I sat in the padded seat, and he took the rolling stool.

"This looks serious," I said.

"It is." He rubbed his hands together. His cheeks puffed up with a breath he blew out slowly. "I've been away from SAFE Security for almost six months."

Motioning to our surroundings, I argued. "You've been back to work for at least a month."

"In a limited capacity. They need me back full time, darlin'."

I knew what that meant. I'd married a man who traveled for work. At the time, I'd known full well what I was getting into, but I'd chosen to concentrate on the love I felt for this man and Bailey. But now the words I'd flung at him so long ago came back to haunt me. Despite my best effort, I was destined to be the woman waiting while my husband went off and fought bad guys.

"Don't go." I closed my eyes as soon as I said it, ashamed at the whining note that had crept into my voice.

"I have to. They need me. Frankie, David, Dean, and Brea have been holding down the fort this whole time, but it's not enough. They're in desperate need of my skills."

A big, fat tear fell onto my wrist. "Can't you just be their tech guy? You could code stuff and make gadgets—and—and—be the person who coordinates missions."

Desperate to keep him here, I searched for options.

He rolled closer and took my hands in his. "Darlin', you knew I had to go back eventually."

I thought about the huge house he'd bought in an exclusive part of the city. My parents lived in the same house, but unless we coordinated our plans, we didn't come into contact with them. Then I reminded myself he'd bought this house so my parents could be here for me when he was gone.

It was an expensive house, and he had to go back to work to pay for it. Was now the wrong time to tell him I'd be happy with a small house in the suburbs?

"Jessica, I won't be gone long. It's a client Frankie and I have been working with on and off for the past couple of years. This is the kind of job that saves thousands of lives and makes the world a better place." He traced his fingertip down the side of my face. "I'll be gone four days, tops. Your parents are here to help with Bailey. I know your seizures have stopped, but they'll be around just in case. And they'll take you to your appointments."

"Have you already talked to them?"

"Months ago, darlin'. That's why we selected this house—Warren, Sylvia, and me."

I knew my parents had done most of the house-hunting for Jesse; this was a clear case of grasping at straws. "I don't want you to go. It's different now. We have a real marriage, and you have a family that needs you."

"It's a few days," he said. "You won't hardly notice I'm gone, except you won't have anyone to gripe at for towels left on the bathroom floor and stuff not put away."

Those things annoyed me, but not too much. I'd known he was a slob when I'd married him. At least he'd hired a housekeeper to come by twice each week.

Though I understood what he was saying, I didn't want him to go. "How about you sell the house, and we get something cheaper? Then you can work on just tech stuff, and my furniture sales are holding steady. We can make it work."

"Jessica, I'd never ask you to give up doing what makes you feel like you have a purpose in this world."

"How is being a security specialist a calling?" I didn't see how a life spent doing dangerous things was a calling. It wasn't creative. It didn't feed the soul. I knew from experience the only thing taking down a criminal did was to make room for more criminals.

He had my hands in his, and he stopped that comforting-rubbing thing he'd been doing. Frozen, he peered into my face. "You knew who I was when you met me."

At that reminder of what I'd been thinking myself, I jerked my hands from his. "Maybe I thought having a wife and a baby would change your priorities." I shot to my feet. "I guess I was just stupid to think we meant more to you than stealing something or guarding something for people who are too wimpy to do it themselves."

I left before he could say anything. I especially left before I could say anything I'd regret. For once I was going on feelings and not logic, and it was wholly unsettling to me.

That night, he packed for the mission. I hovered in the door of his closet, watching.

"You can come in." He looked up from rolling a shirt tightly, the blue in his somber eyes beckoning to me. "I won't bite too hard."

I came in, and I perched on a bench he had in the center of the room. The shelves, racks, and drawers were filled with his clothes, many of them bearing SAFE Security's insignia. He'd founded the company because he'd believed wholeheartedly in what he was doing.

Peeking into his bag, I checked out the contents. "Central America?"

"What gave it away?"

"Jungle fatigues and bug spray."

Straddling the bench, he sat next to me, and he took my hands in his. "Darlin', I know this is hard for you. I'd like to say that it'll get easier or something, but the truth is, I don't know. You got a lot of hormones going on, and our lives have changed a lot. It's hard to cope with."

And this was a bit of *his* normalcy that he'd missed.

"But you've got your art, and this is what I've got."

"You have me." I was not proud that I'd whined. "You have Bailey."

"And you'll be here when I get back."

I glanced away.

"Jessica, don't play these kinds of games. For better or for worse, I'm your husband."

"What if you don't come back?" Okay, there. I said it. I gave voice to my deepest fear.

He framed my face in his hands. "Darlin', I will always come back to you. Always."

That made me feel better. Jesse always kept his promises.

Chapter 19—Jesse

The buzz of the engine drowned out the shouted conversation between the six armed men who'd ambushed Frankie and me in the Guatemalan jungle. We'd been tasked with smuggling out an American ex-pat who was wanted in connection with seventeen deaths and who was a key figure in the Magas drug cartel.

Next to my heart, I carried a small photo of Jessica holding Bailey. Yeah, I'd become one of those guys who drew strength from a picture of what was waiting for me back home.

Frankie's dark eyes roamed the body of the small plane, looking for weak points. I did as well, taking stock of our problem areas as I did so. We were five thousand feet in the air with nary a parachute in sight. Five mercs with automatic weapons kept watch over us while one piloted the plane. Our wrists and ankles were zip-tied together. Two pallets of cocaine took up most of the space in the small hold.

Blowing it up would be fun, but then it would be airborne, and we'd all end up high. And dead. Explosions in a plane were never a good idea.

Four of the five mercs tasked with guarding us were belted into jump seats. They'd ripped out the rest of the seats to fit more cargo, so the fifth one had stuffed himself in the opening between the cockpit and cargo area. Frankie and I were with the cargo, which afforded us a small measure of privacy due to the nature of sightlines.

Something was poking me in the back. I nudged Frankie to check it out, and I leaned forward a bit. When I moved back, I lifted an eyebrow, silently asking if it was a sharp piece we could use to saw off the zip ties. With the element of surprise on our side, we could take out one or two, hopefully find the parachutes, and exit stage left.

She nodded. I scooted forward, indicating she should free herself first. This was not chivalry. Frankie was a lethal weapon. I could kick the shit out of pretty much anybody, but she could kick the shit out of me, so that made freeing her hands the priority.

It took some time—we were probably to Honduras by now—but she got her hands free. Then she worked on her feet while I provided cover by sitting between her and the cartel thugs. Leaning at that angle, I spied parachutes behind the back pallet of drugs.

She finished, and I got to work on my feet. If we were discovered, I was going to need my legs more than my arms. In the meantime, our guards were starting to do their jobs, which meant we were close to our final destination, wherever that was.

"Hey!"

I heard that loud and clear, which meant we'd been discovered. Acting on instinct and relying on years of training, I sprang into action. Frankie's fists and feet were already in motion. Despite the roughness of the flight, she moved as gracefully as a ballerina—she'd kill me for that comparison—and as quickly as a cartoon ninja.

Seeing as how they all went after her, I dove farther back, throwing myself behind the last pallet of cocaine, and I snagged handfuls of parachute. Then I rammed my way forward, taking a header into a man who was about to get Frankie from the back.

She whirled, pulling her punch at the last moment when she saw me. I twisted my body to throw the parachute to her. That's when I realized those handfuls had been one chute, not two.

She was halfway into it when the pilot sprang into action. It looked like someone had paid premium for their mercenaries this time. He raised his automatic rifle and took aim. I pitched forward, knocking Frankie to the deck and out of the spray of bullets. Fire ripped into my ankle and side, but I ignored it. There would be time to take stock of injuries once we were free.

Rolling, I got to my feet with my back against the cargo door. Using all my strength, because opening a heavy door with my hands tied behind my back wasn't as easy as it sounded, I pried it open. The hail of bullets stopped as the pilot reloaded. I didn't know if Frankie was hit or not, but I was, and we both needed to get out of there.

I fell forward, over her body. She was awake and alert, so I took that as a good sign. She buckled the last belt into place.

"You're hit," she shouted.

"Tis but a flesh wound."

"It's not a—"

I didn't hear the rest of what she said because I used my tremendously powerful legs to shove her out of the plane. Now I was alone with six armed guys. Three of them were rousing from the beatdown Frankie had given them, and the pilot was back to doing his job, which was a good thing because we'd hit some wicked turbulence.

179

My leg had been hit, as had my flank, but I was determined to get a parachute and get out of that plane. After all, I had a wife and baby to get home to.

The plane lurched, sending me careening back into the bricks of cocaine. It sounded like we'd lost an engine, which was not good. This thing was going down in the mountains in the middle of nowhere in Central America, and I did not intend to be on it when it hit.

The mercs had figured out the same thing, and they rushed past me for the parachutes. As they did, I lifted a pistol from one of them and fired. I got off three shots before the world went black.

Michele Zurlo

Michele Zurlo is the author of the Awakenings, Doms of the FBI, and the SAFE Security series and many other stories. She writes contemporary and paranormal, BDSM and mainstream—whatever it takes to give her characters the happy endings they deserve.

Her childhood dream was to be a librarian so she could read all day. Some words of wisdom from an inspiring lady had her tapping out stories on her first laptop, and writing blossomed from a hobby to a career. Find out more at www.michelezurloauthor.com or @MZurloAuthor.

Lost Goddess Publishing

The Doms of the FBI Series

Re/Bound (Doms of the FBI 1)
Re/Paired (Doms of the FBI 2)
Re/Claimed (Doms of the FBI 3)
Re/Defined (Doms of the FBI 4)
Re/Leased (Doms of the FBI 5)
Re/Viewed (Doms of the FBI 6)
Re/Captured (Doms of the FBI 7)

The SAFE Security Series

Treasure Me (SAFE Security 1)
Switching It Up (SAFE Security 2)
Unlocking Temptation (A SAFE Security Short)

The SAFE Security Trilogy: Mercenary Hearts

Forging Love (A SAFE Security Novella: Mercenary Hearts prequel)
Coming Fall 2019:
Drawing On Love (Mercenary Hearts 1)
Broken Love (Mercenary Hearts 2)
Shards of Love (Mercenary Hearts 3)

Awakenings

Letting Go
Owning Up
Serving Sophia

Safeword: Oasis Series by Michele Zurlo

Wanting Wilder
Mina's Heart

Paranormal by Michele Zurlo
Dragon Kisses 1-3
Blade's Ghost

MM Romance by Nicoline Tiernan
Nexus #1: Tristan's Lover by Nicoline Tiernan
Nexus #2: The Man of His Dreams by Nicoline Tiernan

Anthologies
BDSM Anthology/Club Alegria #1-3 by Michele Zurlo and Nicoline
Tiernan
New Adult Anthology/Lovin' U #1-4 by Nicoline Tiernan
Menage Anthology/Club Alegria #4-7 by Michele Zurlo and Nicoline
Tiernan
Discovering Desires Anthology by Michele Zurlo

Bear's Cove Series (MM/MPreg) by A. J. Stone
Dak's Omega
Tanzil's Second Chance
Perfect Blend: Kofi's Omega

Draco International (MM/MPreg) by A. J. Stone
Amaricio's Omega
Koren's Omega Neighbor
Zeke's Reluctant Omega

Excerpt from Shards of Love (Mercenary Hearts 3)

Dean

"Brat, that's enough. Jesse didn't do this job for the money. None of us do. We do this because we know we make a positive difference in this world."

"Bullshit," she sneered. "You aren't fooling anyone." She slammed the heels of her palms into my chest.

This was different from when she'd slapped me before. She'd been stunned by her reaction as much as I had, and I saw immediately that she hadn't meant to hit me as much as she'd wanted to smack away the information.

But now she was attacking me. She was in pain and lashing out.

With a neat twist of my arms, I captured her wrists and pinned them behind her back. "Brat, I know you're upset, so let's take a minute to calm down."

She struggled against my hold. "I don't want to calm down. I've been calm for months, and it hasn't helped. I'm tired of being rational and good. I'm tired of feeling all this pain, and no matter what I do, it doesn't go away. I'm tired of pretending for all of you that I'm fine when I feel like I died months ago."

My heart broke at the raw pain written on her features and trembling in her voice. Without further thought, I lifted her onto my lap and held her against me.

Her whole body softened, and she melted into me. I cradled her head, and she rested her cheek against my chest. Her hand grasped at my shirt.

Though the wrong circumstances had landed her in my arms, protectiveness and pure joy surged through me. After all this time, we finally had more than a surface-level connection.